A Thief's Song

Tony Gratacos

© Tony Gratacos 2023
Translated from Spanish by Barry Hudock
All quotations from Scripture are from the
New Revised Standard Version translation.
Cover design by Richard Ljoenes Design LLC

The original work, titled La Canción de Dimas, is registered
in the U.S. Copyright Office at the Library of Congress of the
United States of America

A Thief's Song

Tony Gratacos

Peto quod petivit latro pœnitens
Thomas Aquinas

From Above

Darkness has eaten up the light. I can't lift my head to look up. I can barely open my eyes. I'm dizzy.

Besides, why bother trying? Why should I look up at the sky? Will a prayer save me from this awful death?

Even if I wanted to, even if I had the strength to pull those words out of my mind, I could hardly utter them. My lips are so dry, they cannot even shape their sound.

And even if I could say the words, who would I address them to? Will heaven deign to look down upon me? YHWH has no interest in us. *Eli, Eli...* A vague memory tickles the marrow of my soul, and a new pain runs through my body, from the palms of my hands to my feet.

The bitter, dry taste of blood burns the inside of my throat. I try to spit, a big spit from high above upon the earth, upon the gathering of evildoers below before my eyes close forever.

But not now. Not yet.

From the distance, among the shadows, I scan the figures in the crowd below. No, they haven't come for me. Not even her, in the darkness of the saddest day.

She's not there.

I would distinguish her if she were—her way of tying her mantle over her head, the impatience in her quick footsteps, the warmth of that gaze.

Memories return to suppurate the wounds in my heart and whisper forgotten words that I learned to sing as a child, long ago: *Eli, Eli, lama sabactani!*

PART ONE
A Warning

I.

"Mama! Mama! Dismas took my doll!"

A boy's figure sneaked among the dance of shadows that the trembling fire of the hearth threw on the walls of the house. He fled from the exasperated screams of a girl who sounded as if her soul had been taken from her.

The fire cast shadows and ochres into the boy's wide eyes as he quickly scanned the room, the only one in the house. What was the best place to hide? There weren't many options. He dropped to the floor, sliding his four-year-old self under the table that presided over the room, with the rag doll clutched in his fist.

He sighed in relief. He was safe now from his sister, her cries vanishing into thin air.

All of the sudden, claws clutched at his ankles and dragged his body out from his cover like a sack of wheat. Her sister got over him, pouncing on his chest.

"Give me back the doll! You're going to break it!"

Sara—eyes burning on a face twisted by anger—was not intimidated by the two years that separated her from her older brother. But she didn't dare snatch the doll from his fists, for fear of tearing it to pieces and spilling its straw entrails on the floor.

"I won't!" he resisted, gripping the doll even tighter.

The fight had barely begun when the door opened. It was their mother, alerted by the screams of her children. Sara turned to her for help.

"What's happening here?" Mama cried angrily. "Can't I even step out the door for a moment to talk to the neighbor? Sara, get off your brother now!"

Miriam bent down to her daughter and lifted her into her arms. She sighed; Dismas had been unbearable lately and would not leave his sister alone.

"He took papa's doll from me," Sara said, flying through her tears into the air.

Miriam put her daughter down on the floor and turned back to her son.

"Dismas, give me your sister's doll immediately!"

The boy stood up, his prey pressed against his chest, defying his mother's outstretched hand.

"Promise that you'll play with me!" he turned to his sister.

Sara pointed her graceful chin at him. "I will never play with you again!" she said. "I'm tired of playing the Roman soldier!"

Dismas's lips trembled. His eyes turned to the flames of the hearth, and suddenly he acted without thinking twice.

Sara cried out in horror. She rushed toward the fire, trying to rescue her doll from the flames. Miriam managed to grab her by the shoulders and hold her back. Turning to her son, she slapped him across the face, wiping away his malicious smile.

The girl looked in horror as her doll vanished in the fire. Seized with rage, she broke from her mother's grip and pounced like a wounded cat on Dismas.

"I'm never going to play with you again! Do you hear me? Never!"

A violent shake from her mother separated them both, Sara's rage painted on her lips, Dismas's awe springing from his eyes. He turned from his sister's disconsolate face to the threat that loomed in his mother's. He had the sudden feeling there would be no dinner for him tonight.

He pressed his back against the wall and watched while his mother tried to console Sara, a wave of tears bursting against her lap.

"Don't worry, honey. We'll ask Abba to make you another one."

"My doll! It won't be the same," Sara whimpered. "And Abba isn't home. He hasn't come back yet."

"Come on, come on. Don't cry." Miriam looked up at her son with embers in her pupils. "Dismas, how could you do this to your sister! It was her favorite toy. Would you like it if she did the same to yours? You ought to be ashamed. Wait until your father finds out and you'll see. He's coming today. You know that, don't you?"

Dismas swallowed, taken aback by the news.

"Abba will decide then what your punishment is," her mother continued, with the threat still hanging from her eyes. "Now go up to your bed and wait there."

He sure knew what that meant. His mother was the one with the loud voice, but the one who really had to be feared was Abba. Papa didn't shout; he didn't even raise his voice when he spoke. But his words were the law, and the punishments they expressed were strictly carried out.

Dismas stared at the ground, his hands twisted over his mouth, before taking a few steps towards the ladder that led up to the loft. Despite its scant height and verticality, he had no difficulty climbing to the top. Experience was all it took.

Before lying down on his straw bed, he looked out of the corner of his eyes, from above, at his mother and sister. Sara was still crying. Her tears shining in the firelight caused a tingle of remorse in his gut. He knew this time he had gone too far. A knot tightened in his stomach, and tears of regret would have flowed if it weren't for the fact that there was not going to be supper for him, and because he still remembered vividly his father's last punishment. A slight shiver made his shoulders tremble as he remembered the nauseating smell of those latrines he'd had to clean.

He dropped onto the bed with his hands over his empty stomach. Why did he have to throw his sister's doll into the fire just before dinner? He buried his face in the straw. All he could do now was wait. He imagined the anger on his father's face when he found out that the doll had ended up in flames.

Dismas looked down again and watched as Sara helped to set the table, chatting with her mother as if nothing had happened, as if he did not exist. Fangs of envy and a sting of jealousy grew out of the shadows and made him think better—his sister had *been asking for it*, and if he could go back in time, he would do it again! Wasn't she the one who had stopped playing with him ever since Abba had given her that stupid doll? Well, she then deserved it.

He knew his sister was the favorite in the house, there was no doubt about that. The doll was proof of it. Abba had made it for her before leaving with the sheep he had under his care in the village. "So when you hug her, you won't miss me," he'd told his sister when he said goodbye.

And what had Abba given to him? Nothing. Just a hug and a kiss, because he already had sticks and rods to fight the invisible armies of his imagination, that's what Abba had said.

Tears of self-pity and bitterness wet Dismas's pillow. Did anyone care about *him*? Even his sister had traded him for a straw-stuffed handkerchief. Who would he and his friend

Nathaniel have fun with from now on? Who would play Jews and Romans with them? Who would they take prisoner in their battles against the invading army? That was why he had thrown the doll into the fire! So Sara would play with them again.

And despite everything... Dismas tossed and turned restlessly in bed, his eyes closed. He hadn't realized the tears and sorrows his victorious action would produce in his dear sister. If only he could ask Sara for forgiveness!

All the jealousy, all of his fury, started to dissolve under a coat of repentance that died away in the nooks of a dream.

2.

He opened his eyes, still lost in the mists of his nap. A bang at the door and an unexpected joyful greeting had filled the air and his ears.

Abba was home. And with him, the fears and regrets that had taken hold of Dismas's heart. He got up, restless, from his bed. How long had he been sleeping? He looked down from the loft into the room below. The table was set and untouched, and the cooking fire was still burning, following the same soothing ritual of every meal. But something was different: His father's voice, that playful tone, was unusual.

This was not how Abba usually came home after a week of tending the sheep out in the open, sleeping under the stars, protecting the flock from strays and wild beasts. There was no hint of tiredness in that voice today. Only light. Lots of light.

Miriam turned from the pots she was warming over the fire and looked at her husband with a frown. Her Ezekiel was a sober man; he wasn't one to be fooled into sipping from someone else's satchel. He always returned from his duties with his head over his shoulders, which had earned him a reputation that had served him well; everyone in the village entrusted the sheep to his care. But there could always be a first time, she thought to herself, and the merry tone in his husband's voice told her that that day might have finally arrived.

"My dear, I've been dying to see you again!" he exclaimed, exultant, oblivious to his wife's suspicions.

Reaching her in two long strides, Ezekiel wrapped his arm around her waist and kissed her on the mouth. Miriam was about to slap him for being so insolent and so drunk, but the warmth of that caress stopped her hand dead in its tracks. That kiss had brought her back to their first night, and there was no wine in its taste.

"My beloved! My dear wife! I have seen him! I have seen him! It was him! The Messiah! He has been born!" And then Ezekiel burst into a torrent of words that, like pearls, adorned his wife's face with light and wonder.

Dismas, who was watching the scene from the hayloft, barely heard what his parents were saying. His trembling heart only awaited the moment when his mother would raise her head and, calling his name, make him descend the ladder to face the penetrating gaze of the all-powerful judge and father. He swallowed, while echoes of the conversation below filtered through his ears —cold, fire, splendor, angels, hosannas, child, swaddling clothes, manger.

Suddenly he heard his name called, and he began to climb down like a sheep led to the slaughter. Neither his ears nor his mind had realized that it was not his mother who had called him, and that the tone of his father's voice was very different from the one he'd been expecting —no trace of harshness, kindness taking over instead.

He approached his parents with hesitant steps. Out of the corner of his eye, he saw his sister Sara, standing behind Abba with her arms crossed. His father leaned towards Dismas and, extending his arms, pulled him close, hugging him to his chest.

"Dismas, listen to me, my son. Listen very carefully to what I am going to tell you. Today is a day of joy in this house. In all of Israel! Salvation has come, and you will see its power." Tears clouded Ezekiel's eyes. "You will see it. You, Dismas, my son, will see his power."

Dismas, puzzled, looked up, seeking his mother's face. She was also crying with joy. What about his punishment, then? His eyes wandered to the face of his little sister, who was still behind Abba. She looked as lost as Dismas was, but also delighted to see her parents in that state of happiness. Something inside pushed him to go to her and hug her tightly. Tears sprang to his eyes, but unlike those of his parents, his had the bittersweet taste of regret.

"Sara, sister, I am sorry."

They hugged each other as if nothing had come between them.

That night the family meal was special. It was very similar to the Passover supper. There were songs and prayers of thanksgiving to YHWH. There was wine, unleavened bread, and even half a lamb that his mother had secured from the family of his friend Nathaniel, the richest people in town whose sheep Abba shepherded.

Dismas barely understood anything of what happened that day. He only knew that the little incident of his throwing the doll into the fire had been forgotten and that he had been able to reconcile with his beloved little sister. He didn't know what the arrival of this Messiah, which his Abba wouldn't stop talking about, meant. But he was sure of one thing—the Savior of Israel could not have started on a better footing: He had turned a well-deserved punishment into an early Passover celebration.

In bed, in the still of night, Dismas fell asleep with the singing of the prayers they had chanted during dinner, welcoming this Messiah who was going to save them all, still in his ears:

> Lift up your heads, O gates!
> and be lifted up, O ancient doors!
> that the King of glory may come in.
> Who is the King of glory?
> The Lord, strong and mighty,
> the Lord, mighty in battle.

About to fall into his dreams, Dismas groped for the stick he always kept under his pillow and gripped it by one end with the strength of a warrior. If this Messiah's arrival meant there would be a mighty battle, he was more than ready to fight.

PART TWO
An Arrival

I.

"Dismas! That can't be you!"

The words managed to slip into his ears through the sharp pounding of the hammer. The iron of the lance that he held against the anvil resisted his blows, but the blade was already taking definitive shape.

Dismas looked up with the sparks still fluttering in his dark eyes. It was hard for him to make out the face of the man bathed in the bright midday light that filtered into the entrance of his workshop.

"I can't believe what my eyes are seeing," continued that distant and strangely familiar voice. "Praise God Almighty!" Its owner approached him with open arms, without even waiting for Dismas to put down the hammer.

The floodgates of his childhood opened wide with that embrace, and memories of his began to flood his mind.

"Nathaniel!" he cried. "For all the devils! What are you doing here in Jerusalem, so far from Galilee?"

"For a merchant like me, all the earth is home," Nathaniel answered, a dazzling smile still on his face.

The two friends looked at each other for a moment without uttering a word, absorbing the changes that time had shaped in their features. Behind the beard and the smooth skin tanned by the Galilean sun, Dismas could still recognize his childhood friend, now a man, just like him.

"It's hard to believe it," Nathaniel said, mesmerized. "I go into a workshop looking for someone to straighten the wheels of one of my wagons, and I find you! Do you have any idea how long it's been since you left? Without saying a word since then?"

Dismas looked away from his friend, trying to put an end to the memories that kept flooding his mind. How much time had passed since that conversation with his father? More than twelve years, perhaps?

There had been so much regret and hesitation back then. Those dark nights played again across his mind—arriving in Jerusalem, sleepless wanderings, afraid he wouldn't be able to survive on small jobs that couldn't cover his needs. But it had been his decision to leave Galilee, Abba's home. It was him who had decided to get away from the landscapes and the flavors and the colors of his beloved childhood. It was the price he'd had to pay to be himself and not a replica of his father. He'd long ago known he wasn't a shepherd and that he'd never be one. He loved everything about that land, about his home, except the indecipherable smell of sheep that permeated his father's clothes, his father's soul.

Dismas wanted to earn a living with his hands—to shape clay, temper iron, work wood. He had the talents to create with those. Was there anything more powerful? He had inherited that, ironically, from his father. That doll he'd thrown into the fire as a boy was evidence of that. But what life pushed aside in his father, Dismas was not willing to sacrifice for the demands of the arid and capricious lands of Galilee. So when he turned sixteen, it was time for the decision that his creative soul sought to—leaving home and settling in Jerusalem.

He'd told his mother first. She'd looked at him with sad eyes, but she supported him. Could a mother do anything else?

What he needed next was Abba's approval. Surely, he would understand, too. Despite the hardness of his character and his heart, he would understand his son's reasons.

How wrong Dismas had been about that! The expression on his father's face that afternoon flashed through his mind, and he felt the same old sourness in his soul again. A bitter mixture of anger, pride, and disappointment had flowed from Abba's mouth; he told him that he'd die of hunger if he thought he could live off the work of his hands and threatened to close the door of his home forever if Dismas dared to leave them. Dismas was filled with the same anger, with the same pride and disappointment that his father poured out, and he refused to heed both his threats and the cries and pleas of his mother. Her heart and her insides were broken that day.

Dismas had left for Jerusalem the following morning, leaving behind a world to which he would never return. His old friend Nathaniel had brought it all back with his warm embrace.

"Your mother and your sister Sara told me that you were doing well. But they have never been able to tell me exactly where your workshop was."

Dismas looked away from his friend while searching for a lie with which to respond. How could they know anything about him when he'd not given them any sign of life? "I recently moved to this part of the city, and I have not had time to let them know," he managed to word convincingly.

"They told me that you were a solitary man," Nathaniel said with a smile, patting him on the back. "You are not going to believe it, but I wandered for a while around all the workshops in Jerusalem, hoping to find you. And it's precisely today, when I walk into one, out of need, that I finally find you. It can't be a coincidence. Praise YHWH for that!"

Dismas noticed a special glow in Nathaniel's eyes, and he felt guilty for answering to his friend's warmth with barely a few embers of affection after so many years of absence.

An awkward silence enveloped them. Dismas blushed a little as he struggled to find something they might share in common that could keep the conversation alive.

"And what are you doing in the Holy City? Do you come often?" No better question came to his aid.

"My family's business has grown a lot since you left," Nathaniel answered with that same smile. "We are merchants now, and I have a caravan going back and forth from Galilee every week. I come to the city once a month to see that everything is going well and make sure that my people are well paid, happy, and not stealing too much from me. But this time I have come for different reasons. Bathsheba is with me."

Nathaniel said that name in a way that it was supposed to pull a rope in his head, but no bell rang up there.

"What!" Nathaniel looked at him in surprise. "Have so many years passed that you don't even remember my sister Bathsheba? She is still your sister Sara's best friend."

Dismas suddenly remembered. How could he have forgotten that ugly little girl? He had always thought that giving that name to that creature had been cruel, very cruel. In the Scriptures, the beauty of Bathsheba was legendary; she had driven King David mad. But the only thing Nathaniel's sister had driven mad in Galilee was Sinta, the dog that followed her everywhere, drooling.

"She lives now in Jerusalem. You see, my mother died," Nathaniel continued, lowering his voice.

"Oh, Nathaniel, I'm so sorry. I didn't know," Dismas stammered, unable to come up with any other word of comfort.

He remembered his friend's mother very well—solemn, proud, the kind of person who made the air bend wherever she went. A remarkable woman, indeed.

"Thank you very much, Dismas," Nathaniel cleared his throat, trying to stifle his emotions. "I didn't want Bathsheba to stay there alone; my brother has taken over the business in Galilee, and she has come to live in Jerusalem with an aunt of ours who has just been widowed. Maybe we could meet up before I return to Galilee. How about after the synagogue, on the eve of the Sabbath?" Nathaniel's eyes seemed to burst at this sudden idea.

"Dismas!" A voice behind him interrupted them.

He didn't need to look toward the sunlit doorway to know who had entered the workshop. With a feline movement, he threw a cloth over the spearhead he had been hammering, hiding it from the newcomer's sight. The gesture did not go unnoticed by Nathaniel.

"Gestas wants to know if you have what you promised us." The stranger stood motionless in the doorway, standing in the shadows.

"Hello, Melchiades. Good morning," Dismas answered dryly. "Tell your boss he'll have it tomorrow at dusk, just as we agreed."

"That had better be right, because if not, I will be the one who has to bear Gestas's bad temper. And then you and I will exchange more than words."

The stranger took a step back and dissolved into the white light of the streets.

Nathaniel looked at his friend, who was astonished by the stranger's rudeness.

"Yes, I know," Dismas nodded, downplaying it. "He is an unpleasant little guy, but he pays well. You have to put up with the insolence of some when you are in business. Living in Jerusalem is expensive, you know? This is not Galilee."

"I know, I know," Nathaniel shook his head. "This city is not an easy place to live in without the necessary means."

"Have you been able to visit the temple yet?" Dismas diverted the conversation from Melchiades, the guy who had just left.

"Ah, the temple! It is the only reason I would live in this city," Nathaniel's face lit up, and Dismas grinned. He knew where to press to make his old friend tingle. It was clear that Nathaniel remained a religious man. Unlike him.

"But I prefer the tranquility of Galilee," Nathaniel continued. "There, under its blue sky, I can allow myself to speak with our Creator as peacefully as if I were in the temple of Solomon itself."

"I'm sorry to have to ask you this, but I am afraid you'll have to leave. I have a lot to do if I want to keep my clients happy."

"And I see that you have to finish sharpening a Roman soldier's lance," Nathaniel observed, pointing to the cloth his friend had used to hide the weapon's iron from Melchiades's sight.

Dismas looked at Nathaniel in surprise; his friend was not as naive as he'd thought.

"Are you one of those who think it wrong to put our skills at the service of the Romans?" Dismas defended himself, sarcasm all over his words. "We live in the times that we have to live in. We are part of their empire now."

"Yes, of course, of course. You're talking to Nathaniel the merchant." He pointed to himself, placing the other hand over his friend's shoulder. "But don't forget that we are still the chosen people. So, shall we meet before the Sabbath, at the synagogue?"

Dismas let out a sigh between his teeth. Nathaniel was as persistent as the hammer he wielded in his work.

"I thought you said *after* the synagogue." Dismas glanced at his friend.

"Before, during, after—what does it matter? The important thing is that we meet again."

Dismas smiled.

"Okay. Tomorrow at the synagogue. And now go, or I won't be able to finish this job, either, and the Roman invader will come and crucify me." Dismas took up his hammer and lifted the cloth that hid the weapon.

Nathaniel laughed as he turned back toward the door and the light from the streets behind.

"You needn't feel any guilt about sharpening that lance for the enemy. No weapon shall prevent the arrival of the Messiah."

Nathaniel disappeared and Dismas's hammer fell on the iron. His friend was the same person he'd always been—an innocent little lamb who trusted in the goodness of people and the promises of the Scriptures. Dismas had once been like that; he too, as a child back in Galilee, had been very close to YHWH. But life had turned him into an unbeliever. The Messiah? His hand fell again with a blow on the sharp Roman blade.

He vividly remembered that winter night when his father had come home, dazzled by a baby wrapped in swaddling clothes. He had seen the birth of the Messiah, he said. If that was true, that child should be close to Dismas's own age; and enough time had passed for him to have already manifested himself. But there was no sign of him. No trace whatsoever. Just gossip about his imminent arrival and the final liberation of his chosen people.

Dismas shook his head, snorting. Abba must have had too much to drink on that starry night outside Bethlehem.

But Nathaniel had gotten his way today. Naive or not, his old friend was dragging him back to the synagogue. Did Nathaniel know that he no longer attended religious gatherings? No, he was too innocent to realize that people could grow in life with new and different perspectives. Although Dismas still believed in YHWH, he barely had time for Him. In Jerusalem there was always something to do—obligations, friendships, rest, small pleasures… He'd moved into the Holy City and ceased to be holy, he thought ironically.

Oh, Nathaniel, Nathaniel! The good old days were behind their backs, and they would never return. He had gotten rid of the smell of the shepherd and the synagogue, but his old friend had brought back both of them with him today.

Dismas gave the iron another sharp blow, raising a burst of sparks. Right then he decided that he would skip the meeting at the synagogue with his old friend.

"Goodbye, Nathaniel. We were good friends once, but that time is long gone."

2.

It wasn't hard to find Nathaniel among the crowd that packed the synagogue. He was sitting in one of the seats near the front.

As Dismas made his way toward him, he felt like he was being watched. He read the thoughts in the eyes of the people who looked at him with curiosity: "There goes the stranger." "Isn't that the blacksmith who does business with the Gentiles?"

Nathaniel greeted him with a smile. Dismas was surprised to see that his old friend had saved a seat for him; he'd been certain that he would show up, even when Dismas himself didn't know that when he woke up that morning. What had made him change his mind?

Maybe it was the smell of freshly baked unleavened bread that wafted in from the nearby houses. Or the songs that had been filtering into his ears since the previous evening, and that had gone on until the early hours of the morning. He remembered some of the words of the psalms that he'd heard from the children, preparing to recite them on the sacred day. He had sung them once and could still complete some of its lines. With "Eli, Eli lama sabactani," his memory had flown over the distant notes of the melody "The Deer of the Dawn" to complete the verse:

Why are you so far from helping me,
from the words of my groaning?

A lonely tear had appeared in his eyes then, a tear that reflected the face of his mother kissing him on the cheek while his small hands tried to fasten the belt of his tunic.

"Like that, Mama?"

A sudden melancholy had taken hold of him, something that had not happened since he had moved away from home. It was like a somersault into the emptiness of his own soul, which he'd been unable to fill despite having everything in this holy, eternally sinful city.

Nathaniel had been the cause of that small inner fracture. And there he was now, sitting next to him, listening to the Scriptures as if it were good old times.

While the rabbi read a text from the scroll of Isaiah in which the prophet spoke of a virgin who would give birth to a child, Nathaniel leaned over and whispered in his ear to invite him to dinner at his aunt's house. Dismas tried to hide the horror he felt at the idea. One of the reasons he'd been allowed himself to be dragged to the synagogue was because no talking was necessary during the religious service, and Nathaniel wouldn't have the chance to see how far their paths had diverged in life. He had imagined, at most, a brief chat with him and his sister Bathsheba as they left the temple together. The three would exchange some typical obligatory words that meant nothing, and then they would all go home, each one to his own. And that would be the end of it.

Dismas just nodded to his friend, then spent the rest of the service polishing the perfect excuse that he'd use to decline the invitation. He wasn't good at telling big lies, but if he tried hard, he could be convincing with the little crumbs that fell from the plate of truth.

By the time he left the temple, he had managed to memorize the perfect lines that would free him from the commitment of the dinner with Nathaniel's aunt. But before he could utter a word, Nathaniel had vanished from his side. He reappeared moments later, with his hand hanging on the arm of the most beautiful woman Dismas had ever seen.

"Dismas, I don't know if you remember my sister."

Bathsheba's shyness erased the words that Dismas had carefully drafted in his mind. He remembered Sinta, the neighbors' dog from childhood; only this time that annoying animal wasn't drooling between her skirt: it was him who was.

The dinner at the home of Nathaniel's aunt was the beginning of something very profound that Dismas could never have imagined. The girls he knew in the Holy City were not like Bathsheba. It wasn't just her beauty—there was something else that he could not explain to himself later that evening, as he tried in vain to fall asleep.

Had it been the way she spoke? Dismas, lying on his back on his cot, shook his head. Nathaniel's sister had not uttered a single word throughout the entire dinner. She had been busy going back and forth to the kitchen, serving dinner, making sure no one needed anything, while he, Nathaniel, and her aunt sorted out the world, talking about messiahs, Romans, and narrow-minded Pharisees.

Had it perhaps been a furtive glance thrown out by her, holding promises of a future intimacy with him? Dismas dismissed that idea, so unworthy of her. Bathsheba was not that type of girl. She had even been proper enough to avoid touching his tunic when she leaned over to pour him more wine.

So what could have bewitched him? There was no doubt that he was a good match for a woman newly arrived from

Galilee. His growing prestige as a blacksmith was on the way to making him a rich man and, when the time came, he would have no difficulty choosing the right woman to start a family with. But it was unthinkable that Nathaniel had been planning that meeting all along. It was not his friend's style playing matchmaker.

However, Dismas had noticed that sudden gleam in Nathaniel's eye when he proposed the meeting with her. Had they put something in his food? Dismas closed his eyes, shaking his head again. He could not imagine Bathsheba mixing some secret potion in his cup. She was far, far away from being the kind of woman who wandered through the back alleys of the market in search of impossible herbs that made the most forbidden desires come true. That world belonged to whores and thieves, not to Bathsheba. Her beauty needed no sorcery. She only had to blink those honey-flavored eyes of her to cast a spell.

Dismas finally let the darkness of the room embrace him, and sank into a dream in which a drooling dog ran around its owner's skirts. Something grabbed the hound's attention from her, and when the dog finally stopped sniffing and turned back to its master, she had disappeared. Nervous, the dog managed to spot her in the distance and ran towards her, barking, trying to close the void that separated them. He raced through fields of wheat, but she continued moving forward, unhearing, until she melted into the horizon and disappeared, ignoring his cries. The dog went into a panic, running in every direction, tracking down clues, whimpering and barking in vain. Suddenly the stalks of wheat bent toward him, pressing against his body, suffocating him. In the blink of an eye, they became flaming arrows and set everything on fire. The dog's whimpers turned into howls of despair and, on the verge of madness, when the smoke was about to obliterate everything around him, a pair of strong hands lifted him into the air and held him tight while a voice whispered in his ears: "What are you afraid of? I am."

Dismas woke up exhausted, feeling thirsty, his throat burning. He immediately knew there was only one thing that could refresh the day ahead for him. He needed to see her again. Urgently.

"Dismas!" A shout from the street interrupted his impulse to run to Nathaniel's. By the stranger's tone he noticed he was not the only one who had slept poorly that night. He sighed. Seeing Bathsheba again would have to wait at least until midday.

He put on his work apron before pulling open the curtain that separated the workshop from his home. That hanging piece of cloth was not enough to protect his privacy from the demands of clients who thought they had the right to bother him at any time. It wouldn't be a bad idea to look for a place to live that wasn't his workplace. When he was doing better, he would give it some serious thought.

He hurried to open the door before Melchiades' knocks battered it down. The morning sunshine slid into the workshop along with a cloud of shadows that hovered over the face of the newcomer.

"Where were you? What have you done with them?" growled Melchiades, storming in, ignoring his presence. His agitation stirred up a haze of sawdust that started to waltz with the sunlight that pierced the air of the room.

"Do you know what kind of tirade I had to endure last night? Gestas was furious! I told you I'd be here by sunset, but I found your workshop closed!"

"The sun set with no sign of you," Dismas replied, unfazed. "And today it's Sabbath."

Melchiades turned to him with swollen eyes. "To hell with Shabbat! I didn't know you were a scrupulous Jew." His words dripped with irony.

Dismas stepped toward Melchiades, and his tall frame made the visitor hesitate. "I'm a Jew who has to earn a living, a Jew who doesn't want his neighbors to label him as unfaithful," Dismas faced him defiantly. "I waited for you until the last moment. But you got here late, so don't blame me for your negligence."

Dismas's confidence and poise made Melchiades think twice. He was bright enough to know that, if it came to blows, he had everything to lose against Dismas. Besides, he knew he was the one that had gotten himself into the mess. He had been commissioned by Gestas to pick up the *merchandise* for himself and transport it to Jericho, using the Sabbath as a perfect cover up for their movements. It was his fault that the *goods* weren't where they should be, and they'd had to postpone the plans made weeks ago. Melchiades had tried to blame Dismas when confronted by Gestas, claiming that the blacksmith had not met the delivery deadlines, but Gestas hadn't let him.

"Do you want me to believe that your negligence was the result of the blacksmith's negligence? That man Dismas has a reputation for being the best craftsman in Jerusalem, and you, on the other hand, you"—a vein across his forehead had pulsed in anger—"you are nothing more than a..."

Gestas had to shut his mouth in front of the others present because Melchiades was his cousin, and he had been the one who had introduced Gestas to the gang.

"Okay, okay," Melchiades stepped away from Dismas, forcing a conciliatory smile. "There's no need to get worked up. We all make mistakes. Where do you keep them?"

Melchiades took a quick look toward the back of the workshop, trying to spot the *merchandise*.

"I have the weapons in the—"

"The *tools*," Melchiades corrected, firing a warning glance at Dismas's indiscretion, as he began to search through the objects scattered in the workshop.

"Call them whatever you want, but I know those *tools* are not exactly for plowing fields," Dismas answered fearlessly, following behind Melchiades. "And will you stop handling the things in my place! You're not going to find twelve iron bars with pointed ends hidden anywhere out here. They would raise suspicions."

"Oh, but I can find instead a weapon by the Roman invaders."

Melchiades turned, holding the iron of the lance that Dismas had been forging the previous days. He had in his hands a small little secret of the blacksmith that surely would not please his cousin Gestas.

"My dear Dismas, it is not very sound to work for both YHWH and the devil at the same time."

"I don't know whether the Romans are the devil," Dismas said, snatching the spearhead from Melchiades and returning it to its place without flinching. "But I can guarantee that you are not YHWH's army either."

"I don't think Gestas will like hearing that you also work for them," Melchiades replied with a frown.

Dismas barked out a laugh that dissolved the threat that floated in the air. "The only thing Gestas is going to like is having his merchandise for once and for all." He crossed the room and stopped beside two barrels that rose to his waist. "Here is your order," he said, petting the top of the barrels.

Melchiades shot him a look of disbelief. "And how do you want me to get those out of here?"

"Maybe you'd rather carry the spears out under your arm, parading down the street under the curious look of any Roman garrison you may come across."

"Hmm. I am going to need a cart to take them out of here," Melchiades muttered, scratching the back of his neck.

How the hell had he *expected* to take the weapons with him? Dismas rolled his eyes. Couldn't that mysterious Gestas have sent anyone else to do this job?

"Your revolution will need smarter men than you if it wants to take root." Dismas couldn't help saying out loud what had crossed his mind.

Melchiades stood up, tense, his teeth clenched, trying to pretend the sharp comment hadn't hit its target. He took two steps towards the blacksmith, this time without a hint of fear.

"The only thing the Messiah needs to free his people from the oppression they're under is blood willing to be shed. Are you ready to shed the blood that runs through your veins?" Melchiades asked, his eyes burning.

"Have you ever met this Messiah?" Dismas frowned, stung by curiosity. It was the first time he'd heard someone speaking so directly about that figure.

Melchiades took a step back, "I'm only repeating what is on everyone's lips. The Messiah has already been born, and he is preparing the definitive liberation of his chosen people. He will defeat the Roman invader once and for all, and you will have to choose on which side you'll fight."

"Free us from the Romans?" a voice spoke up from behind them. "Then that Messiah better live a long time, for who will free us from the invader that will come after the Romans?"

Dismas and Melchiades turned, aghast, to see who had spoken.

Both of their hearts sinked in—Melchiades because the one who had spoken was a woman, Dismas because that woman was Bathsheba.

"What's with you, woman?" Melchiades replied, disgust all over his face. "Who gave you permission to interrupt us? You better keep shut and not talk about what you don't know." He turned back toward Dismas, shaking his head. "Some women won't respect the most basic things."

"I'm sorry I interrupted you," Bathsheba replied, her soft voice riding through the air with the confidence of a hundred horses galloping through the desert.

Melchiades turned again, astounded. Dismas did not need to turn toward her because he hadn't stopped looking.

"But I cannot remain silent," she continued, "listening to you defile the figure of the one who Moses and all the Scriptures keep announcing. It is true that he will come. I don't know when it will be or if he has already been born. But the salvation he will bring won't save us from a foreign oppressor. When he comes, he will free us, but he will free us from ourselves."

The silence that followed was as heavy as the words Bathsheba had spoken. The sunlight from outside fell directly on her, and with the motes of sawdust floating in the air around her, she looked more like an apparition from heaven than a mere mortal. Perhaps that was the reason Melchiades did not dare to silence her again. He rubbed the palms of his hands against his chest instead, as if it was dirt that had come from her mouth and fallen upon him. Pointing to the two barrels, told Dismas that he would come back to pick them up.

"This time you'll wait for my return," he snapped as he retraced his steps to the door. As he passed Bathsheba, he glanced at her with infinite contempt. "You have your Messiah, and I will choose mine," he spat, disappearing into the bustle outside as the day was reaching its zenith.

Bathsheba and Dismas remained silent for a moment, wrapped in a delicious daydream. At least that was how he felt, as he finally began to grasp the nature of her charm. He had spent the whole night trying to solve her mystery, and there it was, right before his eyes. The realization had come while she was talking about the Messiah. That warm voice dissolving in the iron certainty with which she had spoken was the essence of what had drawn him to her the night before. She had not opened her mouth then, but her presence alone had projected the same aroma that he was perceiving now: a little slice of eternity breaking into the worldly noise.

With her standing into the frame of his doorway, the sun shining all over her face, the workshop had become—

Dismas swallowed, uneasy; he could not dare to think what had just crossed his heart. But he couldn't *not* think it, even if the thought condemned him forever to hell: Bathsheba's presence had turned his place into a temple for the worship of God almighty.

This sudden fire in his heart ignited his entire body, and he would have knelt before Bathsheba at that very moment and asked her to marry him, if she hadn't spoken first.

"Dismas, I came to find you because the caravan my brother was expecting from Galilee finally arrived this morning. They brought some bad news." Bathsheba lowered her eyes and took a deep breath before looking at Dismas again with a mixture of tenderness and compassion. "Your father has died."

Dismas was surprised to notice his eyes suddenly moist. Tears for the death of Abba? He shook his head; his father was dead to him since the day he had cursed him. No, the moisture in his eyes didn't come from the news of his death; it came from the realization that the bearer of those news was the woman with whom he wanted to spend the rest of eternity.

3.

He didn't have the chance to tell Bathsheba then. Not even spend more time with her. He felt the urge to return home, to kiss his mother, to hug his sister, now that the one who had prevented all that was gone.

Dismas was not going to miss his father. There were few memories of him in the landscape of his childhood—many words, few caresses, no kisses. Only one had really managed to take root in his heart. It was that night when, instead of a punishment, Abba greeted him with a hug and those strange words whispered into his ear.

After attending to the most urgent matters in the workshop and delivering the barrels with the "tools" to Melchiades, Dismas arranged what was necessary to make the trip as soon as possible. He would make the journey from Jerusalem to Galilee under the shelter of a caravan that Nathaniel had arranged. His friend's business was booming, and it was not unusual at that time of year to transport goods back and forth every week between the two points. The wool that was shorn from the sheep before being sacrificed at the Temple was sent to Galilee, and it made its way back transformed into blankets for the wealthier homes of Jerusalem. The miracle had been made possible by Nathaniel's mother, using the hands and the skills of the women of the village. Dismas hoped that, after her death, his friend would find the right person to keep the business going.

Galilee was about a hundred miles from Jerusalem, which could be covered in three days if the caravan left before dawn. The night before, Dismas had summoned up his courage to go to aunt Rebecca's house and say goodbye to Bathsheba. He did not mean to do it directly, of course; he would use as an excuse the more than deserved gratitude he owed Nathaniel for putting all the pieces together—even moving ahead the caravan's departure by a day—so that he could be with his mother as soon as possible.

Nathaniel himself opened the door for him. He was surprised to see his friend again after having said goodbye that very morning.

"Did you forget something?" he asked curiously.

"Hello, Nathaniel," Dismas stuttered, his features tense as he tried to catch a glimpse of Bathsheba behind. "I want… you see… I wanted to thank you very much for everything you have done for me these past—"

"Bathsheba is not here." Nathaniel cut short his friend's hesitations with a grin. "She's gone out. But I'll tell her you came to say goodbye."

"No," Dismas jumped in, blushing. "I don'…"

How could his friend have noticed? He tried to improvise a torrent of words that stumbled in confusion through his lips. He felt so humiliated!

"Don't worry, I will keep your secret. I won't tell my sister," Nathaniel reassured him, amused, patting his shoulder.

On the way home, Dismas cursed himself a thousand times for his naive stupidity. He had behaved like a fifteen-year-old. He had even blushed shamefully. And did he really expect secrets were to be kept between siblings?

As he walked under the starry night of a sleepy Jerusalem, another even more painful thought stung his spirit. Where was Bathsheba? What was a young woman doing outside her house at that hour of night? Jealousy climbed on the shoulders of the humiliation he'd suffered and ended up reaffirming poor Dismas's diagnosis: he was crazy about her. He, who knew no metal so hard that he could not bend it, had melted like straw before the devouring blaze of love.

Dismas didn't think much about love and Bathsheba during his trip to Galilee. Other important issues required his attention along the way. Although his father's death had not caused him any sadness, it had opened a cascade of possibilities that he needed to consider and resolve.

The first was the reunion with his mother. More than fifteen years had passed since he had left home, and they had only seen each other once during that period.

It had happened two years after he left. Dismas had made no attempt to contact them in all that time. He had made that promise to himself. It had been his decision to go against his father's wish, and he did not want to put his mother in the difficult position of having to choose between her son and her husband. He had disappeared without a trace, because he knew that if she found where he was, sooner or later she would come to see him; sooner or later she would expose herself to Abba's wrath; sooner or later Dismas would break her heart again. He had broken it once; he did not intend to do it again. Only time could heal the wounds of the heart

However, it was during Passover of the second year after his departure that he had stumbled upon his sister Sara on the streets of Jerusalem. They had embraced each other, excited, and it had been she who had suggested an encounter with Mother behind Abba's back.

"Leave it to me. He won't find out," Sara reassured him. "We will send him to buy the sheep for the sacrifice, and we will seize that moment to come and see you. Mother will be so happy!"

Dismas had not been able to refuse his beloved sister's proposal, and the meeting took place in the workshop he had at the time, east of the city. It was a neighborhood full of simple and humble merchants, but it did not smell of sheep nor shepherds.

Dismas's vision blurred as soon as he saw her enter. The loss of her beloved son had eaten away years from her and some of her beauty, as well. But there was still sweetness and peace in those black eyes in which Dismas had seen himself reflected countless times.

There were hardly any words. They were not necessary, as mother and son fell into an embrace under Sara's trembling gaze.

"You are too thin. You need to eat more."

"And you look as beautiful as ever," he had answered with his face still resting on his mother's shoulder.

Then everything fell apart in an instant, when they heard Abba's voice behind them.

"I knew it! I knew that sooner or later this would happen."

Dismas let go of his mother and turned to his father with a reconciling smile.

"Hello, Abba."

He didn't even look at him. He approached his mother with such a hard face that it overwhelmed Dismas.

"Choose, Miriam. Choose for the last time: either your son or me." He extended his arm, waiting.

His mother looked at her husband with an expression of infinite pain, and then looked at Dismas, seven knives piercing her heart. Tears ran down her face as her feet slowly crept toward where his father stood.

Dismas took a step towards him, arms outstretched, confident that a reconciliation between father and son was still possible.

"But, Abba," he said, "don't you think it's about time we forget our differences after all these years?"

"Don't come near me, boy. I don't recognize you," his father spat at his face as if he were a stranger.

The words hurt so much that Dismas took a few steps back. He could feel the blood rushing in his veins.

"Don't you realize how stupid this is? Your wife deserves not to have to choose between you and me!" he yelled, standing between him and his mother.

"What parents deserve is obedience and respect from their children," Abba replied, raising his voice. Beside him, Sara tried to hold him back, anticipating the storm.

"And what about what a child needs?" Dismas spilled his words, burning. "Understanding? Support? A little love!" His voice sank into a sea of bitterness, and he couldn't prevent his hands from pushing his father's chest.

"Don't touch me again or I'll kill you!" Fury filled Abba's eyes.

Dismas hit him in the chest again, and his father lunged at him. Sara yelled at them, tried to keep them apart, but they didn't even hear her. It was their desperate mother who put a stop to the terrible shame of seeing father and son come to blows.

"*Enough!* Enough, both of you!" Her powerful scream froze the two men.

During a silence that seemed eternal, Dismas released his father and lowered his face, ashamed.

Miriam covered her head with the cloak that hung from

her shoulders, hiding a look that, if Dismas could have seen it, would have broken his heart.

"Let's go."

The sepulchral echo of her words accompanied her footsteps out the door of Dismas's workshop. Abba followed her averting his son.

Sara was the only one who turned to him, tears in her eyes, but the shame Dismas felt at that moment prevented him from even lifting his face and saying goodbye.

And so he had sworn then that there would not be another "family" reunion. Never. Dismas would not again put his mother in the position of making such a terrible choice.

Yet fate—or YHWH, as Nathaniel insisted—had led his friend's feet to the door of his workshop and had resurrected his family again. The news of his father's death brought him back to a place he never thought he would ever return to.

He was eager to embrace his mother and sister again. And yet he was also scared of the reunion, even though there was nothing that could cloud it anymore.

Nothing except, perhaps, the sudden appearance of Bathsheba in his life. His mother's future had suddenly become a priority, but she was knocking on his heart when it had been taken by another one.

A widow had no means to support herself, and that obligated of him, her only male sibling, to take her under his wings. His plan was to bring her to Jerusalem to live with him, but he knew that dragging her to a new life, uprooting her from the things and the people she'd grown up with, wouldn't be an option for her. She would flatly refuse, and then he would be forced to return home and take care both of her and his sister Sara. He would have to abandon his work as a blacksmith and end up becoming exactly what he had always hated—a smelly shepherd of Galilee.

By dying, Abba had won. His father was ultimately bringing Dismas back to the place he had intended to leave forever. But how was he going to endure leaving Jerusalem behind for good, now that Bathsheba was there?

Irony of ironies! She and her brother Nathaniel were the only ones to blame for this whole situation. If Nathaniel had not entered his workshop that day not so long ago, Dismas would not even have learned of his father's death, there would be no reason to return to Galilee, he could keep on living in Jerusalem. But then, Bathsheba would not have entered his heart, either.

With all that weight on his soul, Dismas heaved a sigh into the evening wind of the third day of travel. At his side, the leader of the caravan, a man with a face modeled in the sands of a thousand deserts, turned towards him and, scrutinizing his gaze, was able to read under the folds of the tunic that wrapped his chest.

"Sometimes life is complicated. But in everything there is a reason," said the stranger in a mysterious way.

Dismas, surprised, did not answer. Both men turned their eyes forward, contemplating the last brushes of a beautiful sunset that painted the face of the Tiberias Sea orange. He had come home, and the crossroads where he found himself were about to rewrite his story. Or not. Everything depended on Mother.

Dismas waited for the dawn of the new day to enter the village. His arrival was less celebrated than he had envisioned. No one he crossed paths with happened to recognize him, and not even the children, always so eager to seek out strangers along the road, crowded around him in circles. He then remembered that it was Yom Revii, market day. The merchants from the surrounding villages gathered in the town of Magdala, by the lake, to sell and exchange food and goods.

Dismas had fond memories of those days where, escaping away from the elders' watch, they climbed as kids onto the clattering wagons that headed for Magdala to enjoy the market day. There the world opened up timidly through the shapes and sounds and tastes of things.

Dismas still remembered the stall of a young carpenter where he always liked to stop by and watch him work. With the craft and skills of his hands, that man was able to carry out tasks as difficult, enormous, and sophisticated as the solid dock extending from the seashore into the water—which the fishermen had demanded a thousand times so they could avoid muddying their feet before climbing into their boats—and as simple as the vibrant and lively figures that he carved from discarded pieces of wood.

"Take it, and give it to your little sister," he said to Dismas one day, bending down before him with his hand extended. Recognizing kindness in the stranger's eyes, Dismas had taken the small carving of a swallow with its wings wide open, defying its stiffness. How had the carpenter known that Dismas had a sister? Sara was too small to accompany him to the market; as a matter of fact, she had only been with him once in Magdala. But even more surprising was that the man seemed to know that he and Sara were angry with each other that day, for he was offering him, with that little statuette, the means to reconcile with her.

As he walked away from the carpenter's stand with the swallow in his hands, Dismas turned around and saw the man ruffling the swirling hair of a boy younger than he was. It had to be his son, because at that very moment the carpenter took the child in his arms and began to kiss him, tickling the boy's face with his beard. That image had stuck in Dismas's memory because he remembered very well what he had thought then: He would have given anything to have that man as a father.

On another occasion, several years later, the Magdala market had also introduced him to other charms of the world, this time in the form of a woman. It had happened on the outskirts of the town, on a farm where he had gone to see some watchdog puppies and negotiate a good price for them. It was his father who had sent him there; he was determined that his son Dismas should follow in his footsteps, but there, in the solitude of that erected stable, everything went south.

The farmer's daughter had come out to greet him, a sweet, beautiful girl with black eyes and a generous smile—too generous, perhaps, to contain what she felt at that moment. The two of them were alone. There was no one else on the entire farm, only the sound of the animals in the stable, the humming of crickets in the bushes, the weight of the heat in the air. It was all very primal—it only took one conversation, three laughs, and two unexpected caresses for the universe to open up and the fire to incinerate all caution between them. In the stable, on an unexpected bed of straw, their two bodies became one with the echo of the horses in their ears and the passion dying as quickly as it had arisen.

Dismas did not return that day with any puppy under his arm, but with a burning ache between his legs, swearing to himself that he would repeat the visit as soon as he had the chance; however, that same night, sitting in the warmth of the hearth next to his mother and sister, he could not help the strange sensation of feeling dirty, very dirty, in front of them.

The little secret he shared with that girl—who in reality offered very little love, some vice, and a lot of unbridled passion—grew bigger and bigger until, overnight, she disappeared. He heard through local gossip that the girl had dishonored herself and her parents, and so they had thrown her out of the house to keep the sin away and prevent it from falling upon them. She didn't even say goodbye to Dismas, but he didn't really care too much either; all he had wanted from her was to quench his passion like horses quench their thirst at the trough.

By then, he had already been stung by one of the fruits of sin—loneliness—and he no longer enjoyed the friendship he used to have with Nathaniel. His friend still had a pure way of looking at the world, and they both began to see life in different tones. Something similar happened with his mother and sister. Even though he had overcome that feeling of dirtiness he felt that first time, something had definitely come between him and the women he cared for. He knew, in short, that the time had come to leave home, go out into that world, of which Magdala had only been a small slice, and live the life he wanted.

Dismas suddenly found himself in front of the door of the house where he'd grown up. He hesitated before knocking, afraid of hearing in response the voice of the one who had forbidden him to ever set foot there again. He had to remind himself that Abba had died, and that was the reason he was there. His hand was already balled into a fist, ready to knock on the door with his knuckles, when it opened. A ghost dressed in black reached out and hugged him tightly.

"My son," she whispered in his ears.

Dismas felt the moist warmth of his mother's cheek against his; she was crying.

He blushed; he had always been ashamed of showing his feelings at home. He didn't quite know why; perhaps it was part of his defenses that had served him well fifteen years ago. He had left then without shedding a tear, despite the heartache of saying goodbye to the woman he loved most in this world. Now, however, he was surprised to notice something crossing his own cheeks, quick and furtive.

Mother and son were suspended in a silent embrace over the threshold of a life that Dismas had never really left behind.

4.

"Mother is sick."

The seriousness with which Sara told him took Dismas by surprise.

"She seems fine, like nothing is wrong with her. But I know there's something she's hiding from us," continued his sister. "The other day I was preparing a bundle of clothes to take to the river, and I noticed the inside of her tunic stained with blood. I asked her about it, and the only answer I got was a good reprimand—Who did I think I was, rummaging through her things when she still had the strength to wash her own clothes without her daughter sniffing around?"

Dismas smiled, imagining the scene.

"Maybe she is not as bad as you think, and it was just a minor wound," he said, trying to convince himself.

Sara shook her head sharply. It was difficult for Dismas to identify the spoiled, ill-mannered girl he had left behind fifteen years earlier with the woman in front of him. Time had not made his sister more beautiful, as it had Bathsheba, because it was difficult to surpass what she had naturally inherited from her mother. Perhaps that was the reason the years had gifted her with the qualities of an exceptionally good wine: presence, body, depth. Woe to the man who got drunk on Sara while she kept sober!

Seeing her now, Dismas understood Sara's friendship with Bathsheba, and how the aromas of one had nourished and enriched the other until they reached perfection, each in their own way. They were both trees planted on a riverbank. Bathsheba was a gentle almond; Sara, a strong olive tree.

Thinking of Bathsheba pushed his heart into an emptiness, and Dismas saw himself standing on a cliff. He looked away toward the window to try to hide the feelings that crowded his heart while his sister continued talking. His fears were crystallizing with each word she spoke; mother could still move around freely, but there were certain symptoms that foreshadowed a slow, perhaps, but inexorable worsening—fatigue, her heavy gait, a sudden forgetfulness of things.

"Mother needs us," Sara concluded, causing a twist of dread in his stomach. He sighed,
closing his eyes to the sunlight that filtered through the window, shutting the doors to the new life he had glimpsed in Bathsheba. His sister's hand on his shoulder brought him back to reality. He turned toward her, silence fluttering over them. Their eyes followed an invisible thread, and she smiled, understanding.

"I'm not asking you to stay here, Dismas. Mother does not need your care. She needs your love. And that of her grandchildren as well."

Dismas blushed. His sister Sara had always known how to read his heart, and that quality did not seem to have diminished despite the years.

"What are you talking about?" He crossed his arms over his chest, pretending not to understand.

"I suppose you will get married someday, right?" she answered in an innocent voice that did not match the sparkle in her eyes. "The caravan that brought you here also brought a letter from Nathaniel. He says you have become one of the best blacksmiths in Jerusalem."

Dismas frowned, biting his lower lip. "And what else has Nathaniel told you? He can't know much more, because we have only just met again in Jerusalem."

"Nathaniel is not the only one who has sent me a letter." Sara's smile made clear to him who her other source of information was. "You forget that she also knows how to write, and I know how to read," she added.

A burst of heat blossomed in Dismas's face. "And what else has Bathsheba told you?" He couldn't help pronouncing her name as if it were a sacred place.

"That look of a slaughtered lamb in your eyes gives you away, dear brother. I would say that the feelings between the two of you are mutual."

Dismas lowered his gaze, confused. Sara reached out and touched her brother's cheek. "You have finally found peace in the Holy City, and Mother and I have no right to take it away from you."

"But how will you survive here without my help?" He shook his head, wrinkling his brow.

"Nathaniel has proposed that I take his late mother's place in the wool business," she replied, her face swelling with pride.

Nathaniel, always Nathaniel, flashed through Dismas's mind.

"From now on, I will earn more than enough to support Mother," Sara continued. "I have been doing the accounting for some time now, and I do it quite well."

Dismas had never doubted his sister's extraordinary intelligence, but above all things, those words were untying the knot that had formed in his soul with the news of his father's death.

"The only thing I ask of you is that, once you return to Jerusalem and decide over the matters of your heart, you don't forget us. We know where you live now, thanks to Nathaniel. But we won't visit if you don't want that to happen."

"Now that Abba is gone, there are no reasons to keep me away from you."

Sara hugged her brother, and Dismas, with that stupid inability to display emotions, could not help feeling his hair bristle like a cat. He felt the weight of his arms on both sides, struggling to respond to her embrace.

"You know," Sara whispered in his ear, "Father missed you very much. He fought hard against himself, trying to reach out to you, but his pride and the shame of forgiveness prevented him from doing it. You two are very much alike."

Dismas was surprised by the revelation. Were they really so similar?

With his arms still hanging at his sides, he felt the blood rushing through his veins, tickling the tips of his fingers. A moment passed that felt like eternity, and he finally managed to hug his sister back.

Sara rested her face on the shoulder of his brother.

"I hope you won't find it so hard to show your affection to Bathsheba".

Dismas stayed a week in his restored home, before returning to Jerusalem. The same caravan that had brought him in was ready to take him back. The day before his departure, he spent some time alone with his mother.

The two of them went together to visit Abba's grave. Since the conversation with his sister, Dismas had been secretly watching his mother, looking for any sign that would confirm Sara's concerns about her health. He noticed nothing unusual, nothing that couldn't be attributed to the inexorable passage of time. Even during the long walk to the cemetery, he didn't appreciate anything extraordinary either. His mother walked slowly, and she had to stop a couple of times to catch her breath and rest. The steep slope up to where the village had decided long ago to bury its dead was a challenge even for young, athletic bodies like his.

It wasn't difficult to figure out which stone his father's body rested under. As they approached it, Dismas saw a small object resting on the grave. It was a small wooden swallow with its wings spread out. He crouched down and picked it up, looking at it with wonder. How long had it been since that carpenter of Nazareth had given this to him? It had lost the color of the freshly carved wood, but it still retained the perfection of its shape, softened by time.

"Your sister put it there on the day of the burial, convinced of your return," her mother said as she sat on an outcrop of a rock. "We've been waiting for you. Your father did too."

Dismas slid the swallow into the pocket of his tunic with a twist of sorrow on his lips. *You were waiting for me too?*

Silence took over as he tried to search within himself for some memory, any hint, that would melt the stone that he felt beating hard inside his chest.

"Abba loved you very much. The day you told him you were leaving, that you didn't want to be a shepherd like him, that day you destroyed him deep inside."

"No, Mother." Dismas turned to her sharply. "It was he who did it. He destroyed me and you and the rest of us. Or are you forgetting our meeting in Jerusalem?"

"Your father was not good at expressing what was in his heart."

Dismas, confused, remained silent. Wasn't that what his sister had told him about himself, in different words? Expressing feelings, knowing how to say what his heart felt… Damn it! Damned be all! What if he didn't feel anything inside his heart, like his father? Wasn't that the ultimate test every man had to face in life—allowing his heart to shape him and guide him? If that was so, his father had failed miserably. Because if his father had loved his son so much—that's what his mother was saying!—he had failed completely in showing any trace of it. Ever! Except, except…

"I want you to know that, before he died, your father made me promise to tell you to keep the memory of that night."

Dismas's stomach churned bitterly, as if he'd been just punched.

"He told me," his mother continued, "that if he had learned to live every day of his life under the same light that he saw that night in that child wrapped in swaddling clothes, everything would have been different."

Bitterness tightened Dismas's throat and rose over his head, forcing his eyes to spill tears that burned. He remembered well that night, when everything had been different, the only warm memory of an Abba who had not known how to be a good father.

He felt his heart beating now in his chest and, despite not fully understanding his father's reasons, Dismas leaned towards his mother and kissed her on the forehead.

"Thank you very much, mother."

They stood silent for a few moments in front of the grave. Then she got up, and they began to retrace their path down the slope, back to the living.

If Dismas had looked back at that moment at the place where his mother had been sitting, he would have seen a small red stain. Blood. It was still fresh.

When they got back to the village, Sara was waiting for them by the front door. Dismas walked towards her, dodging several sheep that were crossing the road, shepherded by the barking of a dog.

"Here," he said, reaching into his pocket and handing the carved swallow to his sister. "The bird flew back home, just as you asked the heavens it would."

Sara smiled.

"Do you remember it?" she asked, stroking the fine edges of the swallow with the tip of her fingers.

"Of course I do. I didn't know you kept it as a treasure."

"And how could I not?" She smiled. "It is the only gift you've ever given me."

Dismas burst out laughing.

"I think it's better for you to have it from now on," Sara said, holding it out to him again. "It will be a reminder of reconciliation, and that you have to return home at least once a year."

He took the swallow back. "I promise," he said as he brought the wooden figure to his lips and kissed it solemnly.

"Now then," she warned him with her hand raised, "when you come home, it will be better you do it with Bathsheba and two children on each arm."

"Do you think she will want to?" he asked with a gleam in his eye, afraid of hearing a negative answer.

"What—getting married or have four children?"

They both laughed heartily under the watchful eye of their mother. Far from interrupting her two siblings, she preferred to keep that moment in her heart.

5.

"Nathaniel, do you think I should try?"

The question hung in the air for a long time, waiting for an answer that never came. It was useless to expect so, as Dismas had uttered it in the darkness of his empty workshop just before closing the doors behind him.

He was going to see his friend, hoping to dispel the many doubts that had tormented him since his return from Galilee. He'd been back two days and spent the two nights since in turmoil, hardly sleeping.

His sister Sara had made it clear to him that Bathsheba had feelings for him. But now he was not so sure.

How could he declare his love to her when he was not certain how she would respond? What was he thinking? Was he out of his mind? Bathsheba had not moved to Jerusalem to find a husband, but to live with her widowed aunt. What right did he have to snatch her away from that old woman now that she had become accustomed to the help and the company of her niece?

Absorbed in these agitated thoughts, Dismas turned the corner of the street and nearly walked straight into the horns of an ox pulling a cart full of saddlebags.

"Hey, you! Watch your step!" yelled the man that was guiding the ox. "You almost scared Jericho and ruined all the merchandise, you fool!"

Dismas was so absorbed in his thoughts that he went on without even hearing the curses. His thoughts continued to churn inside him. How could he love a woman he'd only seen on a couple of occasions? Hadn't he let himself be carried away by a vain illusion?

He halted. No, that was not possible—Bathsheba was no illusion. He had gotten to know other women, had lain with many before. But none of them had been able to clean all the filth that his heart had accumulated since the distant days in that stable in Magdala. No, it hadn't been an illusion that he felt clean in the light of Bathsheba's penetrating gaze.

Dismas shook his head like a dog shaking off fleas. All of this was very difficult to understand! Was he going crazy?

Some laughter brought him back to reality. A few children playing by the fountain had seen him standing there in the middle of the street, talking to himself, and they were making fun of him.

Yes, crazy. He was going crazy.

Dismas quickened his pace again, blending in with the crowd that finally led him to Nathaniel's warehouses. His friend had to get him out of this state of anxiety. He held the answer to this mess.

"No one knows."

Dismas blinked, discouraged.

"No, no one really knows," Nathaniel repeated, stroking the beard on his chin.

Perplexed, Dismas looked away from his friend. Was that it? Had he crossed half the city just to hear that? Was this the only wisdom his friend had to offer?

"Is that all you have to say? I empty my soul to you, and that's all you're going to tell me?" he exclaimed, disappointment written all over his face.

Nathaniel couldn't help but laugh when he saw his friend's countenance; it looked like that of a cow listening to an argument between two farmers.

"No one knows," he said one more time. "You ask me to tell you about Bathsheba's feelings, and that's the only thing I can tell you. Nobody knows. Is anyone capable of deciphering a woman's thoughts?"

"But she is your sister, Nathaniel!"

"That's doesn't make it any easier for me."

Dismas sighed in disbelief.

"All I can tell you is that my aunt Rebecca won't mind giving up Bathsheba, if it comes to that." Nathaniel let a smile slip; he was amused to see his friend suffer. "Ever since Bathsheba arrived, my aunt has constantly been telling her that getting married is the best way to fulfill the plans of the Most High. And besides, if my sister should accept your proposal, we have enough money to find a good woman to take care of our aunt."

Dismas looked up, somewhat relieved. At least he had managed to clear up the mystery of who would look after the widowed aunt, if necessary. But the harder question still remained unanswered.

Nathaniel grabbed his friend by the shoulder and pulled him towards him. "All I can tell you is that it will be a real honor to have you as a brother-in-law, if that is what my sister wants."

"So what then? What do you suggest? Do I have to jump into the unknown, declare myself, and see what happens?" he asked with a shaky whisper.

"Don't make it sound so bad. Calm down! Sara is convinced that it will be a yes, right?" Nathaniel winked at him. "Has she ever been wrong?"

Dismas sighed. His sister had better be right this time.

When he arrived, Bathsheba was about to leave her aunt's house, holding a jar in her arms.

"Nathaniel is not here," she said with a slight smile as a greeting.

"No, um— No—" Dismas cleared his throat trying to hide his stuttering. "I'm not here to see your brother."

Bathsheba nodded as if she knew already why he had come. "You can accompany me to fetch water from the fountain, if you wish," she said. "We'll talk on the way."

That wasn't how he'd imagined it, but Dismas agreed to go along. It was the first time he had seen her since his return to Jerusalem, and he had forgotten the intoxicating effect of that black hair gathered around her eyes bathed in honey, of those lips that kept whispering eternal love to him. Her beauty left him speechless, and that made the whole situation even worse.

They walked for a while in silence. Dismas didn't know how to start. He noticed that someone was following them, sneaking between their feet. He looked down, annoyed, and saw a dog playing with Bathsheba's skirts.

"Get out of here. Go away," he said, chasing the animal off with a kick.

"Leave him alone, poor thing. He just wants a little petting, doesn't he?" Bathsheba said as she bent down to stroke it.

"I didn't know you had a dog." Dismas secretly cursed the kick he'd tried to give the mutt.

"It's not mine, but I seem to attract them all. I had one called—"

"Sinta, I know," he said quickly, trying to make up for his earlier blunder.

"I'm surprised you even remember her name."

"Oh, really?" He swallowed; he was lucky she didn't ask him why he remembered.

"You never paid much attention to us." She stopped petting the dog and stood up, frowning.

"To be honest, I don't like dogs very much. They're too dependent."

"Then you should have one. They expand the heart and soul," she said, resuming her pace, with the jar held firmly against her hip.

Dismas glanced at her, confused. What had she meant by that?

"Give it to me, I'll carry it," he said, stretching his hands towards the jar.

"Why? Don't you think I'm strong enough to carry it myself?" she asked, quickly moving forward with a firm step.

Dismas stood behind, stunned. It was not a good start for the kind of conversation he wanted to have with her. After a few moments of indecision, he caught up with her again.

They were approaching the fountain, and Dismas knew that either he needed to start talking or they would soon find themselves trapped between the hubbub of the children playing in the water and the loose gossiping of the nosey water carriers.

He tried to concentrate, clenching his right fist on the handle of an imaginary hammer with which he was striking the glowing hot iron of his words. He had to choose them with precision, so he wouldn't distort the clarity of the message. But Bathsheba spoke first.

"I wanted to apologize for that day," she started, turning to him without a hint of resentment about his kick to the mutt or his move towards the jar.

"That day?" Dismas asked, bewildered, dropping the imaginary hammer from his hand.

"I shouldn't have interrupted your conversation with that man when I walked into your workshop."

It took Dismas a few seconds to realize what she was talking about.

"Oh! You don't have to apologize! I liked what you said and how you said it. You seemed very confident."

"I just can't stand the revolutionary ideas that some people proclaim about the coming of the Messiah. They take advantage of the Roman occupation of Judea to spread lies. All empires eventually fall, and Rome will too, without the need of a savior to make it happen. No, the Messiah will be something entirely different."

Dismas looked at her with wonder. Bathsheba was a woman with her own ideas, and that made him feel comfortable in her presence.

"The truth is," he said, "I don't know much about the Messiah. But I can tell you something that you might like. Something that happened to my father. One night, long ago, while he was out keeping watch over the flock, he saw an apparition of angels." Dismas glanced and thought he saw a shadow of disbelief cross her face. He cleared his throat, looking for a way to trivialize the story he had just begun. "Yes, I know it's hard to believe, and I don't know if—"

"No, go on!" she interrupted, hugging the jar tightly in her arms. "I'm all ears."

Dismas, more confident now, continued the story, abandoning himself to his memories of that night. He told her everything his father had said about heavenly creatures singing hallelujahs and announcing the birth of the Messiah, and how he and the other shepherds had gone to where the angels had told them and found a young couple with a newborn child in a manger.

He glanced at her again out of the corner of his eye to make sure that Bathsheba still was not put off by his story, and he noted with satisfaction that she was completely wrapped up in his words.

"Sara and I were very young, but I remember perfectly my father's face that day when he came into the house. He was radiant. He seemed like a different person." Dismas gazed for a moment into the empty space in front of him. "He bent down, took me by the shoulders, and said something very strange to me."

He stopped as he brought that moment back, with Bathsheba staring at him, expectant.

"He told me that I would see His power," Dismas finished, feeling again the same astonishment that he'd felt that night, looking into his father's eyes. He turned to Bathsheba.

"Blessed be your whole family, Dismas! Rumors are everywhere that the Messiah has already been born, and your father *saw* him! Sara has never told me any of this!"

Like a dog wagging his tail, Dismas noted the excitement that his unexpected story had raised on Bathsheba's face.

"This cannot be a coincidence. It has to be providential!" Bathsheba opened those eyes that could hold a million different sunsets. "Dismas, I would like to ask you something."

Dismas looked at her expectantly.

"I would like you to accompany me somewhere," she added, mysteriously.

He tightened his jaw, suspicious. "The synagogue again?"

She laughed at his idea. "No, I know you don't often attend. Nathaniel already told me you're not very fond of Pharisees and priests."

And how does Nathaniel know that? a voice inside him protested. His old friend was more perceptive than he seemed.

"I want you to come with me to the Jordan. A small caravan leaves for there the day after tomorrow. It is only a day's journey."

Dismas slowed his pace, confused by this invitation. "Getting to the Jordan from the Holy City is not an easy trip. It will take us more than a day to go and come back. What do you want to see there? Isn't the water from this fountain good enough?"

"A holy man," whispered Bathsheba, with wide eyes and a captivating smile that made him feel prisoner.

"Look, Bathsheba." He didn't know how to tell her without hurting her, but he wasn't willing to deceive her, either. "I am not a religious man."

"I know," she said quickly, undeterred. "That's why I want you to come. You don't expect me to marry you without YHWH first blessing you with His Presence."

Dismas was stunned by her straightforwardness. Bathsheba sure did not mince her words. At that very moment, another much deeper voice interrupted them.

"Hey, you two! Stay out of the way!"

Dismas shot his eyes toward the irritating man pushing by, but he was knocked to the ground before he knew what was happening. He opened his eyes to the dust of footsteps near his face, filling his lungs.

A patrol of Romans continued to force their way through the crowd, pushing aside women and children with equal brutality. Through the cloud of dust and the soldiers' legs, on the other side of the chaos he spotted Bathsheba's purple veil on the ground and several people crowding around it in stupor. A burst of anger washed over him, and he felt the urge to rush to her, to defend her, but he was halted by the tip of a spear just inches away from his face. He clenched his fists in rage and felt his fingernails digging into the ground.

"Don't move until we've passed, you Jewish dog," a Roman standing over him shouted with the arrogance of a man holding a weapon.

Dismas suddenly burst up and threw a handful of sand in the soldier's face; he lunged for the spear of the Roman and snatched it out of his hands. With a fierce look in his eyes, he turned the point of the weapon towards the startled soldier, aiming it straight over his heart. Behind him, a panicked scream surfaced, putting his world into a stop.

"*Dismas, no!* Please don't!"

Bathsheba.

Dismas sighed, relieved. No harm had come to her. He saw her standing on the other side, crossing the ranks of soldiers, running toward him, trying to prevent the worst.

His eyes turned from the pleading on Bathsheba's face to the terror on the soldier's. Blood boiled in his cheeks, his knuckles white from the pressure of his fist on the shaft of the spear. He dropped the weapon, and a brutal punch sent him to the ground again.

"Get down, you dog! That's your place, right there in the mud!" yelled the soldier who had knocked him down as he picked up the spear and handed it back to its owner. "And you—you better learn to hold that spear tighter. With soldiers like you, our empire won't last long."

The soldier, still livid from how close he had come to being impaled like a rabbit, picked up his weapon with trembling hands. His superior turned back to Dismas, who still lay on the ground gathering himself, after the punch to the cheek he'd received.

"You are fast and furious, but do not use your qualities against the wrong side again. Next time she will not be there to save you," he said, nodding towards Bathsheba, who had just reached him and was bending down to his side.

Dismas watched as the two Romans backtracked to the

ranks of their platoon amid the turmoil of the crowds. For an instant he thought he spotted Melchiades among those in the multitude, looking at him with a mix of bewilderment and satisfaction. But then he vanished.

Bathsheba took Dismas's face in her hands, examining whether anything was broken while he licked the trickle of blood that flowed from the corner of his mouth. Everything seemed fine except for that look of a wounded lion on his face; it sent a shiver down her spine. At that very instant she had a strong sense—no, she *knew*—that if he were backed into a corner, Dismas could become a wild and dangerous man. She fondled his face, hoping that the warmth of her touch would melt the ice in those beautiful eyes.

"Maybe it wouldn't be such a bad idea if the Messiah freed us from those sons of bitches," he snorted, clearing his throat before spitting dark blood in the dust.

"So you'll come with me tomorrow?"

The chill she'd felt in her spine had made her aware that it was more important than ever that he went with her to the banks of the Jordan.

"Not even a patrol of Romans can stop you when an idea gets stuck in your head." Dismas winced, half smiling.

"Your sister always says I'm very stubborn," she nodded.

"Do you think I'll be better by tomorrow?" Dismas brought his hand to his sore cheek, still burning.

She contemplated his face for a moment, as if it were a work of art.

"It's difficult for you to become any better." She leaned and he felt the soft touch of her lips on his temple.

Dismas closed his eyes, powerless, happy. Maybe that punch on his jaw had been worth it. Even if it came from a Roman bastard.

6.

So there he was with a split lip, chilled to his bones, and the dawn of a new day upon him, on his way to the Jordan River—though he still was not sure why.

They were traveling in a caravan comprised of four ox-drawn wagons and six men on horseback who brought up the rear. He was among those who had chosen to go by horse; thus it would allow him to travel freely, without the burden of having to talk to anyone. Bathsheba, on the other hand, was travelling in one of the wagons, accompanied by other women who didn't stop talking throughout the whole journey.

He had counted thirty-nine people in the whole group, mostly women accompanied by men who seemed to have been dragged—like him—against their will. Yet, he could see on their faces that—unlike him—these men tried to be accommodating and helpful to everyone else.

Being dragged by a woman was the only thing they had in common. To begin with, he was the youngest of them all and the only one unattached, at least for the moment.... Furthermore, they were all deeply involved with this pilgrimage and hadn't stopped singing religious songs, taken from the psalms of Scripture, throughout the journey. He could barely remember a few scattered verses from his childhood at first, but as the sands of the desert kept rolling under their feet, he got to know them all by heart. With a hundred and fifty psalms to choose from, were there really only five that they knew how to sing? The same ones, over and over again, each psalm about the same obsession with the imminent arrival of Someone who was going to free them all.

They had not stopped talking about it throughout the journey. No matter which wagon he approached, the word *Messiah* kept jumping out like a grasshopper, so Dismas was convinced that that's who they were going to meet on the banks of the Jordan.

He had decided not to exchange too many words with anyone, despite the efforts of the other men on horseback to prompt conversations. That was another of the group's peculiarities that Dismas didn't share either—their excessive displays of friendliness. They barely knew each other and there was little chance of meeting again in the future, so what reason was there to be friendly? And yet, everyone worked hard to do the talking and offer the biggest smile. Exhausting. For Dismas, there was only one person he wanted to talk to, and so far, that had been impossible.

He had approached the wagon she was traveling in several times. On the first, Bathsheba was talking so animatedly with her fellow travelers that when she saw him approaching on horseback, she simply raised her head, greeted him with a smile, and plunged back into the five hectic conversations that were going on simultaneously. The second time there was not even a nod from her, but it was clear to Dismas that the topic of conversation in the wagon was him, after two girls traveling in the back spotted him, exchanged glances, and, after a quick whisper, burst out laughing.

Dismas blushed and promised himself to keep his distance. Why had Bathsheba invited him to come with her if she wasn't going to pay him the slightest attention? Irritated with himself, he decided that when they stopped to eat, he would seek an opportunity to be alone with her in a secluded place.

The caravan halted when the sun reached its highest. The people jumped out to gather around one of the wagons from which the food rations were being distributed. From either side, two women handed out small packages wrapped in cloth. Dismas couldn't help being impressed with the organization of it all.

He looked around for Bathsheba. She seemed to have forgotten him completely, and he mingled with the crowd that was gathering around the cart until he stepped up beside her. She noticed his presence and turned to look at him as if he were a stranger. Disheartened by that look, Dismas thought something was wrong. More determined than ever, he walked over to one of the women who was handing out the food and asked for two portions. Then he turned to Bathsheba and gently led her out of the crowd.

"Shall we eat?" he asked with a dubious smile.

He looked for a sheltered spot and found the slope of a rocky hillside that protected them well from both the sun and the indiscreet curiosity of his fellow travelers.

They sat down in silence, and Dismas unfolded the cloth that wrapped the provisions with the same delicacy with which his mind was trying to choose the right words. Women were a difficult world to explore, and after the unexpected closeness they'd shared—his temple still felt warm when remembering the kiss—he was determined to proceed with extreme caution, taking nothing for granted.

Inside each cloth were five dates, three walnuts, and two slices of dried fish. They provided a good subject to begin the conversation.

"Would you like my dates? I don't like them," Dismas lied, aware that few things were more irresistible than that fruit at the hottest time of the day.

"I would!" two voices answered in unison behind him.

Who the hell—?! Dismas thought, turning around, as his eyes pierced the figures of the two insolent young women who had been gossiping in the back of the wagon.

"Well, only if you're not going to want them, Bathsheba!" one of them added, completely ignoring the murderous look Dismas had just shot them.

"Take them," Bathsheba said. "I have more than enough of my own."

The women didn't even wait for Dismas to give them permission to pounce on his fruit. If that made them skitter away like monkeys, then they were more than welcome to the dates, Dismas thought as he forced his lips into a smile. He waited for them to leave, but as they were about to walk away, Bathsheba's voice stopped them.

"You can stay with us if you want. It's nice here in the shade, and there's space for all four of us."

The girls exchanged glances, nodded, and the flames of anger ignited poor Dismas's insides—he had lost his dates *and* his chance to be alone with Bathsheba.

That was his last attempt to seek her company. Throughout the rest of the trip, back on horseback, there was only one question that remained stuck in Dismas's mind: What the hell was he doing in a pilgrimage of people who only wanted to talk, sing, and wait for a sign from YHWH on the banks of the Jordan?

He had been wrong about Bathsheba, he was now convinced. She had no interest in him.

By the time dusk settled, as they finally reached a small village close to the river, Dismas had made a firm decision.

He would leave the next day at dawn and head back to Jerusalem. This trip he had agreed to made no sense. Bathsheba had asked him to come and, in doing so, had given him hope for a future that he had begun to take for granted; the trip was just a small price to pay for being with her for the rest of his life. But things had worked out differently. Something had changed for Bathsheba to make her avoid him so blatantly all day. It was as if nothing had ever happened between them, or even worse, that she regretted what had happened.

But what had *really* happened between them? Nothing, Dismas answered himself, frowning. Just the Roman's punch and that brief kiss on his temple. He put his hand to his forehead, trying to rub the warm memory off his skin.

The small village where they stopped consisted of five houses that served as lodging for pilgrims traveling to Jerusalem during the Passover feast. The city, though holy, lacked the ability to expand its size to accommodate the thousands of pilgrims who came to offer sacrifices at the temple every year, and there were plenty of people who didn't mind staying farther away if they could do it for a more reasonable price.

The women in the caravan occupied the houses, and the men settled into a stable large enough to accommodate them and to water the animals. After finding a place to lay down, Dismas spoke to one of the men who'd been riding with the group, from whom he'd borrowed the horse. He told him that if it was not too inconvenient, he would leave at dawn back to Jerusalem on the horse. He promised to take care of it and return it as soon as the rest of the group were in the Holy City.

"What? You're not going to meet him?" the man frowned, trying to understand Dismas's odd behavior.

Dismas shook his head.

"Have you told Bathsheba?" he now shot him an inquisitive look.

"Yes, she already knows," Dismas lied. He had no intention of telling her. Would she miss him just now, when she was about to meet whoever they had come to see by the Jordan?

The man nodded and cocked his head to one side, wondering to himself.

Dismas's answer must not have convinced the guy because, a little later, when they had settled in and dinner was warming up in the fire in front of the stable, Bathsheba sneaked in and looked for him. She found him standing next to his horse, brushing it, while he mumbled a conversation with himself in which she thought she heard her name.

Dismas looked over the horse's rump at the person approaching him, not recognizing her; Bathsheba had wrapped herself in a cloak so that no one would notice a woman sneaking into the men's barn.

He jumped when he heard her voice.

"What are you doing here?" was the only thing he could come up with.

Bathsheba motioned for him to leave before anyone recognized her and a small scandal erupted over a silly thing. They stepped out the side of the stable. In the distance, not far away, they could hear the gentle sound of the Jordan flowing.

Bathsheba emerged from the cloak that hid her, and her face shone with fragments from firelight that was burning on the other side of the stable. Dismas could see in her eyes the shadow of the same doubt that he'd glimpsed during the day. A thick silence hovered between them, like a small cloud, before she finally decided to speak.

"Please, Dismas, don't go. It's my fault, and I apologize.

You see," she hesitated before continuing, "the other day I was not good to you."

Dismas was surprised. *The other day?* What had hurt him deep inside had not happened the other day.

"The other day?" He shook his head with a grimace. "Bathsheba, I don't understand you. It's *today* that you ignored me completely—today when I sought your company and you scorned it—today when I wanted to talk to you and found you uninterested. And yet you speak of what happened the other day?" He shook his head again, not understanding.

"Please let me finish." Bathsheba's voice sounded like a plea in his ears, and Dismas fell silent.

"I was playing with an advantage. The caravan with which you returned from Galilee also brought a letter for me, from your sister Sara. She told me." She lowered her gaze, nervously toying with the seams of the cloak in her fingers. "She told me that you liked me. And I like you, Dismas. I've liked you since the day I stuck out my tongue at you and you pulled my braids because I wouldn't give you a piece of my bread."

Dismas tried to remember that distant moment, but there wasn't the slightest trace in his memory. It was hard to admit it now, but he had never seen his sister's friend as a woman until barely a month ago.

"What you mean is that you regret your kiss, then," he said, intending to help her free her conscience.

"How can I regret that?" The glow of her gaze confused Dismas, who was now more lost than ever. "That was the most innocent thing I could offer you as a pledge. But I made a mistake, a terrible mistake for which I don't deserve to look you in the eyes, and it's the reason I've tried today, with all my strength, to correct it. Before that Roman soldier punched you—"

"Before your kiss here," Dismas corrected her, pointing with his finger to the exact spot on his temple.

"Yes, before that," she admitted, lowering her gaze again. "I said some terrible words."

Dismas searched his memory for what terrible words she could mean, but he found nothing. With his spirit frightened, exhausted from so many unknowns, he searched for Bathsheba's hands, chilly and clutched, and gently extended her fingers, as if encouraging her to continue.

"I told you that I would not marry you if YHWH did not bless you with His Presence first." She looked up at him, expectant.

Dismas remembered those words; he had spent the previous night rolling them over in his mind, polishing them excitedly because they had opened wide the doors of Bathsheba's heart to him. But now a small black hole was growing larger and larger, swallowing up those hopes.

"Bathsheba, you don't have to marry me if you don't want to. Don't worry about it."

"But I *do* want to marry you," Bathsheba protested, with her eyes wide open. "But the other day I set conditions on you; and that condition is what has dragged you here today. And that… that is not fair. I— I don't have a right to demand anything from you. That is why I have been cold and distant with you today. Do you understand?"

Dismas would have liked to nod, but he was more lost than if a sandstorm had suddenly fallen upon him in the midst of the desert.

"I have been praying all day that tomorrow YHWH bless you, that you feel the immensity of His love. But that will not be the condition for me to love you. If the Almighty loves me unconditionally—I, who do not deserve to be loved by Him—then how can I put conditions on you for my love?

Whatever may happen tomorrow, I want it to happen for its own sake, and not because you want to marry me. You are free—I release you from the stupid promise, and you can leave if you want now, go back to Jerusalem." Bathsheba swallowed, firm in her decision. "I... I will understand."

She let go of his hands and turned so as not to see his face. Silence fell upon them, but the cloud had completely dissipated.

"And so," Dismas started with a weak voice, "if I decide to stay and tomorrow, as you say, YHWH blesses me, lets Himself be known to me, you will marry me. But if I stay and YHWH does not bless me, you will marry me as well. However, if I decide to leave tonight, you will still marry me. All roads lead me to you."

Dismas put his hands on her shoulders, inviting her to look at him again.

"But what do you gain from it?"

"That you choose me and love me with complete freedom," she whispered, turning to him with a trembling smile.

Dismas embraced her, pulling her against his chest. The contact of her body against his own made him shudder, but unlike the other women he had embraced in his life, that shudder did not arise from the flesh—although there was some of that as well. The origin of this tremor came from much deeper within.

"And a dog too," she added, pulling away from him, holding back a smile on her lips.

"A dog?"

"If we get married, I'll give you a dog. And it will be mine too." She revealed her teeth, happy.

That night, although Dismas did not fully understand Bathsheba's arguments, he did understand, however, that inside that woman was the strongest and most delicate soul he had ever known. And for that treasure, for that treasure alone, it was worth giving up the whole world.

And having a dog.

The shudder Dismas experienced lasted all night, as he felt wrapped in an explosive and infinite happiness. When he finally opened his eyes to a new dawn, he felt so lucky that surely nothing that could happen that day to make it any better. That's what he thought then.

The previous night, at dinner, while the cauldron on the fire managed to fill the hungry stomachs of all the pilgrims, Bathsheba had told him what was going to happen the following day. After the conversation by the stable, she had no qualms about sitting next to Dismas in front of the warming fire, neither of them unaware that, in addition to the succulent soup, they too were the talk of the group. She didn't seem to care at all, as she explained to him who they were going to see and why he was so important.

It was now clear to Dismas that the reason for the pilgrimage to the banks of the Jordan was not to meet the Messiah. That person had not yet revealed himself. But someone who lived in the desert and fed only on honey and locusts had appeared instead. Bathsheba had learned about him through Philip, a friend of her brother Nathaniel. He was one of his disciples, and he'd been organizing nighttime gatherings in Jerusalem to spread his message. Dismas guessed that this must be where Bathsheba had been that evening when he'd gone to say goodbye before leaving for Galilee.

The name of this mysterious individual was John. He preached every day on the banks of the Jordan, inviting people to convert their hearts and baptizing anyone who wished in preparation for the one who was to come.

"Don't you realize—he's a prophet!" Bathsheba had

exclaimed with a restrained emotion that almost made her spill the bowl of soup she was holding in her hands.

Dismas, aware that his dull spirit made him unable to share Bathsheba's emotion, tried to pay as much attention as possible.

"Oh, Dismas, how can you not see it!" she asked, when she realized her words did not set him on fire. "Do you know how long it has been since YHWH sent a prophet to the Jewish people, to *our* people? More than four hundred years! Do you know what this means?"

No, Dismas did not know, but what he did was that after that night, there was no prophet on the face of the earth who could make him happier.

He was wrong.

7.

A frugal breakfast of nuts and raisins mixed in a bowl of milk began the day for the group, which, in Dismas's opinion, had gotten up too early to go see the prophet.

"Hurry up or we won't find any place to watch from," a man next to him had said as he threw his used bowl into one of the buckets that had been set out for them. "Many people come from all over to listen to the prophet John."

Dismas could not help but roll his eyes skeptically.

They set off on foot for the final stretch to the banks of the Jordan. They only had to walk a mile upstream to the place where John, who was also called "the Baptist," preached to his followers and other onlookers every day before baptizing many of them.

The men walked in the front, followed by the group of women, and they began to sing a psalm that Dismas did not remember ever having heard. It was a beautiful melody accompanied by strange and mysterious words about a mistreated man:

"They gave me poison for food,
and for my thirst they gave me vinegar to drink."

The man speaking from the psalm insisted on imploring justice and protection from God and did not hesitate to praise him, at which point the women broke the song's melancholic privation with a chorus full of strength and hope:

"I will praise the name of God with a song;
I will magnify him with thanksgiving."

Dismas recognized Bathsheba's voice among them, as the chorus ascended to its apotheosis:

"I will magnify him with thanksgiving."

Men rejoined the women in that line, and there, in the stillness of dawn, surrounded by silence, all of creation seemed to break out in praise of its Maker. Dismas, who had never been keen on music or songs, was surprised by a slight tingling in his shoulders.

They soon reached the water, which, at that time of the morning when the sun had not yet risen, painted in blue and gray the mist that rose over its bed like a dream. It was a stretch of the river where its banks widened into enormous stones on both sides, creating natural balconies over the Jordan. These stones became silent watchers on a landscape that forced the river to subdue its strength, taming the water into ponds of different sizes. It was a pleasant meeting point between both banks.

This morning there were other watchers as well, and they were not silent. A swarm of gray figures gathered around the river, expectant. The sun's first rays began to dissipate the mist and the anonymity it lent. Dismas was surprised to see a large number of women with children of all ages among the pilgrims. He was good at calculating crowds, and he estimated more than five hundred people were waiting for the appearance of the prophet John. With no village or sizable town nearby, where did so many people come from? They all had their eyes fixed on the center of the river, a thousand shimmering mirrors of heaven waiting for its star to come.

Dismas and the others managed to find room along the riverbank, although the men had to put their feet in the water to allow space for the women behind them. Bathsheba sought him out among the group and stepped onto a rock behind him. She put her hands over his shoulders to balance herself and not lose sight of whatever might be happening on that river. Dismas felt the warmth under her palms.

Bathsheba opened her mouth and resumed the song they had been singing during the descent to the river. Other voices timidly joined in. Little by little they grew louder, and the song finally acquired a definitive body, becoming a pleasant smoke of praise that rose up into the blue morning sky.

Dismas lowered his head and walked his eyes among everyone present, who had magically become one by joining their voices together.

The song broke up into hundreds of voices when a group of seven people appeared at the ford of the river. A murmur spread, and Bathsheba leaned over Dismas's shoulder to tell him that they were John's disciples. Stretching out her arm, she waved to one of them.

"Philip! Philip!" she cried out.

A man raised his head and approached with a smile.

"Bathsheba, it's wonderful to see you! Where is Nathaniel? I don't see him around."

Dismas was taken by the whiteness of Philip's eyes and teeth; they were as pure and clean as Bathsheba's. Suddenly abashed by their presence, Dismas had to look away from them as Bathsheba replied that her brother had not been able to come because work had forced him to return to Galilee. To his left, he peaked at the two gossipers from the previous day, still whispering, not losing sight of him.

"I'd like you to meet Dismas, who is also a friend of Nathaniel." Bathsheba turned towards Dismas, and Philip looked at him as if they had known each other all their lives. He couldn't help feeling strangely welcomed.

"It's good that you could come. Today may be an important day; he hasn't told us anything, but I think he already knows."

Bathsheba grabbed Philip's arm tightly, her eyes wide as burning suns. "We've been praying the entire journey for this! Maybe the Messiah is among us right now."

Dismas looked around and couldn't help smiling to himself at Bathsheba's naivety. He didn't know what the Messiah would look like nor what his intentions would be when he presented himself to the world, but if it were him, he'd be very careful to avoid the company of the people who were gathered here today on the Jordan. Too much glory for this humble and simple herd, men and women bound to earth who did not know to look beyond the clouds over their heads.

A splash behind Philip made them turn their heads. The footsteps of a boy running toward them stirred up the shallowed waters of the river.

"Philip!" he shouted, pointing to the top of one of the banks. "Herod's soldiers are here."

There on the hill that rose above the right bank of the Jordan, the light of dawn outlined the silhouette of eight men on horseback, looking down over them.

"Is there any danger?" Dismas stepped forward, ready to fight if necessary.

"From Herod?" Philip rolled his eyes with a smile. "The

tetrarch is a puppet in the hands of Rome, but people say he takes delight in John's words. That's why he sends his men when he can't come himself, so that they can tell him in detail everything that comes out of his mouth."

"Really?" Bathsheba asked.

"And you wouldn't believe how the Baptist gives it to that bastard when he preaches," Philip bantered in delight.

"Philip, should I tell them something?" The boy who had approached them stood ready for instructions.

Dismas observed him carefully. He was so young that for a moment he'd thought he could be Philip's son. But he dismissed the idea upon closer inspection. He had to be around fourteen, and his manly features had begun to emerge timidly on his smooth and beardless face.

"I'm coming, John," Philip answered. "Tell them that if they want to come closer, they'll have to leave their weapons next to their horses up at the rock."

The young lad nodded and started to set off towards the hill again.

"John? Is he the prophet?" Dismas asked in disbelief. Surely they hadn't made such a long journey to hear him speak!

Philip couldn't suppress a laugh. "Oh, no! His name is John. He's the benjamin of the family. But despite his age, he shows a lot of promise!"

John turned his head as he kept rushing up the hill to meet Herod's soldiers. "Hey, I'm no child! I'm about to be fifteen."

Dismas, Philip, and Bathsheba smiled.

"Well, I have to leave you now. Bathsheba, when John *the Prophet*"—Philip stressed the last word to avoid further confusion—"is ready to baptize, look for me and I'll get you in, if you want, without a problem. Keep in mind that with so many people gathered here today, a few of them will surely be left without being able to be baptized."

Just as Philip walked away, a strange figure drew their attention. He was in the middle of the river, standing upon one of the stones that sorted out its course. Silence took hold of everyone present, and the pleasant burbling of water strolling happily down the river was the only sound.

Dismas looked at him and frowned. That man didn't have the looks he would expect from a prophet. He was too young—though not as youthful as the other John he'd just met—but still not old enough, not serious enough, not imposing enough to be someone whose ears were close to YHWH's lips.

He had imagined a wise man with long beard, a pleated tunic, and hair turned gray by the heaviness and the splendor of God's words. Instead, he found himself before someone close to his own age who shone fire from his eye sockets, a kneaded flesh of veins and muscles, hair chiseled from clay and disheveled into a dark sun pointing in a thousand directions. His attire made his appearance even look wilder—he wore a simple garment of camel's hair that covered neither his legs nor his arms. Could the Voice of God penetrate the ears of someone so outlandish and bizarre?

John raised his face to the sky and, after a few moments of expectation, returned his gaze to earth, fixing it here, there, on each of the clusters of pilgrims who had come to listen to him. When he turned to where Dismas stood, he felt the look of the prophet falling upon him, interpellating him. It was only for an instant, but it felt like eternity. Dismas couldn't suppress a blush from rising to his cheeks, and he had to look away, embarrassed at having been the object of so much attention in the midst of the crowd. But no one seemed to have noticed.

"I see a lot of people waiting today along the shore, up the hill," John began. His voice was strong, deep, serious. "I know some of you have come from very far away, and I thank you for it. I hope that the trip was good and that you were able to at least rest last night."

There was sincerity and kindness in those words, Dismas noted to himself as voices of general agreement rose among the crowd in this improvised auditorium by the Jordan.

"But what have you come to see in the desert today? Me?" John went on, pointing to his chest with a surprised face.

The people looked at each other, somewhat bewildered.

"Yes," a voice spoke up above the crowd before others joined in chorus.

John smiled before continuing:

"Many of you have come because you think I'm the Messiah, the one sent by the Most High, from the line of King David, who will come to free us."

Dismas felt Bathsheba's fingers digging into his shoulders as John humbly shook his head.

"No. I only come to bring you a message that is the dawn of a new beginning."

John stepped down from the rock on which he stood and began to walk around the different surfaces that divided the river ford.

"Be converted, because the kingdom of God is nearly upon us." His tone became less solemn, more persuasive. "I baptize you with water for conversion, but he who comes after me is more powerful than I. I am not worthy to carry his sandals. He will baptize you with the Holy Spirit and with fire."

While he was speaking, a small commotion arose along one of the banks. It came from those who were listening to him from the best places across the shore. Those people had surely spent the night there, out in the open, enduring the humidity of the river, to secure those places, Dismas thought. And they were now protesting because a group of people had come up from behind, forcing them to move aside and make room for them. Dismas recognized the newcomers by their clothing: They were Pharisees, always accustomed to occupying the places of honor in the temple, on the public square, and even here, by the Jordan river.

John, who was talking about the need of a baptism for the remission of sins, stopped and looked at them with contempt for their rudeness. One of the pharisees took advantage of the silence that had emerged, and stepped forward, straightening his tunic, which was somehow still immaculate despite the bushes and the mud.

"And who are you?" his voice rose skeptically, the question falling, impertinent, into the water, splashing the prophet's face.

John took a step towards the Pharisee, and bowing before him, offered such an affected reverence that his mocking tone was unmistakable to those present.

"I am not the Messiah," he answered sharply, amid a murmur of laughter.

The Pharisee looked around, uncomfortable.

"What then!" he demanded with a raised voice, in stark contrast to his short stature, forcing the crowd to fall silent. "Do you want us to believe that you are Elijah?" He looked sideways at his companions, who greeted the question with disdainful laughter among themselves. "Because they say that the prophet Elijah is to come before the Messiah."

The comment raised a shadow of doubt among many of those present. The Pharisees could be arrogant and unbearable in their haughtiness, but everyone knew that their command of the Scriptures was perfect, and if they said that Elijah had to come first, then the imminent arrival of the Messiah that John the Baptist was preaching would have to wait—at least until the prophet Elijah returned to earth, chariot of fire or not.

"I am not him. Can't you see that?" John answered, unfazed, bringing his hands to his face and touching his features.

His gesture prompted a new round of laughter among the people.

The Pharisee, more annoyed than ever, turned to his companions, who clearly felt as insulted as he did, and they began to whisper among themselves.

"Anything else?" asked John, with lightning in his pupils, an impatient smile forging his lips.

The Pharisees stopped talking among themselves, and another figure emerged from their ranks. By his haughty demeanor, it was clear that he was the most important of them all.

"Tell us who you are, that we may give an answer to those who sent us. What do you say about yourself?"

It was a question for which a response clearly was not expected, but that was intended to belittle John in the eyes of the whole crowd. John turned his back on them amidst the murmurs of the people and, stepping again onto the stone where he had begun speaking, he rose his voice with solemnity: "I am the voice of one crying in the desert: Make straight the way of the Lord!"

"Then why do you baptize, if you are not the Messiah, Elijah, or the prophet?" demanded the same pharisee, raising his finger at him.

John lowered his head toward the clear waters of the Jordan, which reflected the blue majesty of the sky. "Brood of vipers," he muttered to himself. He looked up at them once again, and nothing could contain then the voice that exploded into a thousand pieces.

"*Who taught you to flee from the wrath to come?!* Therefore, bear fruit worthy of repentance and do not justify yourselves by thinking 'We have Abraham as our father.' Because I assure you"—he pointed to the great rocks scattered across the landscape—"that God can make children of Abraham arise from these stones!"

"What a barbarity!" cried the Pharisee, turning to his companions. "We have heard enough. Let us leave here."

The others began to retreat indignantly, unwilling to continue being humiliated in front of all the people.

But the storm in John's lungs continued to grow.

"The axe is already placed at the roots of the trees," he shouted, closing his eyes in fury, as if he were seeing it. "Therefore, every tree that does not bear good fruit is cut down and thrown into the fire."

The short Pharisee who had spoken first was in such a hurry to escape John's fury that in his haste he slipped on the wet stones on the shore and fell into the water. Laughter erupted all around him, and a mixture of shame and anger drove him to his feet as he disappeared, dragging the weight of his wet garments through the mud.

The people who had been pushed aside by the Pharisees celebrated their departure as murmurs of approval and appreciation for John bubbled up all along the banks of the Jordan.

Dismas applauded, amused by what he was seeing. He was starting to like this guy.

With John's thundering criticism complete, silence fell again over the crowd, as if nothing had happened, as if everything was starting over. But the words he'd spoken against the Pharisees had also gotten inside the hearts of many of the people gathered. Dismas could see it in the expressions of sorrow and surprise on their faces.

Philip, the younger John, and his other disciples looked at each other. Had their master been too harsh with those Pharisees?

To the left of where Dismas sat, a woman made her way through the front rows with determination. On her back she carried a sleeping baby, while she tried with her right arm to control the impulses of a small girl with big curls who only wanted to splash in the river.

"Stay still for a moment, Sarai!" The woman made a last attempt to keep her daughter at bay.

The girl realized that she and her mother had become the center of everyone's attention and stopped. She looked down and brought the tips of her fingers to her mouth. The mother looked up at the prophet.

"So what should we do to bear good fruit and not be cut down like a useless tree?" she asked him.

John approached her and lifted her daughter up into his arms. He brought his face close to the bunches of curls and kissed the little girl on the cheek.

"Love your children. Take care of them as you do now, and love your husband." John lowered the girl back to the ground with such tenderness that it was as though his previous outburst had never happened.

Beside him, another woman prostrated herself before him, digging her knees into the pebbles of the shore .

"And me? What should I do?" she asked in a trembling but sincere voice.

John leaned toward her and held out one of his hands. When she took it, he helped her stand up again. The elegant scarf with rich brocades that she wore on her head set her apart from most of the women present. John smiled at her and, stepping back with the agility of a gazelle to the stone on which he had begun his speech, raised his voice so that everyone could hear him:

"One who has two tunics ought to give to the person who has none. And one who has food ought to do the same! Take care of one another as if you were brothers and sisters."

A flash of light from the hilltop drew Dismas's attention to Herod's soldiers. A ray of sunshine had lit the armor of one of them, who was stepping away from the rest, walking down towards the shore.

For a brief moment Dismas thought his intention was hostile. But when he reached the Jordan, the soldier raised his voice and knelt. "And us? What should we do?"

Murmurs of admiration broke out around him. Most of the soldiers of the tetrarch Herod were not Jews, and those who were, were far from religious men.

John stepped closer and bowed slightly towards him in a way that contained none of the mockery that he'd shown the Pharisee. He looked at the soldier with an expression that conveyed both respect and affection.

"Do not extort anyone, nor denounce falsely. And be content with your wages."

The soldier nodded at each of John's words. He was about to return to his feet when the prophet's voice stopped him on his knees.

"Oh! And one more thing! Bring a message to Herod." John looked intensely into the soldier's eyes, making sure that he had his attention. "Tell him that it is not lawful for him to desire his brother's wife!"

Gasps of laughter and surprise spread like wildfire all along the shore. It was well known that the tetrarch had ordered the murder of his own brother so that he could have his wife. But to disgrace him there, in public, in front of the common people, gave a new dimension to the sin of this man who reigned as a puppet in Galilee.

Dismas, taken up in the laughter, turned to Bathsheba, remembering the comment that her friend Philip had made to them earlier. "I'm not sure which part of John's teaching Herod likes so much!"

Bathsheba, her eyes lost deep in the emotion of the moment, did not answer, and Dismas bit his lip. He turned back to the prophet, wishing he had not interrupted her attention with such a stupid comment.

"Repent, because a new time is coming. The kingdom of God will be among us, and we will never again be slaves."

As the prophet's words echoed in his ears, Dismas wondered why he couldn't feel the same as Bathsheba and have faith in the coming of a new world in which the Messiah would turn everyone into brothers and sisters.

John the Baptist's speech did not last much longer. The conversion of hearts that he called for, he said, had to take place through the baptism that he was ready to perform next, in preparation for the mysterious arrival of a man who was still to come.

People began to gather nervously in front of the prophet, ready to be baptized. John's disciples stood up and, like shepherds with their flock, they began to organize men and women into orderly rows to avoid any crowding that could harm children or the elderly. The younger John caught Dismas's attention as he watched him confront a man twice his age and height, and ordered him to move back to the end of the line; despite his youth, that kid was not lacking in authority or courage.

Philip, close to the Baptist, made a sign to Bathsheba to come up behind him.

"Come, let's go up there by Philip," Bathsheba said, pulling Dismas by the hand through the waters of the Jordan.

Dismas considered resisting Bathsheba as she led him toward the prophet. The night before she had assured him that she would respect whatever he freely chose today, but the excitement of the moment had made her forget her promise and he didn't want to disappoint her either. Something inside him pushed him to follow her and let himself be led, but another, darker force was fighting to take charge and make him run away from there. Without knowing the reason, something in him hinted that if he let John pour water on his head and baptize him in remission of his sins, his life would change completely.

Bathsheba kept her hand tight around his own until they reached Philip.

"If you stay here with me, I will bring you in behind those people," Philip said, pointing to the pilgrims who were now kneeling before John.

Bathsheba made a move to follow Philip's advice, but then she turned to Dismas and let go of his hand. In that moment, he felt his freedom restored—he could decide whatever he wanted. He had the impulse to run away, to flee from there immediately, but that look of tenderness, those expectant eyes, the fire in her pupils, held him back.

Then he nodded and, taking her hand, followed her. Who in his right mind would have the courage to refuse, seeing her standing so beautiful among the rays of the sun that tamed the waters of the Jordan in white and gold?

Their knees sank into the water, digging into the pebbles that covered the bottom of the Jordan. As Bathsheba bowed her head, Dismas glanced at John, who was baptizing a woman on the other side, next to her. The Baptist then slid in front of her, and Dismas's heart began to pound in his chest. He turned his gaze forward, afraid of stealing the intimacy of that moment from Bathsheba. He barely heard what John was saying as he poured water over her hair, and before he realized it, the Baptist was in front of him, looking down at him.

Dismas swallowed, very nervous.

The prophet extended his arms over his head and, with his eyes raised toward the sky, he whispered words that Dismas did not understand. Then he looked down at him and said solemnly, "I baptize you with water, but one is coming who will baptize you in the Holy Spirit."

The water fell upon him, and Dismas sank himself into the waters of the Jordan. There, beneath a glimmering sea of light, his heart seemed to stop beating in his chest and a sudden peace suffused everything. He felt himself swimming and floating in a void filled with immense light, and a chorus of voices in his ears filling that brightness: "Hallelujah, Hallelujah, Hallelujah," he heard, louder and louder, softer and softer, more and more beautiful. And then, nothing.

Silence.

He felt the weight of the Baptist's hands on his shoulders and his lips leaning toward his ear, a burning fire, a mighty force, an infinite peace. He was no longer swimming in the light; he *was* the light, and everything exploded into a big bang of thousands of crystals disappearing.

Dismas became aware of himself again, with his knees still sunk in the cold river. There was no one beside him. He looked up and saw that the Baptist was now on the other bank, baptizing another group of people.

What had happened exactly? Where was everyone else? And Bathsheba? Where was she? He remained still, motionless, drops of water still running down his face. One slipped over the corner of his lips, and it tasted bitter. He realized it was not water from the Jordan; it was his tears.

"Dismas, are you okay?"

He turned and saw Bathsheba standing beside him.

He got up, still dazed from the dream. She searched his face with fear, trying to guess what had happened to him.

"You have been kneeling there for a long time, alone, without moving."

Dismas looked at her without understanding. She took his hand and pulled him from the shallows and walked with him to the shore. His radiant face told her that something extraordinary had happened.

"What did the prophet whisper in your ear?" she finally dared to ask.

Dismas turned to her and lowered his face, abashed. He felt unworthy of what God had just done with him. But he couldn't hide it from the person who had brought him to kneel before the prophet. At last, he looked up at her.

"'Salvation has come, and you will see his power.'"

His voice broke, and he began to weep. Bathsheba wrapped her arms around him, and they both melted into an embrace from which nothing and no one would ever separate them.

After what had happened on the banks of the Jordan, Bathsheba did not need to ask Dismas anything else. Those words from him had been enough to her. She knew they were the same ones his father had spoken to him that night so many years ago. They were a supernatural revelation, and the scope of its prophecy was a mystery that did not need to be tampered with. Both of them had poured out their hearts during that long embrace by the river, and no further clarification was necessary. When the fulfillment of the prophecy came, he would know.

And if the whole supernatural episode was not enough to convince her that something had happened inside Dismas, there was his behavior during their return to Jerusalem as proof. The old Dismas that the people of the caravan had first experienced was only a shadow of the new man who went back with them to the Holy City. He was helpful, attentive, and never shunned the company of those who traveled on horseback with him. A strange enthusiasm, an overwhelming joy seemed to have taken hold of him, opening him wide to the presence of the others.

He needed no reason to strike up a conversation with any of them. He spoke of YHWH, of John the Baptist, of the Messiah, of the work that awaited him in Jerusalem, of his sister Sara, of his great friend Nathaniel... Some in the caravan even thought he talked too much. The man whom Dismas had told, just the night before that he was going back without seeing John the Baptist wished he had done so after enduring a good stretch of the journey listening to him explain in great detail the best way to shoe a horse. He even insisted several times on shoeing the man's horse for free as soon as they returned to Jerusalem.

Even Dismas himself realized that something had changed inside him when, halfway back, he caught himself sharing his ration of dates with the two girls who hadn't stopped gossiping about him throughout the entire journey.

8.

The wedding preparations began the day after their return.

As soon as he woke up, Dismas heard strange noises at the door outside of his workshop. They sounded like someone scratching on wood, accompanied by the isolated moans of a child. Moved by curiosity, he went down the stairs and opened the door, not knowing exactly what to expect.

Tied with a rope to the doorknob, a straw-colored puppy waited patiently at the threshold of its new home. Dismas smiled and glanced up and down the street, hoping to catch a glimpse of her. Bathsheba was gone, but she had not wasted her time since their arrival.

Dismas crouched down, and master and owner studied each other carefully. The dog did not seem to fear the presence of this stranger, and Dismas decided they would get along well. It didn't try to bite him when he reached out to pet it, and the moment he took it in his arms, the animal settled down on his chest as if he were its father.

"I think we're both going to have a new owner soon," Dismas whispered in its ear as he closed the door behind with his foot.

One of the first challenges was to talk to Aunt Rebecca, but Nathaniel made everything much easier. Dismas didn't have to talk to her; his friend—and future brother-in-law!—

would take care of it, convinced that the old woman would not object to Bathsheba giving up her single life. In the short time Bathsheba had been in Jerusalem, his aunt had grown very fond of her niece—"your sister has the purest and most beautiful soul I have ever known," she had told him on a couple of occasions—but she refused to become an obstacle to Bathsheba's happiness. On the contrary, she had insisted that the ceremony should be celebrated as soon as possible.

Nathaniel, for his part, had not hesitated to congratulate Dismas with a warm and brotherly embrace.

"You didn't know she always had eyes for you. I did, but I never thought it would happen. It's clear that the ways of the Lord are unfathomable. He brought me to your workshop that day, and Bathsheba has won."

"I'm the one who won," Dismas was quick to correct him, pointing to the corner where Atzel was sleeping.

Nathaniel burst out laughing.

"When Bathsheba told me, I couldn't believe it. But hey, this creature is no longer a puppy. It's bigger than I thought," he said as he bent down to pet the dog. "I don't know where my sister got him. If you don't want him, just tell her and I'll keep him for myself."

"No! He'll be fine. We're becoming great friends. He follows me everywhere I go, and he even gives me a little bow every time I stand in front of him. Right, Atzel?"

Hearing his name, Atzel stood up and, stretching out his front legs, leaned his head towards the voice of his new master.

"You see?" Dismas smiled, stroking the animal's head.

Nathaniel put his arm around his friend's shoulders and held him close. There was no doubt that Dismas had won—and a lot. His eyes were no longer darkened by that shadow of skepticism that he'd seen at their first encounter, and his gaze was no longer that of an old man with no room in his soul for wonder. Dismas was the same person that Nathaniel had known before, in the old days. Or even better.

When Nathaniel had entered his friend's house, he had not yet decided whether to bring up the subject, but he suddenly decided it was a good time.

"My sister told me what happened on the banks of the Jordan with the prophet."

Their eyes met, and Dismas couldn't help blushing. It was not that he was ashamed of what had happened to him; rather, he felt unworthy of it all.

"It was—" He paused for a moment. "I don't know. Whatever I say to you, I won't find the right words to describe it. It was as if God himself were embracing me, letting me know how much he loves me." His face shone again as he remembered it. "It was a pity that you couldn't come, because surely something similar would have happened to you."

"I don't know, maybe. I really envy you, Dismas. I've always believed that God wanted something special from me, and now I realize that, in reality, He wants it for each one of us. You are very lucky, and I am happy for you."

Dismas could not help but perceive a certain melancholy behind Nathaniel's sincere words. At that moment, he felt that his friend had not yet found his place in the world.

As a child, Nathaniel had always shown a special sensitivity for the things of God. The teacher of the synagogue in the town of Magdala had discovered that, much to his own chagrin, early one day under the fig tree.

That was the place where all the boys from the surrounding villages gathered twice a month to learn the Scriptures, and old Zechariah, who loved above all things to listen to himself talk, had never come across anyone who undermined his authority—certainly, not a brat who barely stretched five spans off the ground.

That day, standing under the tree with a fig in his hands, the old teacher was telling the children about the arrival of a Messiah who would one day come with a raised sword to avenge the Jewish people and restore to them all the past glories stolen by the Gentiles.

Little Nathaniel had kept his hand raised for a long time while the teacher talked and talked, ignoring him.

Finally, Zechariah had looked at him as if he were a scorpion.

"Yes, Nathaniel."

"Is an upright person a Jew?" the boy asked with the greatest innocence.

The teacher's nose twisted.

"What prompted you to ask such a stupid thing, Nathaniel?" he replied, ready to crush him with his sandal. "An upright person is someone who acts according to what he thinks, and a Jew is someone who is part of our people. You can be a Jew and not be upright, for example."

The rabbi's disdain was echoed in the laughter of the other kids—except for little Dismas, who was waiting with curiosity to see what his friend was getting at.

"So a person can be upright and not Jewish." Nathaniel's careful words put the mocking smiles to rest.

Old Zechariah frowned; the scorpion seemed to be turning into a poisonous snake.

"It would be difficult for a gentile, but certainly not impossible," he acknowledged with a sour smile. "Can I now continue with what I was explaining to your classmates?"

"So, when the Messiah comes, he will not save only the Jews," little Nathaniel persisted, unabashed by the intimidating scowl of the distinguished old man.

His words fell like thunder from above the fig tree they were under. Silence fell even upon the throat of old Zechariah, the wisest man within seventy stadia and, possibly, in all of Galilee.

The storm was gathering around helpless little Nathaniel, but far from being afraid of drowning in it, he kept speaking with the best of intentions. "Psalm 50 of the Scriptures says it very clearly: 'To the one who is upright on the way, I will show the salvation of God.' Therefore, salvation will not be only for the Jews, but for all who are upright."

Nathaniel was expelled from under the fig tree that day without ever understanding why. After all, hadn't they gathered around that shadowy tree to learn? But he had achieved what no one had before: he'd silenced old Zechariah. In fact, the old teacher had found it so difficult to get back on track with his lesson that he decided to bring it to an end for that day. Nathaniel became the hero of all his classmates for having challenged authority, but he didn't seem to care too much about that, because his only intention, far from humiliating the rabbi, had been to resolve a question that had been burning in him since he had come across that verse from Psalm 50. Who would the Messiah save when he came to this world?

The grown-up Nathaniel, however, was up to his neck in the maelstrom of the world. His business as a merchant had made him a very rich man, and that was enough burden to keep him away from religious matters that required time that he did not have. The reason he had not gone with Dismas and his sister to see the prophet John was that he'd had to stay in the city and wait for a caravan that hadn't showed up in days. It was the price he had to pay for his riches.

However, that wandering melancholy in his voice had made Dismas understand that his friend still nurtured that sensitivity for the things of God, still longed for something that the trappings of this world would never provide. Furthermore, Dismas went as far as to think that what he had found in Bathsheba—a flame in the midst of darkness—Nathaniel would never find in any woman. Not even in his sister Sara.

Though Bathsheba's aunt was urging them to set a wedding day, Dismas didn't want to make any decision about it until his mother and sister arrived. Now that he had finally recovered his relationship with them, he was not going to start a family himself without their blessings. So he had requested their immediate presence, and Nathaniel sent the message to Galilee in a caravan that brough them back to Jerusalem.

Dismas's heart was filled with joy at seeing his mother and sister. Nathaniel had insisted that the two of them stay with them at Aunt Rebecca's house, and he was waiting at the door to greet them when they arrived.

Mother and son hugged each other tightly. She was so splendid that Dismas forgot about the conversation he'd had with his sister about their mother's health.

"Not only do I get my son back, but I gain a new daughter—and none other than Bathsheba. I am so happy about all of this" she had said with great excitement.

Dismas, however, had failed to realize the headaches that came with having so many women giving their opinions about the wedding and his future with Bathsheba. The first hurdle happened when Sara entered his house, the workshop, for the first time.

He was working at the forge when she and Bathsheba came in, late in the morning. He had arranged a meeting with them to show them his house.

He left what he was working on by the fire and approached them with a smile, but Atzel ran ahead of him to meet his real master the moment he heard her voice. Bathsheba bent down to pet him.

"You have perfect timing. I was just finishing," he greeted her sister. "So! What do you think of our future home, with a dog included?"

Dismas had noticed Sara's face darkening as soon as she entered, and he tightened his smile. He remembered all too well that, even as a child, she was not one to hide what she was thinking.

Her sister's eyes stumbled across the disorder that reigned in the workshop. Yokes, cages, and other difficult-to-recognize objects were piled up against the back wall, all of it covered by thick dust. To the right, she noticed the gap that revealed the stairs leading up to her brother's lair.

"You don't intend to bring your wife into this, do you?" she barked.

"Of course I do! What's wrong with it? Atzel likes it," he shot back, glancing at Bathsheba.

The dog, back in its corner, barked as well at hearing its name.

"You may be willing to do that to your wife, but you won't do it to my friend, not to Bathsheba." Sara crossed her arms adamantly.

"Don't you realize that I can't change the location of the workshop now that I'm doing so well and everyone knows where to find me?" Dismas said in disbelief.

"There's no need to look for a new place," Bathsheba intervened, coming to the rescue of her future husband. "Dismas is happy here, where all his clients can meet him."

"Then don't change the workshop. Turn this whole house into a workplace and find another place to live."

"Are you out of your mind? That would cost me a lot," protested Dismas.

"Either you look for a new place or I'll tell Nathaniel to save the dowry he's planning to give you."

Dismas faced his sister's outburst with a smile, trying to appease her. "Little sister, you've always been able to see what others won't." He kissed her on the cheek. "Why do you think I wanted you here by my side in Jerusalem?

"Come on, don't give me that. I'm no Atzel you can bribe by throwing a bone. You won't twist our arms with nice words. Let me see the floor upstairs."

"Well, I haven't tidied up much today," Dismas said as he hurried to block her way to the stairs. But he couldn't prevent her from climbing up to his living area and catching a glimpse of the mess that blanketed the floor.

"Do you want your sister's advice, Dismas?" She gave him a harsh stare. "If you're going to live here, don't get married."

He sighed; he couldn't understand the problem that women seemed to have with a little disorder.

"Dismas, I think your sister has come up with a fine idea," Bathsheba said, stepping in carefully, trying to make both ends meet. "If we found a place to live nearby, you could keep the workshop here. You could turn the upper floor into a place to receive your important clients. It would be the perfect way to impress them."

Dismas looked at his future wife with a frown. Had the two women agreed on a plan prior to stepping into his place? There was some truth, however, in Bathsheba's words; he had often complained about his wealthier clients, who thought they were too goo to be attended among the mess and clutter of his work.

Dismas looked at Bathsheba and then at his sister, trying to make up his mind. The eyes of both women had the same veiled supplication, and he finally gave in.

"I can fight with one of you, but it would be impossible for me to take on both of you at the same time. If each of you pulls to one side, I will not make it alive to the ceremony. We'll see if we can find something that is near the workshop and cheap."

Sara opened her mouth to say something, but he placed one finger over her lips, shutting her up before she uttered another word.

"And it will be better," he turned to Bathsheba, "if you be patient with me and put your trust in what Atzel and I will decide." Dismas ended the discussion by placing a kiss on her lips.

Later, as they were all leaving and Dismas turned to close the door, he missed the wink of victory that the two women exchanged. They had achieved what they had come for.

With Sara's help, Dismas launched into the task of finding a place near the workshop that could become the home that Bathsheba really hoped for. A contact that Nathaniel had provided got him the closest thing to paradise.

Isaac was a small guy with short arms and a shrill voice, who knew perfectly—"like the palm of my hand," he said—the wide variety of dwellings that the whims of owners he worked with were leaving available, and, in exchange for a commission, he put them in contact with possible interested parties. Dismas would never have guessed that anyone could make a living out of it, but from the way Isaac looked, it was clear that he did, and a very good one indeed.

The two siblings only needed to see three houses to make up their minds. The first place Isaac showed them, which he had called the "jewel in the crown," was four walls built over a stable that was filled with lambs during Passover and their smells the rest of the year. Sara, never one to mince words, called it a joke.

"We may come from a small village, but we are not idiots," she said with her crossed arms pressed to her chest.

"Okay, okay. I see you are the kind who know what you really want." Isaac adjusted his strategy on the fly. "You should have started there, yes sir. Nathaniel's friends are friends of mine too, of course. They're family!"

He finally kept his word. The guy tried to manipulate them with flattery and coaxing, but it all came off to Dismas and Sara like the hissing of a devious snake that slithered away frightened when Sara showed her claws.

She fell in love from the moment she entered the third house. On the outside, the two-floor adobe was in perfect condition, a preview of what awaited them inside. The main room was large and spacious, and the house had an upper room that opened onto a terrace from which they could see the main tower of the temple.

The negotiations were tough, and Dismas was stubborn, flatly refusing Isaac's initial offer.

"This is the most I can pay," he insisted with a stone face. "I won't go any higher. Take it or leave it."

Atzel, at his side, voiced his support with a quick bark. The dog had also liked the house, but not at any price.

Sara looked back and forth between her brother and Isaac the snake with anguish. The small guy shook his head, as if talking to himself. His face, also inscrutable, foreshadowed the worst, and she swallowed—they couldn't let this opportunity go by. She had already imagined the quiet life that her brother and Bathsheba would share within those four walls, and it couldn't be any other way.

She glanced at her brother again, unable to understand how he could risk losing that house. But Dismas, unflinching, waited for Isaac's answer with his hands clutched at the sides of his waist. She opened her mouth hesitantly, willing to say something, but Dismas's withering gaze stopped her words right there.

The businessman finally took his hands out of the pockets of his tunic and, after crying out to heaven as if a terrible curse had fallen upon him, he accepted the offer.

"I'm losing money with you, but I'm making a friend of Nathaniel happy," little Isaac complained again in the street, while he latched the door of the house that now belonged to Dismas.

Sara and Dismas waved goodbye to him and looked at the two-floor adobe house again with satisfaction.

"Well, it's done," he sighed, still stunned by the negotiation and not very convinced of what he had just done.

Sara wrapped her arm around his.

"Bathsheba is going to love it," she said. "Don't tell her anything yet; let me make it nice first, like a real home, and surprise her afterwards."

"I'm warning you—I'm not going to spend much more money." Dismas furrowed his brow to make it clear that he meant that.

At that moment someone patted him on the back. "Alas! I finally have the honor to set my eyes on you!"

The recrimination fell flatly in Dismas's ears.

"Hello, Melchiades. What a coincidence to find you here."

Sara was surprised to hear Atzel grunt at the newcomer and held him by the collar. Her brother had not been very friendly, either.

"I've been looking for you for several days, but I always find your workshop closed. You're not going to tell me that you've changed location without warning," Melchiades said, pointing to the house he had seen them leave.

"No, of course not." Dismas offered an insincere smile.

"But I've been busy with other matters."

Melchiades took a quick look at Sara and drew his own conclusions.

"I see." He cast a licentious glance at her. "There are rumors that you're getting married."

"I'm his sister, not his future wife." Sara took a step, dispelling any confusion.

Melchiades let out a small laugh and, taking Dismas aside by his arm, he leaned closer to his ear:

"I trust that this won't be a distraction from your business. Gestas wants to offer you a new order. Men like you come handy in our cause against the Romans."

Dismas pulled away.

"You know that I have no problem accepting any order, as long as the workshop is open and I'm inside. Now if you'll excuse me, I have things to do."

Dismas led his sister gently by her elbow, leaving Melchiades behind before he could say another word.

"I must admit," he muttered under his lips as they walked down the street, "it's a good idea to separate the workshop from the house, after all."

"At least Bathsheba won't have to put up with cretins like that," she said. "Who was he?"

"One of my best clients."

"Well, Atzel doesn't like him at all." Sara glanced over her shoulder to look at the strange man again. "He keeps watching us as if you were his property. I hope not all your clients are like him."

"He's a chucklehead, but they pay the best."

"Maybe you shouldn't have treated him like that, then."

"The orders he brings me don't depend on him. And you forget something very important," Dismas added, twisting his lips in an air of mystery.

"What?" Sara answered, ready to hear a confession.

"That you're talking to the best blacksmith in Jerusalem," Dismas said, puffing out his chest and raising his chin like a Greek statue.

Their laughter mingled into the noises that filled the streets of the Holy City, like an echo of the laughter they had shared together as children.

As Sara had suggested, Dismas said nothing to Bathsheba about the house while his sister took on the task of filling it with life. She had also forbidden him the entrance until everything was ready. He gave her complete freedom to choose all the necessary furniture, provided it fit the budget he set—which had been increased four times, and only after as many arguments.

"If you don't have the time to make the things that you need for your house, we will need to buy them elsewhere. And I will not allow Bathsheba to move into a home that is half-finished," she had warned him, ending the last of the arguments.

"It would have been cheaper for me to close the workshop and go work for you," he had sighed, after agreeing to all her demands.

# 9.

While Sara was busy with the furniture of the new house, Dismas's mother had the mission of distracting Bathsheba. She shouldn't suspect anything about her future home; thus, it would become a real surprise when Dismas showed it to her completely furnished. When Sara had to be away for anything related to the house, Miriam found random excuses to keep Bathsheba occupied, usually asking to accompany her to run errands in the parts of the city farthest from the streets close to the temple.

Bathsheba offered no resistance; she liked being with Miriam. Since she was little, she'd always enjoyed the shapes and colors of her friend's mother—the smell of her cooking, the warmth of her gaze, the touch of her hands in her hair as she built impossible braids; they had all played an important part of her little world in Galilee.

But Bathsheba was not stupid. More than suspecting, she knew that her friend's mysterious absences and Miriam's sudden requests to go with her to improbable places had both something to do with her future home. If not so, Why was it that Dismas and Sara had stopped arguing about it after that little scuffle in the workshop?

That day, Miriam asked Bathsheba to accompany her to an alley on the eastern side of the temple, at the other end of the city, where some special embroidery, recently arrived from Syria, was being sold. Miriam thought it might well as part of her wedding dress.

"Are you sure you want to go there?" Bathsheba asked. "It's going to take us practically all day to go and come back, and yesterday you said you weren't feeling very well."

"Oh, don't worry about me! It had to be something I ate, but today I'm feeling much better."

Miriam was used to disguising her sickness behind little white lies.

"Why are you so interested in those embroideries?" Bathsheba asked, looking for a wrinkle in her arguments. "I don't need anything else. Nathaniel keeps piling up fabrics and boxes as part of the dowry, and there won't be room for everything in your son's house."

As she spoke, she cautiously watched the reaction on the features of her future mother-in-law.

"It never hurts to look a little further," Miriam answered with an impassive countenance. "An acquaintance of Dismas told me the other day at the market that those embroideries were worth seeing. And he has found me a person who can take us there. I am to meet him at noon."

Bathsheba could see Miriam's excitement about the shipment from Syria. Few women could resist exotic goods, and her future mother-in-law was no different. She liked to touch some of the fine things that her position in life had prevented her from possessing.

"As you wish," Bathsheba nodded, pretending to be convinced. "If it's fine with you, I will go see Dismas now while you finish getting ready."

"Go to the workshop? Now?" Panic took over Miriam's face. "Then we won't be ready to depart by noon, as expected. Nothing is going to happen if you don't get to see your betrothed for just a few hours, don't you think?"

"But if we go to the other side of the city, I won't be able to see him at all today, and you don't want me to change my mind and decide not to accompany you to see the embroideries." Bathsheba replied, putting a little pressure on the small crack she had just seen on her expression.

"Whatever you wish, my daughter. If you don't want us to go see those embroideries, then we won't go and I'll be fine," Miriam said with a conciliatory nod.

"Oh, you know I will go with you wherever you want, my dear mother-in-law, if you just let me go and hello to your son," Bathsheba replied, giving Miriam a hug.

"Then you better hurry and be back before noon," Miriam replied, giving in to Bathsheba's wish. She just hoped that her son was still at the workshop and had not yet left to see his new home with Sara, as they had already planned the previous day.

Moments later, Bathsheba left the house and headed for Dismas's workshop. She had to admit that her mother-in-law was good—very good—at keeping little secrets. She would tell her that when the truth of this whole masquerade was revealed, and they would have a good laugh together about it.

Deep down, she didn't mind going with Miriam wherever she wanted because she enjoyed her company, she told to her herself as she disappeared around the corner of the street and a long, furtive shadow slipped over the front of Aunt Rebecca's house.

Dismas was striking his hammer upon a plow that was resisting to be straightened. Its owner had begged him earnestly to have it fixed by the following day, and his blows were now savagely accurate, forcing the iron to return to its original shape. He had to hurry if he wanted to be punctual for his meeting with his sister.

It was time to see the new house now that Sara had completed the work. She wanted to show it to him first before showing it to Bathsheba. He smiled at the thought of how nervous his sister had to be, awaiting his verdict. He was not at all worried; he had complete trust in her taste, and he just felt a vivid curiosity to see the final result.

He looked up from his work when he heard Atzel bark. Since Bathsheba had given it to him as a present, the dog had grown day by day, becoming the main attraction at the workshop's entrance. Lying there on his side with all four legs stretched out in the sun, it was irresistible to those who passed by, especially women and children. He contentedly let everyone pet him, but only one person could make him stand up and dance, crazy with excitement, as he was doing now. Dismas raised his eyes, knowing that Bathsheba had arrived.

"Weren't you supposed to be running errands with my mother today?" he asked as he dropped the hammer and went to meet her with the echo of the hammering in his chest, just as he had felt the first time she entered his workshop.

"That's right. But I couldn't bear the thought of letting a day pass by without laying my eyes on you," she answered as she bent down to pet the dog. "Atzel, is your owner good to you? Yes, yes, don't worry, I'll be with you to take better care very soon."

She stood up, radiant, splendid, like ripe fruit about to fall from a tree.

"But I do hope you'll take care of me first," Dismas protested, jealous .

"Well, I don't know! It will depend on whether you are as happy to see me as Atzel is."

"Can't you see it on my face?" Dismas raised his chin and barked five times in the air.

The two of them inclined their heads toward each other, turning their smiles into a kiss.

"I'm very glad you came to see me, but you shouldn't be here. You distract me and then I won't be able to concentrate on my work," he complained between her lips, tasting her.

"Don't you worry, I'm leaving you right away. You've already given me what I needed to survive the day without you."

"Is my mother that boring?"

"You know she isn't. I have a great time with her. It's a shame Sara isn't coming with us too." She frowned slightly, looking for a reaction on his face.

Dismas had not inherited his mother's skills—he didn't know how to pretend those same little white lies.

"So where is it that you are going with her?" he asked awkwardly, trying to change the subject.

"She asked me to take her to the east side of the city, to see some goods recently brought from Syria."

Dismas's face darkened.

"You are not really planning to go to that part of the city by yourselves, are you? You can't go there alone. It's dangerous."

Dismas, who had heard Melchiades talk on more than one occasion about the mysterious goods that were brought in on caravans from remote places, knew that people sometimes got into trouble in that part of the city. In fact, the big cretin had been bragging just a few days ago in his workshop about the imminent arrival of *merchandise* that the Romans would surely pay a fortune to know about. No, that was not a place for Bathsheba and his mother to visit, not today, not any day.

"I will tell your mother, but I don't think I'll be able to convince her," she said, leaning over the dog again and holding his head in her hands, her lips pressed to his muzzle.

"I mean it, Bathsheba." He took her by the shoulders and lifted her gently so that she could listen carefully. "I don't want you to go there. There has been some tension with the Romans lately, and that area is a source of trouble. Tell my mother to cancel that visit altogether."

Bathsheba saw the warning coming from Dismas's eyes, and she comforted him.

"Don't worry. I will tell your mother and suggest we go somewhere else."

"Do you promise?"

"Yes."

"Do you promise?" he insisted again, gazing into the honey in her eyes.

"*Yes*," she nodded solemnly.

"You need to seal it," he said with a frown.

"Do you want me to put it in writing, with my signature?" she said, amused, trying to guess what was on his mind.

"You can seal it with a kiss," he nodded, closing his eyes, waiting.

"Another? I thought one was enough," Bathsheba said, bringing her face closer to him.

Feeling the warmth of her lips on his, Dismas opened his eyes and saw heaven reflected in those pupils.

"That's enough," she said, her lips trembling, separating them from his mouth. "Or something tells me that you won't be able to wait for the wedding night."

Dismas sighed, like exhaling the steam of a hot iron pulled from the fire and plunged into cold water.

"I think you'll like it," he whispered into her ear.

"What?" Bathsheba raised her forehead towards him.

"I don't know, but you are going to like it," he insisted with a knowing smile.

"What are you up to with your sister?" she teased him.

"Ah!" he said, raising an eyebrow. "I haven't said anything, and you don't know anything!" He put his finger on the tip of her nose, and they exchanged a long, smoldering look.

"Have a good day, dear future husband."

Bathsheba turned back to where she had come from, vanishing like a dream. Atzel, the tail between his legs, let out a little whimper and brought Dismas back to reality.

"Yes, my friend, I miss her too. But soon the three of us will be together."

Dismas got back to work and finally finished subduing the damn plow. Then, after closing the workshop, he went out to meet his sister.

"Do you think she'll like it?" Sara asked hopefully as soon as they crossed the threshold.

Unable to answer his sister, Dismas stared open-mouthed at the house he had bought, which had been so dusty and empty a few days ago. How could it be the same place? He barely recognized it. The dog, who had been the first of the three to enter, barked twice.

"Atzel thinks so," Dismas said, reeling with his first impression.

His sister had managed to bring order and color to the empty room that had welcomed them the first time, and the few pieces of furniture that now inhabited the house gave meaning to what had previously been a flat surface. One end was still dominated by the large fireplace he had seen the first day, but the clay pots, the vases, a stack of blue-green plates, and the wooden spoons that hung from above provided the room the warmth and flavor of what was to become the main space of the home.

At the other end of the room, however, he was puzzled to find what at first glance looked like the main bedroom: two single beds covered with fabrics and piled with cushions were facing each other, one table standing between them as a barrier that would need to be overcome if a carnal encounter was to be taken once married… Dismas shook his head. It didn't seem like the right place for those beds, even without the table in between.

He turned to his sister, puzzled. "So that's where Bathsheba and I…?"

Sara burst out laughing. "I don't believe this! You've been in this city longer than I have, and you don't know about Roman customs? It's a triclinium."

Dismas shook his head, his gaze blank; he still didn't understand.

"It's where the Romans *eat*, Dismas!" she answered, half amused and half amazed by her brother's ignorance. "How could you even think I would let you both sleep down here! There, through that door next to the fireplace, you see, will be the children's room, but your bedroom is upstairs. Come on, come up with me."

Sara disappeared up the stairs that led up to the upper floor.

Dismas followed her with a sigh of relief. As he climbed to the room above, he turned to look at the triclinium again. Perhaps that way of dining together was too unfamiliar for Bathsheba's taste.

As he climbed the stairs and the ceiling became the floor of the upper room, his eyes took in the room with wonder. His sister had turned the filthy space under the roof into a bridal bedchamber whose air was rich with the soft and deep and warm scent of freshly carved wood. Dismas breathed deeply—it was the closest thing to home he had ever smelled. Sara had ordered a beautiful lattice carving that now covered the windows, giving the whole bedroom a secluded, magical touch.

Sara looked expectantly at her brother. "Do you like it?"

The latticework that crisscrossed the windows forced the rays of light from outside into a sinuous play of shadows that cast a halo of intimacy and mystery over the marital bed.

"This… this is like an oasis," he murmured, lost in thought, contemplating what Sara had done with the room. "A paradise! Atzel, you're not going to be allowed to come up here. This will be for adults only."

Atzel didn't seem to agree with his master's opinion, but after one bark of protest, he disappeared down the stairs, obeying.

"That dog is incredible," Sara murmured, not quite believing what she had just seen.

Dismas turned his attention away from the blue-and-white striped linens covering the bed and looked at the chests on either side of them. From the top of one of them, the fragrance of flowers standing in a vase mingled with the sweet aroma of the wood in the room. On the other sat the small carving of the swallow, with its wings outstretched to the wind, still aiming to take flight. Sara approached the figurine, picked it up, and showed it to her brother.

"I thought you would be happy to have it here. These birds announce the arrival of spring; that is what is going to happen to you and Bathsheba starting next week: a new life."

Dismas took the swallow and leaned towards her to kiss her cheek.

"Thank you, sister."

"Remember," she said, winking, "it is the most sacred place in the whole house. You said it yourself—it will be your paradise."

A tumult of voices came through the wooden lattice from the street below. Something was happening. Dismas stepped out onto the terrace to see the reason for such a commotion. Below, a flurry of murmurs rose to his ears. He saw concern on the faces of the people. Some pointed toward the east, where the sudden agitation that had taken hold of the city seemed to be coming from.

"What is it?" asked Sara, behind him.

Dismas called down to one of the boys below who was spreading the news like wildfire and asked him what was happening.

"The Romans have forced their way into the eastern quarter!" the boy spat into the air without stopping.

Dismas turned to his sister with an odd blend of concern and relief in his eyes.

"The Romans are attacking the eastern part of the city. Mama wanted to go there today. Fortunately, I forbade Bathsheba from taking her."

Something in his sister's face made his heart sink into his stomach before she even spoke.

"Dismas," Sara had to swallow before she could continue, her face suddenly pale. "Mama and Bathsheba left this morning."

"It's impossible. I told her not to. Bathsheba promised me," he answered, raising the palms of his hands to his forehead.

"I found them by the door when they were about to leave.

They told me they were going there to see some embroidery that had arrived from Syria."

"Damn it!" Dismas's body tensed, and he had to turn around, pacing from side to side of the little terrace, as he tried to control the sudden fear that was taking hold of him. He looked towards the east side beyond the temple that stood out over the rooftops. It took him only a moment to calculate the distance from where he stood to that neighborhood. He could run and get there in time—

In time for what?

Sara seemed to read his thoughts.

"You won't achieve anything by going there right now. Nothing will happen to them. Bathsheba is cautious, and Mama doesn't like to get into the crowds. Besides, they were accompanied by someone you knew."

"Who? What's his name?" His wild eyes looked at his sister, hoping that whoever it was could lead them to safety.

"I don't know!" she cried, regretting not having paid more attention when she'd waved goodbye. "Nothing will happen to them, right?"

The question squeezed his soul again, as he shook his head trying to expel the ghost of the words that Melchiades had spoken in his workshop.

"No." He tried to form a reassuring smile. "You stay here. Don't go out until I return."

He stepped back into the bedroom and disappeared like lightning down the stairs.

"But Dismas, where are you going?" he heard his sister shout behind him.

"You better run to Aunt Rebecca's. Don't come out of it until it's safe! And take Atzel with you! I'm going to fetch them!"

Dismas crossed the house that only a moment ago had

seemed like paradise now transformed into a living hell. He rushed into the street. He didn't even bother to close the door.

Breathing hard through his anguish kept Dimas from drowning in the crowd on the streets of Jerusalem. He felt as though he was swimming against the current of a river, dodging grocery carts, people, animals, all fleeing from the place he was heading. He crossed the esplanade of the temple and entered the eastern part of the city, where chaos had taken over.

On its streets, the crowds had become a stampede, spreading panic in its wake. Cries of horror from the throats of hundreds of people became one big thunder that shook the hearts and the stones of Jerusalem.

Dismas saw objects flying through the air around him—vegetables, clothes, water jugs, even a crutch. The wave of terror grew as he moved deeper against the strong current. He quickened his steps blindly, amidst the tumult that began to rise like a wall around him. Desperation took hold of him. Where and how was he going to find them in the midst of this hell?

"O Lord, please let me get there before it is too late, I beg you! Please let me find them!"

The plea slipped through the seams of his soul.

"Dismas!"

A voice from behind made him turn around, and he saw his mother being dragged away in the raging tide. He tensed all his muscles, and retracing his steps, he fought his way through the bodies towards her.

Finally, he was able to put his arms around her, and making a wall of his body, he opened a fissure in the tide to drag her out of the current, into the porch of a house.

"Bathsheba! Where is Bathsheba?" Dismas shook his mother by the shoulders, forcing her to look at him.

Next to them on the porch, on the shore as the torrent roared by, a distraught little girl was crying for her mother into the faceless crowds that slid downstream.

Miriam embraced her son, sorrow blurring all her features in despair.

"We were strolling peacefully among the merchants' stands. People started running when they heard the Roman soldiers were coming. They pushed against us—"

"Where?" Dismas repeated, his eyes wide.

"Up by the square," Miriam moaned. "Someone came between us, and she disappeared from my side."

Dismas could not contain the anger that had been gathering inside him.

"Mama, I told Bathsheba not to come! Why didn't you listen to me?" A dry sob distorted his last words.

"It's my fault. It was I who didn't want to listen to her. I thought that… I thought—" Miriam couldn't finish her words.

Dismas put his arms around her, biting his lip. It was not the time to cast blame.

"Stay here and do not move. I'll be back," he said.

He bent down towards the little girl, who was still crying inconsolably. "Come with me. Nothing will happen to you."

He pulled the girl to his mother's side, and she held her firmly by the shoulders. Then he turned to the door of the house where they were stranded and knocked hard.

"Please! Open! We need your help!" he shouted with desperation.

"Get out! If I open the door, it will be the end of us; everyone will want to get in," answered a terrified voice on the other side.

"Let my mother and this child in," Dismas begged. "No one else will come through. I'll close the door behind them. I give you my word."

After a few eternal seconds, he heard a bolt slide, and someone cracked the door open. Dismas pushed the two, slipping them through the door, and closed it again, the bolt creaking on the other side. Then he drew back his shoulders and, taking a deep breath, plunged into the horrible tide.

In the distance, among a sea of bobbing heads, he could distinguish the square. It wasn't far, but having to elbow his way through the fleeing people made it a continent away.

Amid the dust and the gasps and the yelling around him, he finally managed to pull himself out of the funnel of the masses, coming out onto the square. Now he could move more easily, but that sense of security didn't last long. A group of Roman soldiers burst into the other end of the square, wrecking everything in its path. They were the cause of the wave of terror that was sweeping down the street, rushing through the city, throbbing into his veins.

He looked around, his heart clenched in his mouth, trying to spot Bathsheba among the people who remained scattered on the esplanade.

"Lord, please let me find her. Let her be alive," he whispered.

The square had become a mousetrap, and he had to move fast if he did not want to be caught between the soldiers before him and the fleeing mass behind.

"*Bathsheba!*" he yelled, the veins in his neck about to burst as he spun around with desperation.

He had to find her before the soldiers took over the center of the square. He ran from one end to the other, searching among the groups that still resisted being swallowed up by the mob— a few were men who *thought* they couldn't leave without first confronting the enemy; many others, all women, who *knew* they wouldn't leave the children and the elderly be swallowed up by the maelstrom that was rushing down the streets.

Then he saw her. Her back was turned to him. She was leaning over an old woman, bringing a trembling bowl of water to her lips. He didn't need to see her face to know that it was Bathsheba; he knew by heart each detail, her every small gesture. His face lit up, and he started to run toward her. He then noticed that another figure, a Roman soldier, was approaching fast across the other side of the plaza, about to confront her.

Later, Dismas would be incapable of sticking together in one piece the nightmare that unfolded before his eyes. He would only recall flashes of it with the sound of his own sharp breaths slashing through the air—of Bathsheba raising her head to the approaching soldier; the soldier grabbing her by her hair and slamming her across the face with his fist; her falling backwards, her head tilted back sharply enough that Dismas could see the terror in her eyes; the heavy Roman sandals stomping over her belly, one, two times; her guttural cry filling his ears; the vicious grin on the soldier's face as he backtracked toward his companions.

With the fury filling the veins of this throat, Dismas was tempted for a moment to go after him, jump on his back, and rip the heart and the soul out of that monster. But his eyes went back to Bathsheba on the ground, still alive, and he rushed to her.

"Bathsheba!" he cried, leaning over her.

She tried to smile when she recognized his voice, but she barely moved her lips. With his heart breaking, Dismas looked up to see how far the battalion had reached across the plaza. He still had time to escape with her in his arms.

"Come on, we have to get out of here." While he spoke, he scanned the perimeter of the square to determine the best way out. He looked down the alley between two houses that led to a dead end.

"I can't move".

Her whisper froze the blood in his veins.

"I'll help you, honey."

Dismas reached his arms under her body, and she couldn't hide a small cry of pain as he lifted her into the air. He felt something warm in his hands, on her back. He looked down and saw a pool of blood where she had fallen. He knew then that he was losing her.

Anguish took hold of Dismas's soul as he hurried with her in his arms towards the dead end he had glimpsed.

"Bathsheba, we'll be safe. Don't worry.... Everything— everything will be right."

He didn't even know what he was muttering.

Her face pale, she closed her eyes. Dismas shook her lightly, completely terrified.

"Bathsheba, look at me! Don't close your eyes, not now! Please!"

He shot a glance toward the alley, at the soldiers, at the avalanche of people fleeing from the square and flowing onto the streets beyond. He was gripped with terror.

"Everything is going to be fine, honey!"

"Dismas—" Her voice was thin and trembling, but its determination pulled his eyes to her face.

"Remember the Jordan," she continued with half a whisper. "You will see his power. Remember the Jordan. Remember the..."

She seemed delirious as her voice slowly faded away.

Dismas clenched his teeth and raised his face to heaven above, repeating those words to himself.

"You will see his power."

He halted and listened—Bathsheba's heart was still beating. He held his breath and suddenly understood. He knelt down with the warmth of her body wrapped in his arms.

The time had arrived.

"O my God, Lord Almighty," he prayed, "you looked into my eyes and I believed. You have wanted me to see your power. Now I understand. That is why I ask you to save her—save Bathsheba so that I may become witness to your power."

Tears ran down his cheeks as he waited for his prayer to cross heaven and reach its Creator.

The chaotic noises of the world around him seemed to be swept from his ears, and the only thing he heard was the beating of her heart, his body pressed to her. Warmth still emanated from Bathsheba's skin and a slight hope shone through. He held her tightly against his chest, certain that he could feel her heartbeat alongside his, the two of them beating in unison, defying the world.

You will see his power.

Could the Almighty God take away from him the light that He had wanted to shine in his darkness?

You will see his power!

Here was His power, in his arms, now! It was time to show it to the world, time to show it to him, Dismas.

"I thank you, O Lord. I thank you for showing me your power."

He opened his eyes, and the sounds of the universe suddenly came pouring back. Screams and chaos returned to his ears, and with hope still hidden under his eyelids, he looked down at Bathsheba's face.

Stone. Pale. Lifeless.

Beauty was the only thing that had not yet abandoned

her. Dismas took a deep breath that made everything whirl around him.

It had all been a lie—Bathsheba's skin was cold, her heartbeat an echo of his own, his prayers nothing more than stupid supplications cried out to an empty sky.

He squeezed his eyelids closed furiously, and two tears expelled that hidden liar from his eyes.

A deep cry arose from the darkness within him, creeping into his throat. He wanted to expel it, to vomit the rage and hatred he was feeling, but they burned so much inside that he could only burst into a hollow, deaf, and monstrous silence.

On the square, everything was stained with blood—blood spilt under the sandals of the invading army.

10.

No one knew anything about Dismas, and Sara was worried. A week had passed since the tragic event, and her brother had shown no sign of life. At first she excused his behavior. Disappearing, grieving, tending to her broken heart was what she would have done in the same circumstances.

But not showing up at the funeral for a last goodbye, not sharing his loss with her brother Nathaniel, were the first signs that something was terribly wrong.

The agony her mother was going through did not help to ease Sara's concern either.

Poor Miriam had not left her bed even on the day of the funeral. She blamed herself for everything that had happened. And although she did not confess it to anyone, she was fearful of seeing her son again, because she was firmly convinced that he would never forgive her. She had lost him again, and this time it was her own fault.

Sara could do nothing except wait for Dismas to be ready to show his face again to the world. A dark idea crossed her mind: What if he had taken his own life? Her soul shook at the idea, like the beating of wings in a cage, and although she tried to dismiss the idea, the possibility became more real as each day passed.

Sara finally spoke to Nathaniel about her fears. Although grieved by his sister's death, Nathaniel was a man of hope and knew that death was not the last word. His friend Dismas was his greatest concern and the reason for his deep sadness. Upon hearing Sara's fears, which he secretly harbored himself, he sent emissaries in search of Dismas in the most sordid neighborhoods of the city, which, despite being holy, also had its sinful corners.

He had even ordered a search of the area around Golgotha, a cursed hillside outside the city walls where the Romans executed criminals.

But no one returned with news of Dismas. The earth had swallowed him up.

It was the merchant Isaac, the little man who had sold them the house, who, inadvertently, offered the first clue about Dismas's whereabouts. He showed up at Aunt Rebecca's house to demand the final payment, according to the terms Dismas had agreed to. Atzel, sitting at Sara's feet, growled at Isaac upon hearing his lack of sensitivity at such a moment.

She tried to get rid of him, cutting him off with a lie:

"I understand what you're asking, but my brother has backed out and wants to return the house to its owners."

Isaac's eyes popped out of their sockets. That was the problem with selling a house to villagers who came to the big city—they forgot that a deal was a deal, not an exchange of blankets for the dowry of an ugly distant cousin. In those cases, you could keep one or the other or return them all, but in the city, business was different—money was involved, and nobody played with that precious metal. So he was more determined than ever: Even if these people were friends of Nathaniel, they had to pay. Of course they did.

"My dear friend, I understand what you're saying, and it is a real pity." As a good businessman, Isaac hid his fury. "But

I find it hard to believe that— He is your brother, right?"

He waited ceremoniously for Sara to nod before continuing:

"—that your brother is not comfortable in his new property, because noises have been heard from outside the house for several nights."

Sara looked in astonishment at Isaac, who rubbed his hands as he spoke. The wings of despair stopped beating inside her, with a new hope. Could it be that her brother was there? Why had it not occurred to her to search the house again? She had done so the day after what had happened, but there was no evidence he'd been there. Who would have thought that her brother would want to escape the world in a house that would never be home?

She got rid of Isaac as quickly as she could. She promised to pay him the next day, assuring him that it was all due to a misunderstanding between her and her brother. She knew that the only reason the little man had left more or less convinced was the protection that Nathaniel's position in the community offered her; otherwise, the city judges would already be upon them, banging on the door.

She waited by the window for Isaac to disappear around the street corner before running out. Atzel stopped her for a moment when she was about to close the door. His barking made it very clear that he knew she was looking for his owner. That dog's sixth sense never ceased to amaze her.

"Atzel, I'm sorry," she told him. "But you're going to have to stay here."

Her heart nearly jumped out of her throat a couple of times during her walk. She had never done it so fast, unable to contain her eagerness to know if Dismas was there.

There was a shorter way, but she wanted to avoid it, because it would take her by the place where she used to accompany Bathsheba every morning to fetch water. The memories of her friend were still painful, but what she needed now was all her strength, not tears, to be able to rescue her brother from the hell in which he must be immersed.

She finally stopped in front of the door of the house where only a few days ago she had poured out all her hopes. Now, although it still looked the same on the outside, nothing was the same. The windows provided no sign of life inside. She closed her eyes before placing her hand on the doorknob. She did not know what she would find inside, but she prayed that God would put the right words on her lips in the midst of so much pain. She swallowed and entered.

The dull echoes of a dead house and the ashes of an extinguished fire greeted her. She gently closed the door behind her, and a gray shadow clouded her face. It had been an eternity since the triclinium had painted her brother's face with astonishment, and now she was shocked to see it shattered in a corner. That was the only sign of damage at the house, but it was an unmistakable sign that her brother had been there. She moved towards the center of the room wrapped in silence and stopped to listen. A slight, brief sound from above, in the bedroom, made her listen warily, like a deer to the rustling of grass.

She put one foot on the stairs and, as she climbed stealthily, a tickling sensation covered her arms. What if, instead of her brother, she found a thief? She tried to reassure herself: If there was someone upstairs, which there was, it could only be her brother.

As soon as her head crossed the ceiling into the floor above, Sara sighed in relief. There he was, sitting on the floor, facing the bed, his back pressed against the wall. With his knees bent high and his forearms resting on them, she could barely see his face. But it was him. Her brother Dismas.

Sara looked around. There was no trace of those sinuous shadows that the wooden lattice had cast in the bedroom a few days earlier. Today they were prison bars.

Dismas offered no sign that he was aware of her presence. His gaze was fixed on something he was fidgeting with in his hands, turning it over and over and over again.

"Dismas."

Her soft voice pierced the silence of the room.

She waited a few moments, but he did not react. His fevered eyes remained focused on the object that his trembling hands kept playing with. How long had he been sitting there? She looked at the marital bed. The linens on it were undisturbed. Sara took a breath as if she were going to submerge her head under water and took a few steps towards him.

She crouched in front of him. Nothing.

Sara looked at the object he was holding and recognized the outstretched wings of the swallow.

She placed her hand on his forearm and gently shook it, but he continued to ignore her. She swallowed, scrutinizing his face while desperately searching for a way to unlock the bolts of that broken soul.

"Do you know what the funniest thing about all this is?"

Dismas's voice echoed strangely among the scents of the fresh wood that still hung in the air of the room. Sara was frightened to hear it. Her brother's eyes seemed to have returned to the world around him, but Sara feared it was not the same one she was living in. She could not find a thread of voice in her throat, so she shook her head

"I never liked spring. I have always preferred winter, the darkness from which I should never have left."

Dismas buried his face between his knees again. Sara reached out and placed her hands on her brother's shoulders.

She wanted to envelop him with a comforting warmth, but instead she felt like she was grasping a bag of bones.

"Brother," she finally dared to speak. "Don't let Bathsheba's fire and warmth go out. She—" Her words broke as his brother started trembling like a wounded animal.

"Bathsheba's fire and warmth." Dismas sighed deeply, his words sharp iron scraping on a stone.

Suddenly he stood, shaking his sister off him.

"Bathsheba's heat and fire," he repeated in a cold, distant tone, unrecognizable.

Then he burst into a thunderous laugh that broke her heart. He seemed to have gone mad.

"Do you know where Bathsheba's fire and warmth should have been?" He turned to her, panting, beside himself. "On my lips, between my legs, in this bedroom, on the bed! Don't you understand?"

Pain twisted his mouth grotesquely and, with a scream, he threw the little figure he'd held in his hands. The swallow flew across the room, striking the back wall.

Mad with fury, Dismas grabbed the bed by one end and upended it, tossing it against the wall with all his strength. Then he turned towards Sara and, taking her by the arms, shook her violently.

"She should be here, warming this home with her fire, every corner of it!" He began to pace back and forth in the room, like a prisoner in his cell. "But that fire, that warmth, have extinguished and her cold body lies buried under the earth, the same earth that the sandals of those Romans will continue to trample—yes, *trample*—until the fire of my anger devours them completely."

A smile crossed his lips like lightning, and Dismas looked up, defying from his shadows to the One who had inspired those same words written in the psalms.

A chill ran down Sara's spine as she listened to him. She tried to look for her brother in those eyes, in those words, in those gestures, but there was no trace of him. Anger had erased everything.

"Yes, until the fire of my anger devours you completely!" He spat out each word, then disappeared down the stairs.

"*Dismas!*" Sara shouted, trying to bring him back to his senses.

She heard the front door slam shut downstairs and stood where she was, helpless. Who could stop the wind from blowing during a storm?

Sara collapsed on the same spot where her brother had been sitting. She felt the weight of the shadows in the room falling on her shoulders, and she burst into tears, salt and fire scorching her cheeks.

She wept for Bathsheba, for the life that she should have shared with her brother that would never be. She wept for Dismas, for the terrible despair and hatred she had seen in his eyes. She wept for her mother, who would never forgive herself for what had happened. And she wept for herself, because she had come to Jerusalem to be in heaven, and instead she had touched hell itself.

The shadows of the lattices slid slowly over the walls of the room, and Sara came out of her reverie when the red of the sunset splashed over her body.

She got up and was about to go down the stairs, when something froze her in her steps. The wooden swallow that Dismas had thrown in his fury had stuck in the wall by the tip of one of its wings, like an arrow. The light of the sunset played upon it, producing on the wall a shadow that stretched in the shape of a cross.

A few days later, Sara passed by her brother's workshop and was glad to hear the sound of the hammer striking orange-hot iron again. She entered feeling as though her soul had been liberated, eager to embrace him and welcome him back to the land of the living.

Her joy was short-lived.

Sparks flew all around him. The blows of his hammer seemed hard, cruel, savage. When he raised his face from the fire and saw her enter, his lips curved obediently in the shape of a smile that failed to hide the unfathomable emptiness of that gaze. Sara knew that her brother was not there.

She approached him and hugged him. Dismas put his arms around her. It was as if her feet were splashing in Lake Tiberias during the winter; she felt cold.

They did not exchange a word. But he had returned, she tried to convince herself when she left the workshop.

For her part, his mother did not dare to go see her son. Since what had happened, she had barely got out of bed, exhausted, defeated. But as soon as Sara told her that Dismas was back, fear and impatience pushed her out of the sheets, and she eagerly awaited his visit, disguised in her best appearance.

He did not come. After three days had passed, Sara decided to visit the workshop again and beg him to come and see his mother.

"I thought she had returned to Galilee. I intended to go and see you both as soon as I finish the work that's been piling up," Dismas said, with that same smile obediently painted on his lips.

Sara knew he was lying.

"Mama and I are leaving tomorrow," she answered, staring into his soul. "You can still come see her tonight. Besides, you'll have to pick up Atzel. Although he's getting used to us, I think he misses you." She hoped that the mention of the dog would light up her brother's heart.

"I'll see what I can do. I need to have this order ready by the day after tomorrow," he answered without looking up, staring at the fire.

"She's your mother."

Sara was surprised by the harshness she heard in her own voice.

"I know. But this is also important," Dismas answered, nodding at the iron in the live fire.

At least this time he deigned to look at her.

"We'll wait for you," she said firmly.

The sound of the hammer continued to ring in her ears as she gave him a farewell kiss. When their eyes met for the last time, she knew she would not see her brother again for a long time.

Her mother aged five years that afternoon as she waited in vain for her son. Sara tried to excuse his absence as best she could, but Miriam was not an easy woman to fool.

That night, the hammer blows that Sara had heard in the workshop pounded in her chest for hours. A few times she had to press her hands against it because she thought she was drowning. She did not want to even think what that early morning must have been like for her mother.

Early the next day, before leaving in the caravan that Nathaniel had arranged to bring them back to Galilee, Sara felt the need to talk to him about Dismas. It was true that when she had last seen her brother, she explained Nathaniel, he'd been better than when she'd first found him; at least he had not worsened. But what was happening now was more uncertain—he had settled for dwelling in a place within his soul where the sun did not reach.

"He has not even mentioned your sister's name again,"

Sara told him, with the echo of her brother's hammer blows still in her ears. "As if it never happened."

Nathaniel looked at her with that kind look that she had once fantasized about. The pain of having lost his sister was still there, but unlike Dismas, he had not lost that spark of life that made his eyes shine.

"Don't worry about your brother. God has his times for each one of us. And of course I will take care of him! Do you think I wouldn't if you weren't asking me to?"

"Thank you, Nathaniel. I don't know what we would have done without you," Sara narrowed her eyes, suddenly moved.

Nathaniel looked away, blushing, and his eyes met Atzel comfortably resting inside the saddlebag of one of the camels. He couldn't help but smile.

"I can look after him as well. You don't have to take him with you; Dismas will need him by his side again soon," he said, petting the dog.

"Atzel is coming with us. My brother and I must have a similar smell, because the poor thing has decided not to leave me alone."

"I would do the same; he's a clever dog." He blushed. "Now go in peace. And don't forget that nothing is lost until the end," he whispered in her ear with a breath of hope, after saying goodbye with a warm embrace.

As she climbed onto the camel, Sara knew that no matter how hard she tried, she would never find a better man than Nathaniel in all of Galilee. But she was convinced that, despite the affection they shared for each other, there was an insurmountable barrier between them. But she couldn't figure out just what it was.

Nathaniel kept his promise to Sara. He stopped by Dismas's workshop every day. He would come in, say hello, watch his friend hammering away for a few moments, drink a glass of water together in silence, and leave.

Nathaniel did not want to force the situation; words between friends come when it's time—no sooner, no later. At some point, Dismas would need to empty his soul, and then Nathaniel would be there, waiting. Besides, he didn't see any reason for concern in his friend's appearance beyond the pain over the sudden loss of Bathsheba, which was to be expected. Perhaps Sara didn't realize that a man is a soul with a more limited range of shades and colors than a woman.

What Nathaniel did agree with, though, was Dismas's noticeable absence despite his physical presence in the workshop. There was hardly any communication between them. He seemed to have no time and a lot of urgency—urgency to finish the order he was working on and that did not allow him to put down the hammer all day.

Then an unexpected complication had to interrupt Nathaniel's visits to the workshop for a few days. It had to do with a small town called Nazareth and the difficulty of finding someone willing to take a caravan there. No one in his right mind was willing to deviate from the trade route that linked Galilee with the Holy City in order to take two camels loaded with goods to that small town, but Nathaniel had personally committed himself to his best client. So he had no choice but to leave Jerusalem to take charge of this small expedition. He hated having to deal with the inconveniences of a caravan; it was something he had done many times in the past, but now he was in command of the whole business, not just a caravan. And yet there he was, doing it in the name of Nazareth. Why on earth would anyone bother to send anything to that lost village in Galilee?

It was two weeks before Nathaniel returned from that trip. He came back changed—a new man.

The first thing he did upon his return was visit Aunt Rebecca. He had to inform her of something important. Then, in the afternoon, after making several arrangements, he met with his most trusted men and told them what he had told his aunt that morning: he was leaving the reins of the business. The shock was clear on the faces of his subordinates when they heard the news. Nathaniel reassured them that none of them would lose their jobs; the business would remain in the hands of his family, and they would report weekly to his aunt until his younger brother arrived from Galilee to take over.

Nathaniel returned to his aunt's, gathered the few belongings he was going to take with him, and distributed the rest among his aunt's servants. After this, he decided to go see his friend Dismas before his final departure the next day.

He was eager to leave; they were waiting for him near Bethany—the eleven and Him. But he could not leave without seeing his friend first. Nathaniel had felt it in his heart after the Teacher had given him permission to come to Jerusalem, and he couldn't leave without speaking to him.

He walked down the narrow alleys that led to Dismas's workshop. He had passed this way many times before, but today he saw them differently. In the evening light, the sun folded its shadows in a different way, making the street narrower, darker, sadder. What strength and power the light had to cast opposite views of the same landscape!

As Nathaniel approached, he found a wagon with two yoked oxen waiting in front of Dismas's door. It was loaded with barrels. Without knowing why, something twisted his insides, warning him that he was late.

Then Dismas came out of the house, accompanied by another man. They embraced before the stranger got into the wagon.

Dismas noticed his arrival, and Nathaniel waved to him; he could see in his eyes that his presence made his friend uncomfortable. The man with the cart took the reins and the oxen started to leave, but Nathaniel still had time to recognize in that face the rude client who had walked in on that first day he'd visited the workshop. Melchiades.

Dismas invited Nathaniel to enter, and he was startled to find the place empty. Only the extinguished forge stood as a silent witness of a workshop that was no longer there.

"I have sold everything. I am leaving here," Dismas said when he saw the astonishment on his friend's face.

"But I don't understand. What about the order you were working on like crazy before I left?"

"I have already delivered it," Dismas answered dryly.

Nathaniel knew then that the man with the wagon was taking the delivery, and with it, his friend's soul as well. He tried to smile as he stretched his arm over Dismas's shoulders. Dismas shrugged out of his embrace and, taking a step back, walked away from him.

"What happened, Dismas? What have you done?" Nathaniel asked from the bottom of his soul.

They had known each other for too long to ignore the elephant that stood there, in the middle of the room, between them.

Dismas offered only a cold and dry smile. He picked up a rag that had been left on the forge and wiped his hands without taking his eyes off it.

Sara had been right; there was nothing on that face that reminded Nathaniel of Dismas. He turned his mind to the Teacher and, lowering his gaze, gathered new strength with which to penetrate his friend's heart. If his had been set afire, it could also happen to Dismas.

"I have found him," he said, starting over, his chest warming again at the memory of his encounter in Nazareth.

Nathaniel's words caught Dismas off guard and, for an instant, the same spark of curiosity that he'd shown as a child chasing his friend through the dusty streets of Eilabun appeared on his eyes.

"The Teacher," Nathaniel added before Dismas could ask. "The Messiah."

Dismas blinked, and the boy disappeared from his eyes. In its place, he offered a mocking and condescending smile that hurt Nathaniel. But he decided to continue, unabashed. What he had to say was too important.

"Philip introduced me to him. You met him, didn't you? Philip. When you were at the Jordan to see the prophet John."

Nathaniel felt the sudden sting of pain in Dismas's heart, and he cleared his throat to push away the words that had inadvertently evoked Bathsheba's memory in his friend.

"Philip, he's a good friend of mine. I met him when I was about to leave Nazareth. There was something special about his face, a smile that went beyond his lips. He told me they had met the Messiah. I answered him with the same skeptical look that you're giving me now. Then he simply said, 'Come and see.' Don't ask me why, but those words were enough to spur my curiosity—"

Nathaniel had to stop for a moment, overcome by emotion as he remembered. He gazed at his friend. Dismas flipped the rag he had in his hands over his shoulder and simply nodded.

"Then I saw him," he continued. "There was nothing special about him or his appearance. He was a normal man, like you or me. But when he looked at me, it was as if he had known me all his life. He told me that before I met him, he had seen me under the fig tree." His eyes widened like two shining stars.

"And what were you doing under the fig tree, you little rascal?" Dismas spat rudely.

Nathaniel raised his eyebrows with sadness at his friend's skepticism.

"Don't be a fool, Dismas. Of all the people on earth, you're the only one who can understand those words," he insisted with renewed impetus. "Don't you realize? You should have been there!"

Dismas put the rag he'd been tossing back on the forge and, resting his hands on its edge, looked at Nathaniel intently.

"I have found him too," he said.

Silence fell over them both like night over the desert. Nathaniel looked at his friend, confused, and suddenly remembered the man with the wagon at the front of the workshop.

"But I have the strange feeling that we're not talking about the same person," Dismas continued, going around the forge, standing in front of Nathaniel. "Mine calls himself the Son of the Father. And he has promised to free the people of Israel from the oppressive hand of the Romans. What is yours going to do? What army does he have?" Dismas flung each of the questions at Nathaniel, full of irony and anger.

So this was his way of dealing with the loss of Bathsheba? With revenge? A feeling of pity gripped Nathaniel's heart, but he could not and *would* not give up—not yet. He had to try one last approach.

"Do you remember that day with our old teacher Zechariah?"

Dismas was taken aback by this unexpected moment from the past.

"When he looked at me, he was referring to that day when old Zechariah kicked me out of class. We were under the fig tree, remember? It was the place where the teacher liked to meet for his classes." Nathaniel swallowed, his skin suddenly prickling as he recalled what had happened to him a few days ago. "Zechariah kicked me out of class that day because I was convinced that the salvation promised by the Messiah could not be just for the Jews; it had to be for everyone. But after the death of my sister, of Bathsheba, I began to question that idea of the savior all over again. Shouldn't salvation be ours alone? After all, *we* are the chosen people, aren't we? Why should we share it with the Romans? They... they deserve death! And our duty is to defend ourselves as the Maccabees did, as the Zealots want to fight today. That has been the confused state of my soul during these days—not knowing what to think after the death of my sister."

Nathaniel stopped again, taking a breath as Dismas waited quietly.

"And then—and then He appears and tells me that He saw me when I was under the fig tree, when I insisted to old Zechariah that the Messiah had to come to save us all." Nathaniel couldn't keep two shining tears from running down his cheeks. "Don't you think that is a definitive answer to my doubts, an answer that only someone who saw me then could have given me? That man is the Messiah, Dismas!"

"And what is your Messiah willing to do for our salvation?"

Nathaniel saw a faint ray of sunlight breaking through the clouds over his friend's mind, and he placed his hands on his shoulders.

"I don't know, Dismas, I don't know. But he will do something, for certain!" he answered with the confidence of a child who knows he is safe in the arms of his father. "Do you think someone who was already watching over me that day under the fig tree can ignore our longing for freedom?"

With a slight movement of his shoulders, Dismas shook off Nathaniel's hands.

"Such bad luck then! He could have been watching when I begged for his help in the middle of the street, with your sister's dying body in my arms. No, he didn't even need to watch! He could have just deigned to listen to me! That would have been enough—listening to my pleas to save your sister." Dismas's voice shattered into a thousand pieces. "He couldn't bother to save one person in the world, and you say he'll save us all!?"

"Dismas, you can't be like that. You can't let hatred eat away at what's left of your life."

"And what do you want me to do? Join the cause of your Messiah and sit around a campfire solving riddles about what we were doing twenty years ago? Do you forget that your sister is dead?!"

A sharp slap on the cheek cut Dismas off. He blushed with anger and raised his fist, ready to return his friend's affront. But he was stopped by that gleam in Nathaniel's eyes, the same one that he'd seen in Bathsheba's gaze that day by the fountain.

The two friends looked at each other, defiant, without recognizing each other.

"Go with your Messiah and be happy," Dismas finally said, turning. "Meanwhile, I will be avenging your sister's death with the strength and the power of my messiah."

He went to the door and walked out, disappearing into the bustle of the people who were moving up and down the street.

Alone, Nathaniel lowered his head and sighed. They had both suffered the loss of Bathsheba, but the light that illuminated their souls cast radically opposite visions. Like the sun in the alleyways.

He cursed himself. He had ruined everything. He had found the Messiah, and he had wanted so much to allow His face to shine on Dismas, to convince him, to save him! But all he had managed to do was drive his friend away.

He would tell the Teacher as soon as he had the chance. Surely He would know what to do about Dismas. Because if it depended on Nathaniel himself, it was clear that his hopeless friend was a lost cause.

11.

Dismas imagined his feet crossing an unfathomable abyss, until they finally touched the ground.

He descended from the camel in the darkness that enveloped him. It felt strange to be back on earth after travelling all day on the animal's bony back. He heard mocking laughter behind him, and he turned nervously, forgetting that he still wore the cloth that covered his eyes. He heard footsteps approaching and, fearing for his life, raised his arms to protect himself. Fingers played on the back of his neck, and when the blindfold finally fell from his eyes, his blurry gaze again fell upon the guy who had blindfolded him before they'd left Jerusalem that very morning. "It's better for you not to know where you're going," the guy had said when he noticed Dismas's hesitation about the blindfold. "That way, if you change your mind, at least he'll let you live. Although that's no guarantee either; the last one who backed out hasn't returned yet," he had added with a malicious smile.

Now Dismas looked around. He had no idea where they were. He had spent the whole day trying to calculate where they could be heading; a day's journey was halfway to Lake Tiberias. However, the aridity and ruggedness of the terrain were not at all familiar to him; they had probably traveled south, deep into the Judean desert.

The place where he found himself was as gloomy as the few souls that inhabited it. The flames flickering among the embers of a campfire that refused to die away played with the darkness on the faces of the three men who sat around it. Their shadows were projected, imposing, on the limestone of the mountainside behind them.

Dismas couldn't discern the reason those guys were there. If it was really because they were waiting for him to arrive, they didn't seem to show much interest in his presence.

He let time pass, confused. Had he been traveling all day just to be greeted by this indifference? This was not the welcome he had anticipated after what he had agreed with Melchiades. He had expected to be led to the person organizing the resistance to the Romans. In exchange, he was willing to provide a large number of spears and swords. At first Melchiades had strongly opposed his proposal, but, in the end, he'd backed off from his initial refusal, and he agreed without consulting anyone. Of course, they would do it his own way—first he would take all the "tools" that Dismas had been forging day and night, and then, only then, would he give him the instructions needed so he could meet his boss.

There was such urgency coursing through Dismas's veins that he hadn't minded accepting Melchiades's conditions: the stranger, the hungry camel, and the blindfold. But now that he had reached the end of the journey, he saw no reward: not in the bored faces of those men by the fire, not among the dark shadows that had taken over the evening.

He turned impatiently to his traveling companion, who seemed absorbed in pampering and hissing to the two quadrupeds on whom they'd had their asses glued all day.

"Melchiades told me I would meet your boss. Where is the one you call Gestas?"

Without taking his eyes off the animals, the guy pointed to a stone among the men warming themselves by the fire.

"Make yourself comfortable. You'll have to wait."

Dismas snorted, annoyed, and advanced toward where the three men sat. He felt the menace of one of them peering at him, and although he didn't really care anymore, he feared for his life; he didn't want to die there, deceived in the middle of nowhere. He pretended to ignore the look, but he clenched his fists, hidden under the sleeves of his tunic, ready to jump if it was necessary, as he sat by the fire.

He glanced around. The man had stopped looking at him, and Dismas took the opportunity to scrutinize his face. Looking at the glow of the embers in his black pupils was like plunging into an abyss. He, the youngest of the three, extended his leg towards one of his companions and kicked his foot. The latter reluctantly bent toward the fire, took a branch with some meat stuck on its end, and passed it to Dismas. He bowed his head slightly in gratitude to the man in command, who looked away, ignoring him.

He was hungry, and he took the piece of meat in one bite while he looked at the steep rocks that surrounded them above. Later he learned that those rocks were riddled with caves and crevices. In one of them a young David had taken refuge a thousand years before, the same cave where his pursuer, King Saul, had entered to relieve himself. That day David could have killed Saul and taken his place, but the arm of YHWH had sprinkled mercy upon his heart and he'd spared Saul's life.

Many of these openings in the rock were still good hiding places for bandits and criminals chased by the law. They were less royal asses, no doubt; with hearts lacking in mercy, perhaps; but their shit still smelled like it did in the time of King David.

At last a fire appeared in the distance, approaching from the same direction they had come. The flame of the torch shining in the darkness surrounded its arrival with anticipation, but the magic of the moment dissipated as soon as the light revealed that the figure approaching was Melchiades.

"You arrived early. I was expecting you tomorrow at dawn," he gruffed, with the crackling of the torch as a background.

"You shouldn't be surprised, considering how quickly you took all the merchandise from my workshop." He stood up from the fire, and after a slight bow to the three men seated around him, he approached Melchiades. "I hope Gestas is not too far away. I don't like having to walk with you through these places at night, with that flame as the only guide for our steps."

"Not so fast, my friend, not so fast", Melchiades answered, holding the torch between them as if defending himself from a vermin. "Tomorrow we will decide calmly whether or not you will meet Gestas."

"That is not what we agreed upon," Dismas replied, the flame of the torch heating his face.

"He is a busy man and—"

Dismas moved fast, snatching the torch from Melchiades's hand while he wrapped his other arm tightly around his neck, cutting off his breathing.

The men by the fire stood, ready to defend him, but Dismas brandished the torch at them.

"Stay where you are, or I'll send him to the very gates of hell." He leaned his head slightly so that his lips were close to Melchiades's ear. "Now, you better take me to Gestas, if you don't want me to lose my patience and end your life now for your lies."

He began to loosen the muscles of his arm to allow some

oxygen back into Melchiades's lungs. The man struggled to inhale, red with anger, cursing Dismas between stammers.

"Gestas doesn't let himself be seen by just anyone," he muttered in ragged breaths.

"I'm not just anyone, Melchiades! I've given you twelve swords and fifteen spears. I don't think there are many in Jerusalem who would do that without demanding money in return. The only condition I asked was to meet your boss face to face. And I won't leave here until I do."

"I'm Gestas. Let that wretch go."

The voice rose loudly among those present, and Dismas obeyed. He turned to the one had spoken, the man in whose eyes one could plunge into an abyss, but he had no time to see no more—a powerful punch landed in his face, dropping him to the ground.

"Don't ever threaten me again, you impetuous bastard!" Melchiades's words died in his ears with the fire of the torch on him, and everything faded into darkness.

Dismas awoke, face down, in the rocky belly of the mountain. Sunlight filtered in from the outside, timidly licking the walls of the cave he was in. He tried to get up, but his bones were numb and his wrists were tied behind his back. He felt his cracked lips with his tongue. A trickle of blood was dried in the left corner. He scratched off the bitter taste of it with his teeth, when a sudden voice behind him made him raise his head.

"It took you a while to come to. I didn't know our soft Melchiades could hit so hard. Bringing down a rearing horse isn't easy."

Gestas, the man with the abyss in his eyes, stood between him and the light from outside.

"Even the weakest man can bring down a bull if he takes

it by surprise," replied a hoarse voice that Dismas had a hard time recognizing as his own. "Where is Melchiades?"

"I sent him back to Jerusalem, to avoid another misunderstanding with you."

Gestas pulled a knife from his belt and approached him.

The threat made Dismas forget the stiffness of his body and he stood up defensively. Gestas offered a friendly smile.

"Relax. If I wanted to kill you, you would already be dead. You came here to talk to me, didn't you? So let's talk."

Leaning towards him, he cut the rope that bound Dismas's wrists.

"But first, a good breakfast. Life looks different with a full stomach."

The drippings of the sound of an unseen waterfall filled the silence as Dismas devoured the honey-filled cake that a woman had laid at his feet. A gulp of goat's milk helped wash the last bite down his throat, and, wiping his mouth on his sleeve, he finished the breakfast.

Gestas, who had been watching him as he ate, shook his head in disapproval.

"It only happens three times a day."

Dismas looked at him without understanding.

"You should learn how to take your time and enjoy a meal." Gestas gestured to the empty plate. "It's one of the few things that distinguishes us from dogs."

Dismas stood up and took a quick look around. Gestas perceived his disappointment on his face. Hundreds of holes opened in the rock walls that surrounded them, stretching upwards, behind their backs, on the sides. Many of them seemed large enough to be dwelling places, like the cave they were in, but apart from two women Dismas saw laying out clothes at the other end, on the sunny side of the wall, there was not a soul. Where were all the men of the resistance that Melchiades boast so much about?

A sudden splash drew his eyes to a stream that must have flowed from the bottom of that unseen waterfall he could still hear. Two children were fighting playfully in a life-or-death battle over the water channel that disappeared into the pine forest beyond, sheltered by the rocks.

Seeing the boys giggling and scuffling together increased Dismas's impatience. If this was all there was of the camp that he'd imagined when they blindfolded him, he had wasted his time. Where had Melchiades brought him?

"Melchiades has told me a lot about you," Gestas said, drawing his attention back. "He has been trying to convince me for some time that I had to meet you. And I have resisted until now. I am not going to lie to you—if it had not been for your generous contribution to our cause, you would not be here today. You have managed to arouse my curiosity. But before our relationship can continue, I need to understand why someone like you would abandon his job, his position, his place in the world, for something he didn't even believe in just a month ago."

"I have my reasons, but I don't think they matter. My generosity and commitment should suffice," Dismas replied curtly.

"You are the master of your silences, and I of their consequences," Gestas said in the sudden void that had opened between them.

"Are you saying that if I don't tell you my reasons, you won't let me join you?" Dismas asked incredulously.

"Understand that if you refuse to speak, our paths will separate here and now. The shadow of the Romans stretches too long." He looked at Dismas gloomily. "Melchiades has warned me that you've done some work for them, and we want to avoid any conflict of interest."

"Melchiades is an idiot." Dismas was unable to contain himself any longer. "Look, I think this was a mistake. I shouldn't have trusted him or what he told me I would find here. I won't lie to you either—I expected more than a hive with no swarm." He pointed at the caves in the rock that surrounded them with the veins in his arms pumping fire through his muscles. "It takes more than words and good intentions to cast vengeance upon the Romans!"

Something inside him broke, and Dismas sunk to his knees, crushed to the ground under the weight of the rage and sadness that had been consuming him for days. The grand blood-stained expectations he had placed on this encounter had suddenly collapsed, and with them, his entire body succumbed to the wrath of the moment.

Gestas's eyes lit up. He let a few moments pass. That pain, that anger, was perfect fertilizer for the soul of this bleak man. Then he leaned toward him, surrounded his face with the palms of his hands, and, holding it gently, fixed his gaze on those two sparks of fire.

"Ah, at last I understand, brother! There is nothing more powerful on the face of the earth than the seed that sows vengeance. It can grow into a tree full of leaves, heavy with fruit, but you have to know first how to water it, carefully, slowly, letting its roots sink into the heart until it drinks the last drop of blood it finds there. You and I can become strong, very strong. The time t has come to be so, and to free ourselves from the yoke."

Gestas put his arm around Dismas's shoulder and helped him to rise. The despair and hatred that he'd seen crossing those eyes like lightning at sunset had been sufficient explanation.

"As you said, our hive is empty," he continued with his lips pressed to Dismas's ear. "That is our advantage over the enemy. We don't have a burrow, but they do. The Romans, they all gather together under one roof. We, on the other hand, are thousands walking separately under the sky, scattered in the streets of Jerusalem, over the fields of Judea. That makes it very easy to attack them when the time comes. We will strike their hornet's nest and, when they emerge, we will devour them, hundreds of thousands of ants upon them. But all in due time, like your thirst for revenge."

Gestas's words had the strange effect of a balm on Dismas's heart.

"So, what can I do now?" he answered, strangely comforted.

"I want you back in Jerusalem first thing tomorrow morning."

"What!" Dismas's eyes bulged again, but Gestas restrained him by placing his hands on his shoulders.

"I just want you to wait there, five days, until my return. It's not much time."

"Are you out of your mind?" Dismas erupted, "Where do you want me to go? I no longer have a workshop, and I don't want to stroll the streets of that city again, not yet."

A slight fear accompanied his words.

"You can go to my house, if you want." Gestas didn't raise his voice as he spoke. "Wait for me there, and I'll introduce you to someone. Five days is all I ask of you."

Dismas looked up at the sky, undecided. This man was asking him to wait while blood called for blood; it was difficult to contain. He looked again at Gestas, who poured those black eyes again upon his soul.

"Five days," Gestas repeated, extending his hand in the air with urgent energy. "I'll take you to meet the scourger of the hornet's nest. His name is Yeshua, but he likes to call himself Son of the Father. Bar Abbas."

Hearing that name, Dismas took a step back, confused. *You will see his power.*

Damned. Damned be all if Gestas was referring to the same man who had snatched Nathaniel.

"Are you talking to me about the Messiah of Galilee?"

"Oh, no!" Gestas burst out laughing. "That's a lunatic from Nazareth who likes to pet people, comforting them with words of forgiveness and love for one another. But people will grow tired of that charlatan, and when they do, the time will come to present them with someone who will comfort the Romans with fire and sword."

Gestas's figure, outlined against the light of a pale sky, suddenly looked strong, powerful, even invincible to Dismas. How could he say no to someone who spoke with words that his heart longed to hear?

That night, before leaving for Jerusalem, it took Dismas a long time to fall asleep inside the dark cave where he lay. His life had undergone a shattering change, and his heart was still beating wildly, due to the course of events for which both the Romans and the Messiah were to blame—the former for their brutality, the latter for his absence.

Bathsheba's beauty had led him to green pastures where to lie down, and he had found happiness there. But the grass had become stained with her blood, and without her at his side, there was no path forward except revenge. He felt the sweet taste of it in his mouth now. And if all he had to do to grasp it with his hands was to wave the figure of the Messiah before the masses, he would do it. Didn't the people want liberation? Well, they would get it.

His thoughts began to fade away, one after the other, cascading in his mind until blackness covered everything. And there at the end, he saw himself reflected in those eyes, clinging to the edges of the abyss, falling.

PART THREE
A Miracle

I.

Her mother's life was slowly fading away and no one could do anything to stop it. The bloodstain that Sara had discovered that day in the bundle of dirty clothes had been a first sign. But that was a long time ago now, and everything had been getting bigger and wider since the terrible accident.

Her mother had left Jerusalem with her heart broken into two pieces—one half because she blamed herself for Bathsheba's death, and the other because of the dark abyss that threatened her son's life. His absence the night before their departure had been more than obvious proof of it.

And her mother had carried all that pain and anguish back with her to Galilee. Sara had seen it reflected in her face during the trip. The night after their return, when she hoped that her mother would finally be able to rest, Sara had heard her groaning, gripped by nightmares that shook her soul. Only with the light of dawn did the laments cease, as she seemed to fall asleep.

Mother gave no sign of life all morning and Sara decided to let her rest until the sun was at its peak in the sky. Finally, she went into her room and had to shake her several times to get her to open her eyes. When she managed to get out of bed, a large streak of blood had stained even the mattress under the sheets. She stayed in bed throughout that day, her strength exhausted by a stream of blood that flowed from her like tears for the lost life of her son.

From that day on, the flow of blood that her mother had been hiding became more and more acute. They visited several doctors, who, apart from emptying their pockets, did very little to ease her. The one from Magdala had suggested as a remedy the stupid superstition of applying ointments on nights of the full moon.

But it was the last doctor who had given the most painful diagnosis. After charging them a shameful sum of money, he'd had the nerve to suggest that being an impure woman—that's what he had dared to call her mother—was a difficult problem to solve, since the cause was surely to be found in sin. Sara came out of that consultation fuming, and, although she did not manage to get him to return the ridiculous amount they had paid him, she was at least satisfied by the shouts and insults she hurled at the imbecile until they lost sight of him.

Miriam, however, remained silent for several days after that visit, churning in her mind the harsh words the doctor had spoken. She had understood perfectly what he had meant—her life was slipping away from her in torrents because she was to blame for her son's sins.

If she had obeyed what Dismas had ordered through Bathsheba that day and had not visited the eastern part of the city, she would still be alive, and her son's life would be very different. The accumulation of the effects of that terrible decision fell upon her, and therefore, the sins that her son committed from then on would be hers as well.

With the useless visits to doctors behind her, Sara had settled for the weak embers of a fire that would never burn again. That was what her mother had become, and the only hope left for her was that she would go out gently, like a log consumed by the flame that collapses into a mound of ashes and dust when fire vanishes.

Of her brother Dismas, Sara assumed everything, but knew nothing. Atzel was the only thing they had left of him. She held in her memory the image of his face full of anger emerging from the shadows of the bridal chamber. Although she had wanted to return to Jerusalem to see how he was, her mother's delicate health prevented her from doing so. She could not leave her alone for so long, and she decided instead a message through Nathaniel's caravan service.

The news that it brought to her could not have been more disturbing. His workshop was abandoned, and the newly acquired house had fallen back into the hands of the original owner when the last payment had not been made. There seemed to be no one in the city who could say where her brother was. Not even Nathaniel.

Mystery also surrounded Bathsheba's brother. It was as if he had been swallowed up by the earth after giving up the family business overnight. Sara was hurt that he had not even said farewell to her, first because he had promised to look after her brother, but above all because, even if she would have never admit it, always had thought there was something deeper between her and Nathaniel.

For a time, Sara secretly harbored the hope that wherever Nathaniel was, Dismas was with him. Nathaniel's brother, Jacob, let her know how wrong she was in this supposition.

He had taken over the business after his elder brother's sudden resignation and spent most of his time travelling between Jerusalem and Galilee, trying to patch up the wounds that Nathaniel's absence had opened in the reputation of the caravan service.

One afternoon, as Sara finished tallying up the wool that

the most recent caravan had brought with it from Jerusalem, she overheard a conversation between him and one of his customers. They were talking outside the door, and there was a certain nervousness in Jacob's voice.

"Caleb, please reconsider it. You have always used our service to move the merchandise from your boats in Tiberias to Jerusalem. Why should it not continue to be that way?"

"Jacob, you know that I have always loved your whole family, and I am very sorry for the misfortunes that have befallen you in such a short space of time. But I must look after my fish; I cannot risk having thieves attack your caravan again."

"Come on, that has only happened once with your merchandise, and I can assure you it won't happen again."

"But it has with other expeditions of yours. I am sorry to have to tell you this, my friend, but it seems that the bandits have taken particular liking to attacking your caravans."

Sara raised her head from the numbers she was writing and looked towards the door. What she had just heard had made Jacob's back tremble.

"Come on, Caleb. Don't exaggerate it so much. It was all bad luck." Jacob smiled, trying to stifle the obvious irritation in his voice.

"I am truly sorry, Jacob. The decision has already been made."

Caleb the fisherman said goodbye, and Sara returned to her numbers, letting out a sigh of worry. The client was right; Jacob was a good man, but his lack of experience and poor business acumen had led him to some bad decisions. Reducing the number of porters traveling in each caravan, for example, had saved them money in every expedition, but it also had left them with fewer men to defend it in case of an attack, and that had attracted thieves and bandits like flies to honey.

Jacob came in and slammed the door. Sara tried to stay out of his bad mood, focusing her eyes to the accounts.

"If others follow Caleb, there will be no caravans very soon," he muttered to himself before turning to Sara. "Do you have the numbers done for the last expedition?"

Sara had feared that question. She looked up and nodded.

"Are we that bad?" he asked when he saw her face.

She hesitated a few seconds before answering.

"I'm afraid so, Jacob."

He pounded the table with his fists, unable to contain his anger.

"If things continue like this, I'm going to have to contact Nathaniel and ask him to implore his Messiah for the salvation of his own family," he said through clenched teeth.

Sara pretended she hadn't heard what Jacob had just said, but his words made her heart skip a beat.

The Messiah? So that was the reason why foolish Nathaniel had abandoned everything? All of Galilee was in turmoil over that word. The Messiah was the subject of discussion by the inhabitants of all the towns spread around Lake Tiberias. Rumors of miraculous healings and news of miraculous catches of fish kept eavesdropping throughout the region. When she heard them, Sara shrugged her shoulders with skepticism.

She was not inclined to believe in extraordinary events. In fact, that was precisely one of the few things that she and her dear friend Bathsheba had never agreed on. Her friend always liked to see a divine hand behind every unexplained event. Sara could still remember the day when, as little girls, they were returning from the market in Magdala on foot, starving because they had not eaten all day. Bathsheba made her kneel in the dust of the road to implore Almighty God to raise his hand and make some food appear before their very eyes. Nothing happened, of course, but then, as they entered the village, they found two loaves of bread by the side of the road. Bathsheba's eyes lit up and Sara had no choice but to acknowledge the wonderful miracle that YHWH had done for them.

However, the next morning, on her way to the river with a bundle of dirty clothes on her shoulders, she passed in front of the baker's house at the very moment when he was complaining about the petty thieves who, the day before, had stolen several loaves of bread that he'd left to cool on the windowsill. At that moment, Sara knew that Dismas and Nathaniel were the perpetrators of this misdeed, but, more importantly, she was absolutely certain that YHWH had had nothing to do with the miracle of the two loaves of bread. He had more important matters to attend than feeding two little brats like her and Bathsheba.

"Sara, you cannot be so unbelieving," Bathsheba had replied after hearing her reasonable explanation of the previous day's miracle. "Don't you realize that Almighty God can use any ordinary means to grant us what we ask for?"

Could it be that Nathaniel, having the same naive spirit as his sister Bathsheba, had left everything to go after a fraud who pretended to be the Messiah? Sara tried to conjure up his image before giving an answer. She recalled that special look of his, full of tenderness and wonder, that had captivated her since they were children. But even then, she'd understood that eyes like his could only be destined for something much greater.

But now it turned out that poor Nathaniel had become tangled in a fisherman's net.

Sara shook his head, not knowing what to think of it. But of one thing she was certain—it was absolutely impossible that her brother's destiny was tied in any possible way with Nathaniel's. Dismas could not have become a follower of the Messiah. All the more after what had happened. Had the death of Bathsheba made her brother lose his faith? Sara did not dare to answer that question.

For a moment she wished that her brother had fallen for the same deception that had ensnared Nathaniel, because even if this Messiah were a fraud, perhaps the fantasy of His kingdom coming would have torn from Dismas's heart that thirst for vengeance that she'd seen in his eyes that day.

All this ruminating led to an inevitable question with no answer in sight: Where had her brother gone?

"Sara, I need to talk to you."

Sara looked across the room, towards the unexpected voice of Jacob, who had just slipped through the door in the evening light. More than six months had passed since the previous conversation, but the scene was the same. She had just returned to the cupboard the tablets where she recorded the quantities of blankets and wool, and was preparing to return home, where her mother waited, as every night, with a forced smile on her face and a delicious meal on the table.

There was an uneasiness on Jacob's face, unlike the peace that his brother Nathaniel had usually conveyed, and Sara was greatly troubled. Had the time come to say goodbye to the world of caravans?

"Please, sit down." He pointed kindly to one of the chairs. "I spoke this morning with Abdomeneo."

Sara nodded, her eyes widening. Abdomeneo was the leader of the caravan that had arrived from Jerusalem the day before. Since Nathaniel's departure, he was the most trusted man they had to lead the expeditions between Jerusalem and Galilee every week.

"You see, I don't know if you've heard, but the caravan was attacked again."

Sara looked at Jacob, confused.

"It can't be possible. The list of goods from Jerusalem matches what I counted this morning in the warehouse. Nothing was missing. I saw it myself."

"It was attacked, but they didn't take anything."

"What do you mean? I don't understand," she replied, shaking her head in disbelief.

"Abdomeneo saw them coming out from behind a dune, and they fell upon the caravan before there was time to escape. There were seven men. Two of them stood in front of him and forced the caravan to stop. They had their faces covered, just like Abdomeneo."

"Why are you telling me all this?" she interrupted, surprised.

"The other five men had begun to get their hands on the goods on one of the camels, when Abdomeneo, mad with rage, confronted the man who was in command of the thieves. He pulled the turban off Abdomeneo's face, and when the thief saw him, he stopped dead and ordered his henchmen to return all the goods they were stealing."

"Why? What did Abdomeneo do to stop the robbery?" Sara asked, intrigued.

"Absolutely nothing, except show his face. That was enough. When the bandits were about to leave, Abdomeneo asked the leader why he had stopped the caravan if they weren't going to steal anything. The man, who in all that time had kept his face hidden under a turban, answered that they did not attack caravans that belonged to Nathaniel's household."

Sara looked at Jacob, trying to figure out exactly where was all this leading. Her heart began to beat fast.

"The leader insisted that they were not thieves," Jacob continued. "They were only working against the enemies of Israel, to establish the reign of Yeshua the Messiah."

"So you think those robbers knew Nathaniel and that's why they did not raid the caravan?"

"The Messiah that everyone is talking about, the man from Galilee, is called Yeshua," answered Jacob, narrowing his eyes.

Sara thought quietly, trying to comprehend what she had just heard. So Nathaniel's Messiah was ordering the raid on caravans in order to finance the establishment of his reign against Israel's enemies? Praise the Lord and pass the ammunition. Hmm. This Messiah's approach was interesting, very different from the one she had forged initially.

"But I haven't told you everything." Jacob's voice broke the brief silence that had befallen upon them.

Sara returned her attention to Jacob.

"Your brother, Dismas..." Jacob tried in vain to find the most delicate words. "He was the one who led the band of the attackers."

"*What?*" Jacob's words crashed inside her head. "How does Abdomeneo know? He didn't even see his face, and they don't know each other!"

"They travelled in the same caravan, when Dismas came after your father's death. Do you remember? And he recognized him by his voice, by his eyes. He is sure it was Dismas."

Sara was speechless. Jacob's words were like a sudden source of water in the desert.

"You seem happy about it!" Jacob was astonished. "That your brother is a bandit?"

"No, of course not. I'm not happy about it. But he can't be such a bandit or so bad if your brother Nathaniel is also involved in what he's doing, don't you think?"

"My brother Nathaniel's decisions have only brought us misfortunes, and I assure you that not all of them happened after he left."

Sara was hurt by those last words—Jacob was obviously referring, without naming her, to Bathsheba's death. How could he seriously think that it had been the fault of his brother Nathaniel? Was the human heart so dark as to never stop looking for someone to blame for anything bad that happened?

That same night, when she returned home, Sara said nothing about what she had heard about her brother. Her mother couldn't take any more blows.

It wasn't that Sara was afraid of telling her that her son was a thief—nobody could truly be a bandit if he were working alongside Nathaniel. It was the shattered expectations of an encounter that she could not guarantee that she wanted to avoid. First she had to figure out where to find this Messiah and his followers. Only then would she not only tell her mother but run along with her to the place where her brother was.

During dinner, it was hard to contain her excitement, but she stoically endured. It was only as they finished and had already collected the dishes that Sara was about to give in and share her secret. Then Miriam began to talk about her sister, Aunt Judith.

"That crazy woman has sent me a message from Capernaum, saying we should go to visit her. It seemed quite strange to me."

More than strange, Sara found it delusional. Aunt Judith didn't bother to send messages to her sister very often, much less invitations to her magnificent house in Capernaum. She had married an ambitious fisherman who, by force of sacrifice, hard work, and emptying Lake Tiberius in the process, had filled his home with luxuries and wealth that Sara and her family could never afford. Mother had not been as lucky in her marriage.

"She must be very lonely in that house now that she is a widow and her children are married," Miriam added thoughtfully.

"We could go see her someday," Sara said, taking advantage of the unexpected opportunity to explore her mother's willingness to travel.

"My dear one." A quiet anguish touched her words. "Your aunt knows nothing, and I want to keep it that way."

"But the trip there is not long," Sara persisted without digging too hard.

"Daughter, you know I get exhausted as soon as I wake up in the mornings, but even if I didn't, you know sleeping in someone else's house is out of the question."

No one except Sara knew the truth about her mother's illness. Even if in the village neighbors were aware that she was not feeling well, they did not know the details of her affection. She had insisted on keeping silent about her situation. According to Jewish precepts, a woman was considered impure during her menstruation periods and had to lock herself in her home so as not to contaminate anyone. One could imagine how people would respond if they found out about her chronic blood flow. Miriam did not want to end up like a leper, avoiding people, or worse, having them reject her when they saw her approaching.

No, that would never happen; she preferred to stay silent. The frequency of her blood flows, their irregularity, condemned her to spend most of the time inside her house, but keeping it a secret allowed her at least to enjoy a few rays of sun each day, of feeling alive herself.

"Well, I don't know," Sara insisted, pushing just a bit harder. "I think one of these days we should venture a small trip."

"Bah!" her mother dismissed it without even looking away from the tub of water in which she sank the dirty dishes.

Sara was about to tell her that such a trip would be worth the effort and its hardships if it allowed them to see her son Dismas, but she bit her tongue. First she needed to find out where she could find that group of enlightened disciples of the so-called Messiah.

Every day, Sara kept her ears open, listening for any news about the Messiah's whereabouts. She knew that he and his followers moved along the western shore of the Sea of Galilee. On its shores, Capernaum and Tiberias were the biggest towns. Both were the same distance from Eilabun, barely a day's journey, so it would not be difficult to travel there when the time came. The only difficulty was knowing where to find this Yeshua, and Nathaniel… and Dismas.

The answer came a dozen evenings later, when after inventorying the number of wool blankets that were to be loaded onto the caravan to Jerusalem, she passed in front of the house where Alon, the baker, lived.

She was surprised to see his cart full of loaves of bread at that time of day. It seemed strange to her. It was Yom Revii, market day in Magdala, and the cart had returned bearing the same merchandise it had left with that morning.

She was still looking at the bread, more curious than hungry despite the sudden pang in her stomach, when Alon's heavy figure—"Alon weighs a ton" was one of the favorite rhymes of the children of Eilabun—emerged from the doorway of his house, accompanied by his wife.

"I'm serious, dear. Look for yourself! I didn't sell *any*," the man said pointing to the cart full of bread.

When his wife, thin and dry as a stick, saw all of the unsold bread in the cart, her sallow skin turned red with fury, like a chameleon.

"You're useless!" she shouted, still not believing what her eyes where seeing., "I shouldn't have let you go without me! I knew you weren't going to sell anything on your own."

Alon's beefy body seemed to catch fire from the flames she spewed from her mouth, and he threw his arms in the air, looking for a way to defend himself.

"Shut up and listen, woman!" he shouted at last from his magnificent corpulence.

She stopped short. She knew perfectly well when her Alon was angry, and at those times it was better to keep quiet and wait for him to burn and deflate himself out.

"There were very few people in the market today," he went on with excitement on his face. "It was nearly deserted. From early in the morning, news had spread that this Messiah was in Taghbar, on the shores of the lake, and everyone went to see him."

"And what does that have to do with our bread?" she asked, frowning, not understanding the connection between the bread and the Messiah.

"That's how the morning passed, very boring," continued Alon without listening to his wife, his tongue on the verge of burning. "I had sold only two loaves, but I said to myself, 'Calm down, Alon. The afternoon will be better. People will return hungry, and with a bit of luck you will sell everything.' Then something incredible happened!"

At that point Alon couldn't help being carried away by the story he was narrating.

"People returned, yes, as I predicted. They came back from the shores of the lake, from Taghbar, full of wonder. And they all came with a loaf of bread under their arm!" he exclaimed, beside himself with a combination of astonishment and anger.

"So who is the scoundrel who dares to compete with us?" his wife murmured, tapping her chin as her mind rushed through a list of possible candidates.

"Don't you understand yet? It was Yeshua the Messiah!" Alon's excitement was now palpable in every inch of his flesh. "There were more than five thousand people gathered, listening to him, and he fed them by *multiplying loaves for everyone!*"

"You must be out of your mind. Completely mad!" She shook her head, trying to imagine an oven large enough to accommodate five thousand loaves of bread.

She shook it sharply once again, dismissing the probabilities.

"You can say whatever you want, Alon, but if you want to hide from me the fact that you spent the day in the market drinking with your friends, you don't have to come up with such nonsense."

"But darling, smell me, smell me!" insisted Alon, opening his mouth and breathing heavily into his wife's face. "No trace of wine. How could I make up something like this? If you want, we can go to Capernaum tomorrow. I heard the Messiah is going to be there for a few days, and we'll be able to see him. Then you will be convinced. Maybe he will do more miracles."

"And what do you want to do with these?" she turned to her husband with renewed fury, "Two more miracles like this and our business will be done. Go on, come in and close the door! We will decide later what to do with all this bread. Maybe we can sell it in Tiberias at half price," she added thoughtfully as she went back inside the house.

Alon and his wife disappeared behind the door, and

Sara could no longer hear them. Nor did she need to; she quickened her pace and ran back to her house, her heart on the verge of exploding.

When she entered, Atzel was already on his feet, by the fire, waiting for her. He jumped and barked with joy when he saw her, like he did every afternoon.

"Mama, I have good news and bad news," she said to her mother as she bent down to pet the dog, breathing heavily.

Atzel lifted his snout and sniffed her, more curious and insistent than usual, as if he suspected what she had to say—though it could also have been due to the aroma of Alon's bread on her clothes.

Her mother turned away from the steaming pot of dinner to pay attention to the sparks in her daughter's eyes. Something in her face told Miriam that her son Dismas was behind them.

"Tomorrow morning we leave for Capernaum."

Her mother looked at her, unsure how to respond.

"Dismas is there!" Sara cried, unable to hide her enthusiasm any longer. "He is with Nathaniel! They are disciples of the Messiah."

Miriam had to sit down. With her back to her daughter, a faint silence enveloping them.

Sara slowly approached her. She put her hands on her mother's shoulders and leaned her face against her cheek. A tear fell, fleeting. Sara waited a few moments before facing her. Then she kneeled in front of her, lay her head on her lap, and they both wept in silence.

"We will leave tomorrow and stay overnight at Aunt Judith's house," her mother finally said, standing up.

There was strength and determination in her voice, but also fear.

That night, it took Miriam a long time to fall asleep. A

window had opened in her heart that allowed a ray of sunlight to pierce through so much darkness that had gathered for so long. She was going to see her son! This time she didn't care whether or not he wanted to see her. She would hug him, ask for forgiveness, love him. Wasn't that all a mother had to do? Besides, the news that Dismas was with Nathaniel drove away like a storm the worst forebodings that had cracked her soul all these years.

However, something continued to pinch her insides. If Dismas had not been dragged into a life of hatred, a life of resentment, a life of revenge, what was the reason for her flow of blood?

Whose sin was it that made her bleed?

2.

"So, you won't say anything?"

"I won't say anything," Sara said, tired of repeating the same answer for the fifth time.

"And you brought it all? Didn't forget anything?" Miriam insisted with a fleeting glance before knocking on the door again.

Sara nodded as they waited for someone inside Aunt Judith's to open the door. She had brought extra sheets and towels to absorb the traces of blood on the bed or anywhere in the house where her mother might sit. She hoped that the four bundles they had taken along would be enough for the two days they planned to spend in Capernaum and, above all things, that Aunt Judith would not scream when she saw them unexpectedly appearing with all that luggage by her front door.

Fortunately, they had also brought the goat that was scurrying around their skirts. The animal had been a last-moment addition to the luggage before leaving. Despite Aunt Judith's repeated invitations in the last few weeks, it would not hurt to bring a gift that would serve to temper her unpredictable mood when she saw them arriving without notice.

The only thing they had not dared to take was Atzel,

much to their regret. Bringing a dog to Aunt Judith's was incurring too much risk.

They heard footsteps inside, walking along the corridor that bordered the orange garden that Sara still remembered. Mother and daughter swallowed together nervously before the door opened.

Aunt Judith's reaction upon seeing them could not have been more disconcerting. A face of genuine joy greeted them, as if she had been expecting them to arrive at any moment.

What was going on? Sara was aghast. What had they done with her aunt?
She had always thought it impossible to find a colder and more uptight woman that her aunt in all of Israel. And there she was instead, throwing herself into her sister's arms.

"Just yesterday I was thinking about you, and here you are today!" she exclaimed with uncharacteristic joy as she hugged her sister for the second time.

"What a coincidence!" Sara managed to express as she received the same bunch of kisses.

"Coincidence? Nonsense! This can only be a miracle," Judith replied. "Come on, come inside, don't just stand there! Jonah!" she called over her shoulder when she saw all the belongings they had brought with them. "Please come down and take my sister's cart to the stable."

Then she noticed the small goat that was tangled now between the legs of the mule.

"Oh, how generous you are! But don't even think for a moment that I'm going to accept it as a payment for your stay," she said, waving a warning finger. "Well, although it won't hurt for dinner tomorrow, either."

The goat bleated at the thought, and Sara smiled. Her aunt seemed like a different woman, that was true, but her spendthrift ways remained intact. That had to be the indispensable quality necessary to accumulate wealth, she thought as she crossed the threshold behind the two sisters who, arm in arm, stepped into the interior of the well-lit courtyard.

Shortly after her arrival, mother and daughter were sitting at the table eating a delicious, freshly prepared fish, as if Aunt Judith had known they would be arriving at any moment.

"Fish is never lacking in this house," she smiled when she saw their satisfied faces. "My sons always make sure to send me some of their catch. But do I ever see even a hair of them? Never. They are always busy with something. That is what happens when you become a fisherman. Their father warned them on more than one occasion: 'The boats—look and touch them from the outside, but never step in.' But they didn't want to listen and there they are, tangled up in it." She nodded to her sister. "You, however, became luckier—YHWH favored you with a girl, and it's clear that Sara knows how to take care of you."

She gave her niece a look of genuine affection, and Sara blushed.

"Thank you very much, Auntie. Taking care of mother is a great gift."

"And Dismas—how is he doing in Jerusalem? Is he still a blacksmith? I haven't heard from him in a long time."

There was no malice or hidden intent in her sister's words, but Miriam looked down at her plate, trying to avoid that awkward moment. They had never told anyone what had happened to Dismas. It was no secret, but the wound hurt less if it remained covered.

"Oh, Auntie, this bread is delicious!" Sara quickly diverted the conversation, grabbing another piece of the loaf in a basket at the center of the table. "It has come right out of the oven, hasn't it?"

Aunt Judith opened her eyes with a sudden emotion that was difficult to contain.

"Have you noticed it too?"

Sara, confused, did not know how to respond to that. What was she referring to?

Aunt Judith reached for the loaf and, tearing off a small piece, put it in her mouth. She closed her eyes, and Sara and her mother looked at each other in surprise. Aunt Judith's face transformed as though she was tasting the most exquisite delicacy in the world. She finally opened her eyes with a sparkle still in them.

"You said yourself that it seemed freshly made, right? You are not going to believe it, but this bread is from yesterday!"

Sara reached for the loaf again and pressed it gently. It still had that crispness of bread only recently out of the oven, and she thought she could even feel just a bit of the heat from baking still left in it. She looked at her aunt and shook her head.

"Come now, Auntie! Our Alon makes the best bread in the whole area, and everyone knows it. But even he can't make bread like this. It can't possibly be from yesterday."

"This bread is special." Judith paused, her face shining as she tried to choose the right words. "It is... It is from the Messiah. I saw it with my own eyes. I watched as he made them—*five thousand* like this."

Sara and her mother Miriam looked at her as if she were crazy.

"Don't look at me like that. I was as skeptical as you are now."

"But Aunt Judith, it's impossible to make bread out of nothing, and feed five thousand people."

"And yet here it is, right under your nose." She pushed

the basket of bread towards Sara with a sign of triumph all over her face. "His disciples were handing it out from baskets as if it would never run out."

Sara couldn't help wondering if this was why her brother was stealing from the caravans—to deceive people like Aunt Judith.

"Look," her aunt continued, relentless. "I've been hearing a lot about the Messiah for some time now, and I used to make the same faces that you're making now. But I don't know if you remember Simon, a friend of my son Daniel, who is one of the best fishermen in all of Galilee?"

Sara and Miriam shook their heads, not willing to interrupt what Judith was telling them.

"Well, Simon had spent the whole night fishing in the lake without catching anything. When the boat returned to shore, this man, Yeshua, told him to cast his nets one more time. The incredible thing is that Simon listened to him, cast the net into the water, and when he went to retrieve it, there were so many fish that they almost capsized the boat. I refused to believe that story myself, so the other day, when news spread that the Messiah was in Taghbar, I decided to go see him with my own eyes. I was amazed at the number of people who were waiting for him on the shore. But when the Teacher arrived, the moment he opened his mouth, everything fell silent."

"Teacher?" Miriam's voice shook. "Why do you call him Teacher?"

"Oh, Miriam," Judith turned, casting her warmth over her sister. "If you had heard the beautiful things I heard yesterday, you too would call him Teacher."

"But Aunt Judith," Sara cut in, skeptical, "with all the people crowding the shore and the surrounding hills, it would be impossible to hear anything he said."

"And you are absolutely right, my dear!" Her aunt looked at her with a gleam. "I was very far away myself, but I swear to you that I could hear every word he said as if he had whispered them into my ear. He told me about the kingdom of God, that it is small like a mustard seed before growing into the largest of trees. And then I remembered us, Miriam—"

Aunt Judith turned to her sister with moistness lightning up her pupils.

"Do you remember when we were kids? The day Abba showed us the size of the seeds from which the tree we climbed on grew? He told us that in order to become big like that tree, we first had to be small like those seeds." Tears welled up in Judith's eyes now. "It was the same thing the Teacher said.... And He was whispering it into my ear!"

Something stirred inside Miriam. For a second she thought, terrified, that the cramp she had felt in her insides was the prelude of a new flow of blood, but she discreetly felt underneath her seat and found that it was dry.

Sara glanced at her mother; this conversation was not doing her any good. She couldn't allow what Aunt Judith was saying to generate false expectations about Dismas. She had not told her mother the whole truth about her brother—that he was a thief who raided caravans to help establish the reign of the Messiah. And precisely in that detail lay an incompatible duality between the portrait of the Teacher that Aunt Judith was drawing and that of someone who sent his followers to rob caravans in the desert sands.

No, her brother was a bandit, and his messiah a fairy tale.

"Auntie, but then how exactly did he multiply the loaves?" Sara pressed with disguised innocence.

That's what she wanted from her aunt: break down the details to unmask the lie.

"When it was well past noon, the people began to get impatient, because there was nothing to eat. You know how people get when hunger strikes," she added, rolling her eyes. "Then someone brought five loaves to the Teacher, and He blessed them, put them in baskets, and told the disciples to distribute their contents among all of us who were there."

"So what was the miracle? Surely all the baskets that the… the Messiah"—Sara was reluctant even to say that word—"ordered to be distributed were full of loaves of bread from the start."

"But that's impossible." Aunt Judith turned to her niece with an assurance that disarmed her. "I was at the back of the crowd. And when one of his disciples came up to me and handed me this loaf of bread"—she pointed to the bread on the table—"I saw with these very eyes that the basket was still full to the brim."

Sara could not keep her disbelief from showing on her face, and her aunt turned to her sister for her approval.

"Dear Miriam, you have tasted this bread. Give me one good reason why it still seems freshly baked after a day."

Miriam reached out for the loaf and put a new piece in her mouth. It seemed softer and more tender than the first time she had tried it. She chewed attentively for a few moments and suddenly its flavor and sweetness made her a little girl again, the same girl who waited by the roadside for her father to arrive, with a crust of bread in her hands. It was a little secret that both father and daughter shared: her mother let her go out to offer her hungry father the first taste of the family bread, but she—impatient, hungry—inevitably gave it to him nibbled and crumbled, with shame on her face and the promise not to do it again. And he would receive it from her hands with a kiss, a smile, and the certainty that, the next day, the same thing would inevitably happen again.

A tear welled up in her eye, making the image of her

sister Judith blur and tremble. She could make out a smile crossing her lips and, when the tear finally fell down her cheek, alone, into the void, she saw that Judith's arm was reaching out toward her, gripping her hand tightly in her own, the two of them becoming one single heartbeat.

"Judith," Miriam said with a tremble of emotion, "we have come here to find—"

"Aunt Judith," Sara stopped her mother from continuing, standing up from the table. "Do you think we will find him here tomorrow? Him and his disciples?"

Judith disengaged herself from her sister and turned to her niece.

"Oh, yes! It's very fortunate that you've come. I know they'll be here, because one of the women who accompany them told someone I know that Yeshua has to attend a family wedding. Some of his disciples are staying at Simon's mother-in-law's house, by the lake. My guess is He will be with them."

"How good it would be to meet them!" Sara offered a pretend smile while glancing sideways at her mother, who had chosen to remain silent. "We'd better go to bed then. Mama, you must be very tired."

Her mother nodded, and then Aunt Judith clapped her hands in the air twice. A young woman with a dark face and a kind smile emerged from the shadows of the next room. She was one of the servants that Judith had in her service.

"This is Deborah." Judith greeted the newcomer with a warm nod. "She does so much to make me feel comfortable in my own home. She has taken care of your room on this very floor so that you don't have to climb stairs," she said, biting her lip in sorrow as she watched her sister get up from the table. How much Miriam had aged since the last time they had been together, an eternity ago!

Sara inspected the servant Deborah's face. It was clear that her air of affection toward her aunt went beyond the strict servile relationships she had seen in that house over the years. She had the strange feeling that Deborah had a lot to do with the noticeable changes in Aunt Judith's life. Kindness was a virtue one could rarely obtain without help.

"Why didn't you want me to tell your aunt that Dismas is a follower of the Messiah? She would have liked to know."

Miriam scrutinized her daughter while she spread two towels on the bed and covered them with the sheets they had brought with them.

"Mama, it was not the right time to tell Aunt Judith the whole story about Dismas. Besides, first we have to make sure that he really is among the followers of the Messiah."

"Why? What makes you think he might not be one of them?"

Sara was frightened by the sudden shallowness in her mother's voice, and she was quick to put her doubts away "Of course, Mama, Dismas is with Nathaniel, and Nathaniel is with the Messiah. We'll most probably meet him tomorrow. But let me go first find them and prepare the way."

Sara snuggled up next to her mother and kissed her goodnight.

She had time to catch one last glimpse of her face before turning to her side of bed and blowing out the candle. She heard her sigh under her breath. There was certainly something strange about mother, she thought, and it had to do with being away from home and the fear of staining the bed with blood. What would Aunt Judith say if she found out, if she knew that she had given shelter to an impure woman, even if it was her sister? Would the new presence of the Messiah in her life do anything to appease her anger?

The foam of those thoughts dissolved quickly in the darkness of the room, and sleep came upon her with hardly any surprise.

But Miriam was slow to follow her daughter. Yes, there was a strange restlessness inside her, but it had nothing to do with the flow of blood. She had suffered it intensely for a few days now, and her experience had taught her that it would probably not recur during the time she was at her sister's house.

That restlessness came from the sudden thought that had stricken her after their conversation during dinner. What she had heard over the table raised her hopes. Was it really possible that her son had found peace at the side of this man who could multiply loaves and who spoke of seeds and mustard trees with the same kind of simplicity that her father had used? If that were true—and it was, she was sure of it—a soft voice seemed to have taken hold of her, stirring, promising that her flow of blood would end the moment she held her son Dismas back in her arms again.

This tangle of thoughts that run through her as she lay in the darkness managed to sneak into the depths of her dreams. From the shadows rose hundreds, thousands of loaves of bread. She held them in her hands and saw that bites were taken from each one of them. Tears started to roll down her face, tears that turned into rain as she walked along a path traced by a ray of light that wrapped her, and swallowed her, and threw her into a void of blood

In the morning, when she woke up, the first thing she did was to feel the bedlinens below her hips. They were dry. She sighed with relief and turned to wake her daughter. She was gone.

Sara had awakened very early, before anyone at Aunt Judith's house and when most of Capernaum had not stirred yet. She checked that everything was fine with her mother—that there were no traces of blood on her bed—and left the room without a noise.

In the kitchen she met Deborah. The young servant offered her a bowl of goat's milk that was still warm. She thanked her and, as she sipped it between her hands, she watched her pulling the first layers from a cabbage. She looked at her features. She did not know the woman's story, but she surely was not Jewish. The dark color of her skin and her large, jet-black eyes gave her away. There was beauty in that gaze, so absorbed in the peeling of the leaves of the vegetable. Sara asked Deborah if she knew the location of the house of the man her aunt had mentioned last night, Simon. A bright smile that she did not understand then crossed her face, and she told her to follow the road that went straight down to the lake. There she would see it.

"But how will I know which one it is?"

"You can't miss it. You'll know when you see it. Wherever He is, there is always life around him."

Sara was surprised by the description Deborah offered, and the feeling she'd had the previous evening came back to her—the smile on the face of that servant had a lot to do with the changes she'd seen in her aunt.

"Tell my mother that I've gone to do my errands. I will be back by noon."

Sara left the house as the rays of the sun began to paint the first silhouettes on the dust of the streets.

3.

A string of humble buildings bordered the shores of the mirror over which the sun was peeking. The soft murmuring waves licked the bottom of deserted boats. Few had gone out to fish that day.

It wasn't difficult to figure out which house was Simon's. In front of one of them, on the narrow beach, she saw a group of men sitting together. They seemed to be waiting. As Sara walked up to them, she counted seven figures contemplating the sunrise. The silence of the morning enveloped them. She tried to make out their faces as she walked forward, her heart in her throat. None of them looked familiar to her.

For a moment she thought of going back and not to interrupt something that, though she didn't understand it, seemed important. She had to remind herself that what she had come to do was more important and, steeling herself, she approached the man who was nearest to her.

"Good morning. I'm looking for Simon's house."

The man turned to her and, with a slight smile, nodded without saying a word.

"You see, I'm looking for someone."

"He's not here now. You'll have to wait."

He returned his face to the sun.

Disconcerted, Sara followed the man's gaze across the

waters of the lake, hoping to see what he seemed to be looking at with such delight. But she saw nothing. Then she realized that he'd thought she was asking for the Messiah.

"No—wait." The man turned to her again, this time without a smile. "I think you've misunderstood. I am not looking for him. I am looking for someone else—his name is Nathaniel."

The man sighed reluctantly and, shaking the sand off his hands, placed them on his knees and stood up. He walked away, without even looking at her, to another of the men, who was lying on the trunk of a tree stranded on the shore. She watched as he leaned toward his ear and whispered a few words.

Sara waited impatiently for him to return with some news, but he didn't bother to; instead, he shouted from where he stood with a voice cracked by the wind:

"Woman, there is no one here called Nathaniel!"

His words struck Sara's heart. She looked confusedly at the other figures, who had turned to look at her with curiosity.

Suddenly another voice spoke from further away:

"Of course there is! I am Nathaniel."

A man stood up from behind a sand dune at the end of the beach, and Sara's pulse raced beneath her skin as she recognized his voice.

"What? You—Nathaniel? But your name is Bartholomew!" protested the man who had just assured her there was no one here by that name.

"Judas, will there ever be a day when you really know something?" another voice joined in the exchange with amusement. "Bartholomew was called Nathaniel before the Master changed his name.

"And how did you want me to know, Philip?" Judas answered defensively. "He never changed my name; I thought he only did it with Peter." On his lips, the complaint sounded bitter.

New voices joined in, and laughter swept away the silence of the dawn, but Sara only heard Nathaniel's footsteps in the sand, coming closer, a timid ray of sunlight that had just broken over the lake illuminating his face.

"Sara? Sara! What are you doing here?" He greeted her with a smile that competed with the sunrise.

He looked quite unkempt. His beard had become one with the tangled hair of his head, pointing in all directions. However, the seamless tunic he was wearing still gave him that elegant and distinguished air that she remembered so well. Where and how did these men wash their clothes? The trivial thought in such serious circumstances helped to distract her mind in that expectant moment.

They embraced each other in silence. She felt his heart beating next to hers, and all the resentment she might have felt about his inexplicable flight disappeared.

"I see you are as beautiful and as young as ever," he finally said.

"And I see you are more of a man."

"Is that good or bad?" he asked with a joy that seemed impossible to contain.

"I suppose it is good. You look different though, but very happy!" she quickly added, as she wondered about the cause.

Nathaniel returned the compliment with another smile in which Sara could see all the sunrises of the world. A commotion behind them interrupted them. At Simon's house, there was a sudden cry and wailing. Someone had stopped at the door, accompanied by a large group of men and women. A man came out to greet him and bowed deeply.

Sara and Nathaniel looked at each other; it must have

been someone important. The newcomer seemed to be pleading, and after listening to him, the other man ran to where Nathaniel and Sara stood.

"Listen!" he exclaimed, panting. "Jairus, the leader of the synagogue, is looking for Yeshua. His daughter is dying. Where can I find him?"

"Philip, will you go look for him?" Nathaniel intervened, pointing to one of the disciples on the shore who had just come to his side. "He left early this morning with John, James, and Peter. He is where he always likes to go."

Nathaniel turned to the messenger, who was still catching his breath.

"Tell Jairus that the Teacher will be on his way home soon."

The messenger and Philip took off in opposite directions. Still running, Nathaniel's friend turned and called back to him:

"Don't worry. You stay with her and send the others to Jairus's house. I'll take the Master straight there."

He disappeared in a cloud of dust behind the dunes to the north, and Nathaniel went to his companions to pass along the instructions. Sara watched him, remembering the Nathaniel she'd known—neat and distinguished, giving orders, moving busily from one place to another, directing caravans, collecting merchandise. What had become of him? Had the change he had given his life really been worth it? That smile, that happiness she had glimpsed on his face, made her think that perhaps it was so.

"Come with me. Let's sit over there." Nathaniel returned and pointed toward the dunes. "We can sit down and talk about whatever has brought you here. Although just seeing you has made your trip worthwhile for me, I assure you."

Sara responded with a hesitant smile as she looked

around, unable to find the one reason why she had come in the first place. Where was her brother Dismas?

Miriam had the habit of not having breakfast until she had everything tidied up. Of course, here at her sister's, she wasn't going to do that. Everyone had their own quirks, and she wasn't going to impose her way of cleaning a house. All she could do was put some order in the room where she and her daughter had slept.

As she spread the sheets on the bed and tucked in their edges, she tried to imagine how long it would take her every morning to have everything under control in such a large home. "I wouldn't sit down for breakfast until well after noon," she thought, horrified by the idea.

Today, however, she wished she had any task to keep her mind occupied, protected from the gale that was whipping at it. Had Sara already found the followers of the Messiah? Was she with Nathaniel? Had she learned anything of Dismas yet? Would her son be happy to see his sister? And would he have forgiven her? Would he want to embrace her again, or would he leave forever, out of her reach? Hundreds of questions, doubts, and radically opposed hypotheses swam around inside her, bending her heart from side to side.

Impatience and uncertainty began to eat away at her heart as if it were wood, and Miriam sat down on the bed when she realized that her legs were weakening. She swallowed and closed her eyes, trying to expel the worst forebodings that now invaded her. What if he continued to cry out for revenge? What if resentment had laid its foundations in her son's heart, building an impregnable fortress around it? Miriam bent like the stem of a flower, overcome by pain, until her forehead touched the bed. She remained like that for a few moments, trying to conjure away the tears that threatened to flow.

"Enough, no!" Something moved inside her that made her sit up again.

She rose with renewed impetus, defiant. An unexpected image had come to her rescue once again: the Messiah her sister had spoken of yesterday.

Could she possibly fear a son who had given everything to follow a man like that? No one with resentment in his heart would waste time feeding so many people with a miracle bread; no one thirsty for revenge would take up weapons in the name of someone who defended the virtue of being small; no one consumed by anger would have the patience to wait for a small seed to grow big. If her son was with this man—and he was!—there was nothing to fear.

With a sudden peace on her face, she bent down to pick up the empty sack of sheets from the floor and a tongue of fire licked the insides of her abdomen. Her moan echoed in the silence of the room, and Miriam felt the need to sit back down on the edge of the bed to keep her balance. Then the intense pain faded.

She touched her stomach, trying to find a sign, a possible swelling or blood stains between the folds of her skirt.

There was nothing.

She felt relieved but strange. The blood flows did not usually start this way, much less a just few days after having experienced an intense cycle.

Miriam waited a few moments until she stood up again. She felt a slight dizziness, the urgent need to look out the window and breathe fresh air.

She opened it, anticipating the feeling of the breeze on her face, but instead she was greeted by excited noise coming from the street. She looked out and saw the remains of a crowd hurrying by in a cloud of dust.

The sound of the door behind her brought her back into the room.

"Good morning, sister," Judith said, poking her head in. "I've been waiting for you for breakfast for a while, but if you don't come now, I'm going to start eating without you."

"What's all that noise in the streets?" Miriam replied as she closed the window.

"The head of the synagogue, Jairus. His daughter is very ill, and they have gone to let the Messiah know. Poor thing! She is such a sweet and loving girl. I hope they find Yeshua in time! Anyway, are you coming, or should I tell Deborah to save your breakfast for you?"

"I'll be right there. Let me finish making up the bed and I'll be right out."

Judith closed the door and Miriam, alone again, felt her stomach once more, looking for some sign of the sting of pain she'd felt. Nothing. It must have been a false alarm, no doubt the result of the anxiety that was consuming her. Thinking about the Messiah had calmed her down. Hopefully Jairus, the head of the synagogue, would find Yeshua and he'd cure his daughter in time, as he had done with her son Dismas.

"No, I don't know where Dismas is. He didn't come with me. I wanted him to, but our paths separated that day. And I haven't seen him since." Nathaniel knew that no matter how sweetly and gently he tried to convey those words, they were knives in the soul of his dear Sara. But there was no other answer he could offer to the surprising, hope-filled question she had just asked him.

They were still seated by the shores of the lake with the sun on their faces, but Sara couldn't appreciate the beauty of it all; Nathaniel's words could not be clearer, but neither could they be more confusing.

"But it can't be, Nathaniel!" Her pupils only needed a spark to set them on fire. "Abdomeneo, that man you trusted, told your brother. He recognized him despite the turban he had over his face. Maybe he is part of another group of disciples, and they have changed his name, like you!"

"Sara, he is not here. I would love to tell you that yes, he is with me, among the other followers, but it's not so." Nathaniel tried to inject gravity and regret into his gaze, wanting to convince her and console her at the same time. "Dismas is not among us."

"But he went with Yeshua! Abdomeneo heard it from his own lips," she repeated to herself stubbornly.

"Are you sure he said Yeshua?"

Sara nodded against all hope.

Nathaniel let his forehead fall on his knees, which were raised to his chest like a wall, and heaved a sigh. Pieces of the conversation he'd had that day in the workshop mingled with the image of the man waiting outside on the cart, and he was afraid of breaking Sara's heart any further. *"Oh, Dismas, Dismas,"* he thought, *"why didn't you want to follow the path I showed you? What you would have discovered!"*

He raised his face, determined to speak. She had to know. Even though it would hurt. But he looked straight ahead, avoiding her face.

"I went to see Dismas that day, to tell him that I had found the Messiah. I invited him to come and see with his own eyes. I was convinced that the man I had just met could soothe his pain, relieve his thirst for revenge. But I was too late. He told me that he no longer needed me."

Sara looked at Nathaniel's profile against the blue sky, unable to open her lips. She let him continue.

"There has been talk for some years about the imminent arrival of the Messiah. These are messianic times, and people see what their hearts tell them. Your brother is with Yeshua, Yeshua Bar Abbas," he said, looking into her eyes again.

"They share the same name, but they are not the same men."

"Yeshua. 'YHWH saves,'" she whispered to herself the meaning of that name for the Jews. "Two messiahs ready to save the world. With one, Dismas; with the other, you. It seems like a bad joke. How pretentious you men are, always ready to do anything for a spark of immortality!"

"A lot has been said about this Bar Abbas, but it's not true. There is only one Bar Abbas, 'son of the Father,' and that is Yeshua of Nazareth."

"*Your* messiah, of course." She couldn't keep the bitterness out of her voice. "You are very sure of what you say, but Dismas will believe that his messiah is also the true one."

"Judge for yourself, dear Sara." Nathaniel could not contain himself and had to stand up. "The deaf hear, the blind see, the lame walk! He goes around the villages proclaiming love for one's neighbor, unmasking the hypocritical Pharisees, forgiving prostitutes, curing the sick! The other day he fed more than five thousand men with five loaves and two fish! Who can do that but God?"

"Good words, miracles, do not save man from himself, from his stupidity, from pride," Sara let the words flow with disdain.

Nathaniel looked at her with a wounded soul. How could anyone deny the obvious?

"Did Abdomeneo tell you what *that* Bar Abbas does, why he recruits an ever-greater number of disciples? He wants to expel the Romans with a bloody uprising. Do you know how he is getting more and more power? His followers rob caravans, seizing everything they carry as taxes for their revolution. That man is a criminal who knows how to feed rage and anger in wounded hearts—like Dismas's!"

Nathaniel stopped, regretting the words. Sara's eyes

shone with tears, her figure shrinking, getting smaller, almost devoured by the sand.

"Forgive me, Sara. I shouldn't have told you this way. I'm such a fool. I got carried away by— I'm truly sorry."

Nathaniel bent and wrapped his arms around her. She let her head fall on his shoulder as tears fell in torrents.

They sat there for a long time, silent, watching the Sea of Galilee stretch out under a sun that was now burning over its waters. In the distance, some fishermen were throwing their nets into the lake, and the sky on the surface broke into a thousand reflections.

The trill of swallows overhead brought them back to their senses, and Sara rose from the sands and pebbles at the shore.

"Everything you've said I saw in his eyes the day I said goodbye to him. I hoped and trusted that you could change him, as Bathsheba had done before. And then he disappeared. When I heard that he had joined the Messiah and that you were also a follower of his, I was relieved. Even if that Yeshua had turned him into a bandit, you were behind him as well; 'If Nathaniel follows this Yeshua, then he can't be so bad,' I kept saying to myself. You were always better than my brother."

A slight smile cleared the mists of her pain.

"Don't talk nonsense." Nathaniel blushed. "Dismas always led the way. Always the first in everything, and I followed in his shadow. Don't give up on anything yet. Dismas will return. You'll see."

"If he's still alive." She sighed.

"I'm sure he is. YHWH won't let him go to Sheol without you and your mother hearing his voice again. You'll see. Trust."

"What am I going to tell my mother? I brought her to

Capernaum with the hope of meeting Dismas again. The truth is going to cause her a lot of pain again."

"I can introduce you to the Teacher," he answered, holding her by her shoulders. "I assure you that it will change your day."

Sara smiled.

"It's hard for me to understand you. What made you leave your home, your business…" Sara looked away from his gaze and swallowed before continuing. "…Everything! To follow a stranger?"

The question took Nathaniel by surprise. He bit his lower lip, thoughtful, digging into his soul to show her the treasure he had found that day.

"It's going to seem crazy to you, but it was his look. I stood before him and just by looking at him, I was pierced by his love. It sounds corny, I know."

Nathaniel blushed, glancing at her reaction, checking that she wasn't laughing at him.

"I know it's hard to understand, but I assure you it's much harder to explain." He looked around, searching for something that would serve as inspiration to express what was burning inside. "Look! Do you see the sky reflected on the water? It's as if they are the same sky. That's how I saw myself reflected in his eyes. It was very strange—he had just met me and it was as if he'd known me all his life. But when he told me that he'd been watching me under the fig tree, then I realized that he'd had his eyes on me from all eternity. At that moment, I felt an overwhelming desire to weep!" he remembered, embarrassed.

"To weep?" Sara interrupted, taken up in his story.

"Yes, but not from sadness or pain, nothing like that. It was like a rain of happiness falling from my eyes. He was so big that I had to empty my soul to fit him in here." He pointed to his chest. "Something similar has happened to each one of us who are with him—very different in each case, but all very special, nonetheless!"

Nathaniel noticed the look of astonishment on her face. Did she believe any of the words he was saying?

"Hey, but don't just stand there looking at me like I'm a freak. There are women, too, who have left everything to follow him. You still have time to join us, if you want!" he added, teasing her with a welcoming smile.

The invitation floated in the sea breeze that caressed their faces, and Sara lowered her head.

"Don't be angry with me, but right now I don't feel like following any messiah. I have to go back to my Aunt Judith's house."

She was already thinking about what words she would use when she saw her mother.

"How could I be angry with you for that? Besides, if He wants, He will find you first. He did it with me," he added with a sparkle in his eyes. "Give your mother a big hug from me. Tell her that I always remember her when I smell celery in broth!"

Sara felt a pinch in her heart as she remembered the battles of a much younger Nathaniel over her mother's soup every time Dismas invited him to dinner. She wished she could go back in time and stay there forever!

She walked back to Aunt Judith's house with a heavy heart. She didn't care whether Nathaniel's messiah found her first or not. What she really cared about was how to find this other messiah that her brother was following and demand that he leave Dismas alone.

And telling her mother.

How was she going to do that?

4.

Her mother and Aunt Judith were having breakfast in one of the galleries that bordered the orange courtyard. The scent of orange blossom filled the air, but Sara didn't even notice it, because the expectant look on the face of her mother, who stood up immediately when she entered, blocked out her other senses.

"What? Have you seen him? What did he say to you?"

She was so excited that Judith turned to her sister, quite surprised.

"But Miriam, what is happening here?" Judith looked from mother to daughter, trying to discern whether it was good or bad; her niece looked like a cloud about to storm, and Miriam, a big ray of sunshine.

"Judith, we didn't want to tell you yesterday, but we came to see Dismas," Miriam exploded, unable to hold back her tongue. "He is one of the disciples of the Messiah you told us about." She pointed to the bread that was still in the center of the table.

"Mama!"

More than a cry, it was a lamentation.

Miriam's heart stopped beating for a second. She inspected her daughter's face and realized there was nothing good written on it. How could she have been so stupid as not to have read it?

Something twisted again in her depths.

She had to sit down, slowly, by the table, her eyes lost, wandering between an orange tree and the ray of sunlight on the floor, between the colored ceramics on the wall and the bare feet of Deborah entering at that moment.

"Is something wrong, mistress? I thought I heard a cry," said the maid, approaching the table.

With a slight smile, Judith shook her head quickly and Deborah discreetly vanished again. She turned her attention back to her sister and Sara, who were still standing there, motionless, facing each other.

Sara swallowed hard before approaching her.

"Mama, I saw Nathaniel."

The words were heavy on her tongue.

"Nathaniel." The name was a distant echo on Miriam's lips.

"Dismas isn't with him." Sara fidgeted nervously with the edge of the table that stood between them.

"I don't understand."

"He's not one of the followers of the Messiah that Aunt Judith was talking about yesterday," she exhaled, waiting for her mother to say something.

Only silence filled the void.

Judith took the hand that her sister was resting on the table in hers. It felt cold.

"He is part of a group that follows another man, one who calls himself the same name." Sara heard the echoes of her own voice coming from her lips.

Life returned to Miriam, a small window opening again in her soul.

"Then we can find him!" she said, clinging to a small hope. "Maybe that messiah is not as good as Nathaniel's, but—"

All the anger, all the frustration that Sara had kept tightly bound inside her broke loose without warning.

"Mama, the man Dismas follows is planning a rebellion against the Romans." She could not hold back her tears now. "They kill and steal with the sole purpose of seizing power!"

Darkness fell like a stone upon Miriam. Her worst fears about Dismas, those that the hope of the previous day's dinner and that bread had managed to chase from her heart, returned to their place, even stronger now. Her son had been carried away by the resentment that *she* had caused. His sin was also hers. The blood that he had spilled, the blood that he would spill, were upon her own hands as well.

She slipped her hand out of her sister's and picked up the bowl of milk that was in front of her. Her mouth had gone dry. She drank some of it, and as she put it back on the table, she saw next to her arm a piece of bread that she had been eating before her daughter came in. She brought it to her mouth instinctively, but as she was about to bite it, an idea crossed her mind. It was a wild, crazy, superstitious idea, perhaps, but it made her return the bread to the table, uneaten.

She did not feel clean enough to eat it.

With all the strength she could muster, Miriam held back the sob that the sudden thought had produced inside her. She looked around again at her daughter, at her sister, who were each watching her with lumps in their throats.

"Mama, are you okay?" Sara drew closer, sagging under the weight of regret. "Forgive me for speaking to you like that. I shouldn't have said it like I did."

Miriam caressed the hand her daughter had placed on her arm.

"Don't worry, Sara, darling. I'm fine, really." Her face barely formed a smile that cracked her soul.

Sara rested her cheek on both their hands, hers and her mother's, and they remained like that for a few moments, mother and daughter, without words. Judith looked away, aware that there were spaces she shouldn't enter, even if they were in her own house.

"If you don't mind, I'm going to go to the bedroom for a moment," Miriam managed to say with the same determination with which she had painted the smile on her face a moment ago.

Pushing out the chair she was sitting on, she stood up, and Sara stood up with her.

"Do you want me to accompany you?" she asked.

"No, please, daughter. Sit down and have breakfast. You got up very early. Sit with Aunt Judith."

Miriam left the gallery, dragging with her the terrible weight of her thoughts. She was not worthy of eating the bread that man had made. With each step she took, she felt the same sting in her heart. *I am not clean.*

Judith made her niece sit down with her at the table.

"There is a lot of fuss in the streets today, isn't there?" she asked, trying to dispel the heavy atmosphere that had fallen upon them.

"It was impressive," answered Sara, trying to recover her spirits. "Everyone was walking down the street in expectation of the Messiah."

"Yes, Jairus's house is along the public square next to the synagogue. His poor daughter is very ill, and everyone is hoping for the Messiah to cure her."

Sara nodded while she watched her mother turn the corner of the gallery and disappear.

"I was with Nathaniel when they came looking for him. Will he arrive in time?"

"Oh, yes! If poor Jairus has done everything possible to look for him, he will arrive in time, as expected, don't worry."

"But will he cure him?" Sara narrowed her eyes, dazed by her own curiosity.

"That depends on Jairus," her aunt said with a mysterious air. "But I don't think someone capable of making this bread for more than five thousand people would have any problem doing whatever he wants."

Aunt Judith took the loaf of bread from the center of the table, tore off a piece, and offered it to her niece.

"Is it still as fresh as yesterday?"

"Try it yourself."

Sara was again surprised by the tender feel of the loaf. Another day had passed, and it was still so soft. She caught a glimpse of the satisfied expression on her aunt's face.

"Aren't you going to go see how he heals Jairus's little girl?"

Her aunt shook her head.

"I don't think going just for the sake of satisfying curiosity would do any good. Some things are not necessary, and if we go, we will be one too many. There are moments that concern only those who seek the Teacher."

Deborah's bare feet stepped onto the gallery once again, and Judith raised her head before Sara had time to notice her presence. Only her aunt was capable of hearing her servant's silences and discretions.

"What is it, Deborah?" Judith asked as soon as she saw the tension on her face.

"Mistress, your sister has just walked out the door," she answered, glancing at Sara.

"My mother? From her room?"

"No." Deborah cleared her throat. "She has left the house."

Sara stood up with anguish on her face, but Judith held her gently by her arm.

"Why did you let her go?" her aunt asked Deborah, without any hint of recrimination in her words.

"She said she needed to see the Master. She begged me not to say anything." Deborah looked at Sara, knowing that she wouldn't understand.

"And you let her go?" Sara barked, astounded. "I have to go find her!"

"Sara, be calm. Your mother will be fine."

"Auntie, do you know what the streets are like this morning? Any push could—" She bit her lips; her aunt knew nothing about her mother's illness. "I'm going out to fetch her."

Sara crossed in front of Deborah and felt the force of her gaze upon her. She raised her head, and their eyes met. She ignored the mixture of compassion, encouragement, and hope that saw in those black eyes and continued through the end of the gallery.

"Shall we go out to look for your sister?" Deborah asked uneasily when Sarah disappeared. Perhaps she had made a mistake by allowing her mistress's sister to leave.

Judith raised her head, surprised to hear that question coming out of her servant's mouth, as they both heard Sara closing the front door behind their back.

"But Deborah!" Her voice, a loving reproach. "You let me go by myself when the time arrived! My sister will find him. Both of them will. As you found him first, and as I found him afterwards."

Deborah smiled at the words—she had done well to let her go alone.

Miriam's pace through the alleys that wove through the heart of Capernaum was slow but steady. She knew where to go; she only had to follow the noise of the crowd. It soon led her into the public square where the synagogue stood.

After listening to her sister, the resolution had struck her as a wild idea. If she was unclean, if she felt unworthy of eating the bread on Miriam's table, only He could cleanse her of all the sins that her son had brought upon her.

Between the backs of the crowd advancing in front

of her, she could see the old religious building. It was surrounded by a swarm of people waiting. All of Capernaum had been alerted to the illness of Jairus's daughter, and they were gathering at his house, next to the synagogue, to await the arrival of the Messiah.

As she walked, she listened to snatches of conversation from the people passing by.

"Hurry up. We won't get there in time," one woman said to another as she hurried by nervously.

"Mama, do you think he'll cure her?" asked a boy who was holding his mother's hand.

"If Jairus has sent for him, he must think he has the power to heal her," said a man passing by who pushed her out of his way without the slightest apology.

"I think he's a fraud," replied his companion, who also paid no attention to the old woman his friend had nearly knocked down.

Miriam lost her balance; she only managed to stay on her feet by grabbing onto the basket that someone was carrying on his shoulders. The stranger gave her a threatening glance and then looked back to make sure nothing was missing from his basket.

"Woman, be careful," he snapped as if she were a common thief.

Miriam stepped to one side of the street to avoid being run over by the crowd that continued to hurry toward the square. She had to compose herself and gather strength.

She gritted her teeth with determination. "I have to see him. He can make me clean," she repeated to herself before plunging back into the crowd. She was ready for anything.

Sara left Aunt Judith's house and ran into the crowd. She tried to make out the familiar figure of her mother between the overlapping backs that were moving down the street. It was impossible to distinguish her among the multitude.

"Mama!" she shouted nervously, surrounded by the indifference of those who passed her by. Distressed, she began to move quickly, ignoring the murmurs that gathered around her. There seemed to be more people here than she had even seen during Passover in the streets of Jerusalem. She began to fear for her mother's life. What had she been thinking, to leave Aunt Judith's house in that way?

"Mama!" she called again as she made her way through the crowd.

Miriam was just a few steps from the entrance to the square, but the crowd prevented her from advancing any further. On tiptoe, she tried to see whether the Messiah had arrived yet, but it was impossible to see above all the heads in front of her. She was filled with impatience, afraid of not getting to meet him.

I have to see him; he will cleanse me, she continued to hear inside her, unable to silence it.

"He hasn't arrived yet," she heard someone say amid the murmurs around her.

"Well, if he waits much longer, he won't see her alive. I've been told the poor girl is in very bad shape," another answered, with an air of knowing everything.

There was still hope, Miriam told herself as she calculated how to move through the spaces between the people that blocked her advance. After a few moments of indecision, she threw herself between the gaps and the jostling of the people before her. Her fragile and harmless appearance was an advantage here, but it was also a great risk—a simple shove, a sudden squeeze, could throw her to the ground and she'd end up trampled by the crowd.

She began to feel the oppression around her, people pressing against each other, looking for an inch, an opportunity to see that man up close. She felt the sweat of the people sticking to her body, and a trickle of her own rolling down her forehead, all of her wrapped in hot air difficult to breathe.

Suddenly she felt it again to her—that stabbing pain in her abdomen, like a knife pushed into her and twisted by an invisible hand. Her vision blurred and she saw herself falling into an abyss.

And then everything closed in.

A distant sound returned to her ears, slowly transformed into intelligible voices that forced her to open her eyes.

"Get away! Don't touch her!"

"An impure woman!"

"Sinful slut! Go back to your lair! Don't touch her!"

From the ground, Miriam saw only a collection of angry faces blocking out the sun. She noticed something wet between her legs; she didn't need to look to know that the blood was flowing, giving her away. Frightened, she feared for her life. Outrage burned on the faces of the men who surrounded her. They seemed ready to kill her. But to her surprise, the opposite happened: they stepped away from her, as if an invisible barrier kept them away from an animal, afraid of being contaminated by its impurity.

I have to see him! Before it's too late! He will cleanse me.

Something inside her was building more intensely now, on the verge of exploding.

Sara reached the edge of the square, where the crowd was practically impenetrable. She jumped up several times, trying to spot her mother between the shoulders and heads in front of her. Desperation took hold of her. Where was she? It was impossible for her to have slipped through that human tide without anything happening to her.

She looked to her sides, about to ask those around her if they'd seen a middle-aged woman, when she heard someone complaining, "Those women should be with the lepers! How disgusting!"

She turned to the man who had spoken, certain that he was referring to her mother. She grabbed him by the arm, gripped by fear.

"What happened?"

The man looked at Sara with disgust still in his eyes.

"A madwoman with blood flowing down there," he said, nodding toward the waist of Sara's tunic.

"She was on the ground a moment ago, and now she's vanished." A woman pushed herself between them, shouting in Sara's face.

"Where did she go?" Sara asked, turning around desperately, seeing no trace of her.

"She's in the middle of the commotion ahead, among the people," said a third person, joining the conversation.

"I don't know how she can be so shameless!" added another voice as Sara disappeared in the direction her mother had apparently slipped away, without waiting for further comments.

"I have to find her. Please, Lord, don't let anything happen to her," she whispered. As she did, someone demanded those around her be quiet.

"*Shh!* The Messiah is coming!" She heard in unison from different directions.

A wave of silence immediately spread throughout the square, and Sara's face contorted in an expression of fear and shock.

Miriam found it increasingly difficult to push through the crowd as she approached the center of the square. She was still stunned, with lingering traces of the pain and the stain of shame on her skirt. With everyone pressing so close to her, she had the advantage that no one could see her blood. A single thought in her head—*I have to see him, I have to see him*—forced away the voices around her, impelling her to keep pushing forward. Suddenly she got stuck in the tumult and could move ahead no farther. The anxious crowd began to push impatiently, shoulders shoving against her, and the ground began to disappear under her feet.

She felt like she was floating. It was a sensation like the one she had experienced one day as a child on the shore of Lake Tiberias, when she'd been caught up by a wave. Terror filled her now; it was impossible to regain control of her body among the human tide that swept her away. She raised her face to find some air to breathe; a white and dusty light reminded her of the violent foam that had swept her away that day in the lake. Once again, she did not know where the wave would break or where she would be thrown by its force. She stopped resisting. She had to surrender to the imminent fall, with the desperate confidence that the jolt against the ground would bring her back to life.

She felt herself growing stronger, moving away from the earth, reaching for the sky. The shouting around her rose, wild, unbridled, as the wave intensified and finally spat her forward.

By the shore. In the dust of the road. At the feet of a group of men.

Time went still.

Immersed in a golden cloud, she heard the cries of the people as if in the distance. But here, kneeling on the open path that the crowd had opened up, flecks of gold hung in the air around her in an infinite stillness. She looked ahead, and sandals disturbed the cloud of dust. She could make out the feet between the folds of a white-gold robe, and she knew, without knowing it, that it was him.

"Wait, you have to make me clean, please," she heard herself cry out.

She raised her head even higher, upward, to see him, but a blinding light prevented her from making out his figure. She tried to speak again, to shout for Him to please wait, but the dust clinging to her palate muffled her lips. No words came out of her. Then she realized, terrified, that the man was not stopping, that he was passing by, that he had not seen her, jostled among the crowd that besieged him from all sides.

It doesn't matter. You will be made clean if you touch Him. You will be made clean if you touch Him. You only have to touch him—

The voice was not coming from anyone around her but within her.

With the Teacher's firm step advancing, the folds of his tunic rustled the air and a soft breeze caressed Miriam's face. Obeying the voice, she stretched her trembling arm towards that passing cloak, and she touched its hem with her fingertips before it disappeared from her sight.

Something golden dazzled her then, and she had to close her eyes before the blinding glow. For a very brief moment, she felt the fluttering of thousands of butterflies around her, and she lay prostrate on the stones of the square, with her forehead touching the ground, grateful, filled by an infinite peace.

The shouts and the shoving of the people rushed back to her ears, and Miriam raised her face, not knowing where she was. The golden cloud was once again merely the stirred-up dust on the ground of the square. What had happened?

The sandals, those feet.

To her left, a white tunic disappeared among those who accompanied the Teacher, protecting him from the crowd.

A shiver ran through her soul as she stood up again and looked at herself. She was still a fragile and trembling figure, but something had changed. Her gaze slid timidly towards the folds of her skirt. There was no blood. The stain had disappeared.

The tingling of His cloak between her fingers, that flame of fire sailing through her veins!

She was clean. She was healed. She was made pure without anyone ever learning, not even her sister, the shame of the illness she'd borne, the origin of so much pain. All of the shame was held between her and the cloak of *that man*.

"Who touched me?"

His voice rang out over the crowd. The Teacher had stopped, and with him the whole entourage that was accompanying him. Miriam froze, and with her all those in the crowd around her.

On his right, one of those accompanying him, the oldest, was startled by his question. He turned toward him, raising a calloused hand to his furrowed, sun-worn brow.

"Teacher, what... what do you mean?"

Peter had been in his company for more than two years, but the Teacher still had the ability to surprise him. How could he ask who had touched him? Didn't he see that everyone was rushing at them, making it almost impossible for them to pass?

Yeshua turned to him.

"That someone touched me."

The Teacher's words, his gaze, were so direct, so simple, so clear, that Peter was speechless, not knowing how to respond. He discreetly nudged the person to the other side of Yeshua, and with a quick movement of his eyes, begged him to intervene. The man, the youngest in the group, came fast to his aid.

"Lord, our presence has caused a great stir in the streets of Capernaum, and everyone is crowding around us to see you pass."

The Messiah looked with burning eyes at his young disciple and spoke firmly:

"John, I noticed that healing power has gone out of me, and it's because someone has touched me."

Yeshua diverted his eyes to the people gathering around him and looked at each of their mute faces.

John and Peter looked at each other, expectant. What was going to happen now? The Teacher always kept a surprise up his sleeve.

"Who touched me?" he repeated, sweeping the people with His gaze.

Miriam, who had been hidden behind the figures of Peter and John, was about to blend back into the crowd and disappear, when she heard Yeshua's voice behind her for the second time.

He was speaking directly to her—there was no doubt about it. But she was afraid of being discovered in front of everyone. Her guilt had been erased and there was no need for anyone else to know about it. Everything was between her and the healing power of the Messiah. Had she not been cleansed, just as she had wanted? She only had to take one more step and she would disappear into the crowd. She raised her right foot, ready to vanish, when a sharp bite of heat sank into her back. It was as if someone had brought a torch to her skin, but she didn't scream; that fire did not burn: it compelled her to turn around.

Their eyes met.

She saw in his eyes the spark of someone who is glad to see a friend after a long time, and she blushed. But he said nothing, waiting. Something moved her completely and, dropping to her knees on the ground, she prostrated herself before him with a loud sob.

"O Lord, it was me, it was me." Her words rushed trembling from her mouth. "I did not know you, but I tasted your bread. I tasted your bread, and I didn't feel worthy to eat it. No one is worthy of you, Lord, but I knew that just by touching the hem of your garment I would be healed. Don't ask me why. I only know that after so much shame, after so much pain, you alone could cleanse me. I have had a flow of blood for twelve years. No doctor has been able to cure me. And this morning I discovered why. My son, sir, my son.... I am to blame for my son's sins. I was the one who took away from him what he loved the most, and because of me, he... he..." Miriam's weeping prevented her from continuing.

Yeshua, visibly moved, leaned towards her and, gently taking her by the arms, helped her to stand up.

The silence around them was absolute.

Tears clouded Miriam's eyes, so she could barely make out the blurred face of the Teacher, but she did notice the warmth of his hands on her cheeks, holding her face and drawing it closer to himself.

"My daughter, your faith has saved you. Go in peace, and be cured of your illness."

The words were like embers of fire upon Miriam. Everyone around her heard them, and when it seemed that he was going to let her go to continue on his way, the Teacher brought his lips close to her ear and whispered:

"You are not to blame for your son's sins. Do you hear me? This has happened so that the works of God may shine forth in you. Let me take care of him."

And kissing her on the forehead, Yeshua let her go.

Behind the Teacher, the world trembled in John's eyes, and he brushed the tear from his cheek. He looked at Peter and was surprised to see that the eyes in the weathered face of the veteran fisherman were also glassy. John avoided meeting those eyes. He would keep to himself that moment of weakness in Peter, who was not as tough as he seemed. After all, who was capable of remaining unmoved when one was near Yeshua? That man was capable of making all things new. This thought hit John as the Messiah turned back to them, and they set off again in the direction of Jairus's home.

The crowd dispersed after the group passed, but no one dared to approach Miriam. The Teacher's words still echoed in her ears, and she sat there on the stones, with her eyes lost and an unexpected joy painted on her face. "Let me take care of him," he had said of her son. How could she not trust the word of the one who had healed her just by touching his cloak?

"Mama!"

The cry of her daughter Sara brought Miriam back to the square in Capernaum. She saw her running toward her with the cry of anguish still in her throat.

"I thought something had happened to you!" she continued, unable to contain a sob, happy to have her back.

"And it has happened, daughter. It has happened!"

Her mother's voice was nearly unrecognizable, and Sara searched her face, bewildered. She had seen that the Teacher had stopped, but because she'd been engulfed in the crowd, she didn't know that her mother had been at the eye of the storm.

"He... he healed me," Miriam said, nodding, still amazed by what had just happened. "Just by touching his cloak, he healed me."

Miriam held her daughter so tight between her arms that Sara felt embraced as no one had ever been before. She breathed a sigh of relief, as if she had returned home, to her mother's lap.

Then her mother sought her ear with her lips.

"He told me that he would take care of Dismas."

The words scampered like a lizard in the summer shade, raising goosebumps all over her skin. Without yet knowing quite why, Sara began to cry and laugh and let out whoops and cry again, all her feelings made one with her mother's.

Still cradled in her arms, she smiled. Nathaniel always turned out to be right; the Teacher had found her first by bringing salvation to her mother and to the whole house. And Yeshua Bar Abbas, her brother's messiah, was nothing compared to the power of Him.

PART FOUR
A Curse

I.

Dismas opened his eyes to darkness, his body bathed in sweat. He had awakened with the same force as someone who is drowning under water and desperately needs air.

He drew a large breath of the fresh night into his lungs, and his heart stopped dancing in his chest. The nightmare, again; it wasn't the first time it had come to visit him without warning. But lately it had been doing so often.

Maybe it had something to do with what was about to happen. They had been preparing the assault for months, and the plan was so thorough that it could not fail. Or everything could fall apart due to the smallest detail. The tension was so high that Bar Abbas had decided to give all his "generals" a break until it was time to execute what, according to him, was going to change everything.

Dismas rested the back of his neck on his arm, on the pillow, dismissing the possibility. The coup that would free Jerusalem from the Roman yoke once and for all had little to do with the strange nightmare that, after visiting him, left without a trace. He knew, however, that it had the form and scent of a woman.

His face turned toward the body beside him. She was sleeping peacefully, with the sheet coddling her skin with pleasures untold. Susanna was fresh and juicy, like a summer fruit. He sated himself between her thighs in the hope of forgetting, but every time he did, the nightmare stood in the way, jealous, bringing with it distant memories veiled by time, of which only he knew the name.

His heart leapt into the void one more time when he heard it again inside him.

He had made real efforts to forget her. During the day he had managed to cover her absence with blood, Roman blood, to the point of having forgotten the reason for his hatred. He could no longer tell whether he killed because he hated or hated because he killed. The two words had been feeding on each other in a spiral of corpses that, if he had kept count, could easily amount to a full centuria of the invading army.

The one that had given him the most pleasure was the first. He hadn't stopped looking for him until he found him. It was shortly after he'd returned to Jerusalem, after having met Gestas. He was dying to be introduced to Bar Abbas, but he was obliged to wait in the house that Gestas had lent him. Five days, he'd said.

He had sworn to himself that he would not leave the house during that time. He was afraid of running into Sara, Nathaniel, someone he knew, of having to give explanations, having to lie. He was already another person; his life was starting anew.

But there was one image that he could not get out of his head; it was etched in fire. The pig that had pushed her to the ground. The one that had bled her dry. The one that had ended her life. And now it was Dismas's turn to end his.

He decided to go out very early every morning and stroll cautiously around different parts of the city. He walked through its streets, in the markets, around the temple, in front of the prefecture—the places in Jerusalem where there might be a detachment of Roman soldiers, however small; the places where he might see his face.

And he did.

Dismas saw him coming out of a brothel. There were a few in the Holy City. They were not seen in broad daylight, but everyone knew where they dwelt. And Dismas knew which ones were the Romans' favorites.

It wasn't hard to find the prostitute the soldier slept with. Dismas arranged the meeting in the only place where one could talk to one of those women in broad daylight without getting tainted: by the fountain. All he had to do was learn on which one did that brothel filled its water jars.

He spoke to her; they connected quickly. He was an attractive man, and he had money in his pocket. But he gained her cooperation without paying her. She hated that soldier as much as he did. She didn't like what he did to her and how he treated her. Dismas didn't have to explain the reasons for his hatred, the reasons for the revenge he sought. He would have lied to her, but she didn't even ask. She told him to come to see her the next day, at her "house."

"I won't charge you anything, but come well equipped," she said, pointing to the knife he had on his waist, above his crotch.

The next night, she let him into her bedroom at the appointed time. It was one among many in the house, and the echoes of pleasure penetrated through every crack in the walls. Dismas felt uncomfortable in the presence of that half-naked woman waiting for him in bed. He had come to kill, not to frolic on her bed, and although he would do it gladly, spilling that man's blood came first.

"Come, puppy," she said, taking his hand and pulling him towards her.

The two of them looked into each other's eyes; there was no sex in the gaze of either one.

"When he is about to get on top of me, you'll come out from under the bed and cut his throat."

She brought her warm lips to his cheek and gave him a kiss; she trembled like a little bird about to be freed.

He hid himself under the bed, and then they waited. He watched her feet pace nervously from one side of the room to the other. A while passed until they heard footsteps outside, approaching. They stopped in front of the door. Over his head, the cot sank under her weight, and someone entered. The smell of wine filled the room.

"I was beginning to think you weren't coming anymore," he heard her say seductively.

A pair of Roman sandals dragged themselves to the edge of the bed.

"I see you're ready," the Roman spilled out the words at her.

The cot creaked under the new weight, and the wooden boards supporting it bowed dangerously over Dismas's face. He closed his eyes, afraid they would break on his nose.

"You know you're my favorite whore, right?"

Dismas felt the tingling on his skin of the two bodies rustling against each other; he reached for the hilt, ready to pull the weapon from his belt.

"But today we're going to do something different," the Roman hissed with disgust.

The bed creaked violently, and the boards tightened again, away from Dismas's face. He heard her scream in pain and the soldier spitting out a laugh; her beauty dragged across the floor, an iron fist pulling at her hair.

Dismas shuddered. His blood boiled under his skin, his hand tense on the hilt, not knowing what to do. He saw her knees settle on the floor in front of the Roman's sandals, as he stood over her, and Dismas winced, undecided. If he came out of his hiding place now, the soldier would see him and defend himself before Dismas could slaughter him like a pig.

"Not so fast!" Dismas heard her object, regaining control as she backed away from his enemy's feet. "Take that off first," she added in a playful tone.

There was a tense silence, followed by fingers unbuttoning, and then Dismas saw the armor fall to the floor behind the soldier's feet. The legionary's sandals took two steps towards her, his tunic falling now over his hairy legs.

"I'm the one who gives the orders here, bitch!" his voice burst out, followed by a thud and a scream.

She rolled on the floor in a swirl of hair and blood, and Dismas saw the same terror fill those eyes that he had seen on Bathsheba when she fell.

The bed flew away in the air with the cry of a caged beast, and Dismas pounced on his naked prey. The Roman didn't even have time to blink before his life began to drain away, blood spurting from his gaping throat.

By the time Susanna realized what had happened, a crazed Dismas was standing over the dead soldier, stabbing him repeatedly in the chest. She counted twelve stabs before he threw the dagger to the floor, burning with hatred, as the pool of blood expanded around the corpse. Then he slipped in the blood, onto the corpse, crying with the same fury with which he had killed the man.

Voices bursting into the hallway outside her door, asking what was happening, forced her to act quickly. She grabbed him by the hand and, pulling him along, led him to a trapdoor that opened to the stable below her room, a safe escape route for compromising situations.

The two of them disappeared together into the darkness of the night, not ever returning to that place.

She never asked him why. But she knew that despite his anger, despite his rage, he had not been able to extinguish the fire that seemed to consume him with each stab. Even to this day, two years later, when the capricious mists of dusk fell upon him and sleep bound him helplessly, the stabbing continued in a nightmare that threw him to the edge of the abyss, onto his bed with tears in his eyes...

At that moment, Dismas turned onto his side beside her, awake.

Susanna reached out her arm and, without even opening her eyes, let her hand rest on his chest. He felt the warmth of her body, and the remnants of the nightmare disappeared with the heat of sudden desire. Sex was a good substitute for longing and nostalgia while it lasted.

Dismas leaned gently, covering her with his naked torso, searching for her lips with relish. Susanna opened her eyes and smiled.

"Didn't you have enough last night?" she murmured, still sleepy, her eyes clouded with pleasure.

Dismas smiled. Susanna knew what to give and when, without the need for further questions. She was still the best in all of Jerusalem, the muse of the coming revolution. He was lucky to have her at his side, but even more so, not to be in love with her: jealousy would kill him. Besides, could one be content with splashing in a puddle when he had swum in a deep blue sea?

The wooden floor behind him creaked and with a flash of metal from under his pillow, Dismas disappeared from between the sheets. With the swiftness of the wind, he materialized with a leap behind the intruder who had just entered, pressing a dagger against his throat.

"It's me, damn it!"

Recognizing Melchiades's voice, Dismas relaxed the muscles of his arm and lowered the weapon.

"You shouldn't come in without warning. One of these days I'll kill you accidentally."

"You can be sure that on that day, we will die together, you and I, my friend. And cover yourself, by all the devils, because seeing you like a dog disgusts me a little, you know?"

"Maybe what you really feel is envy," Dismas answered, wrapping a cloak around his waist.

The words splashed like oil burning over the skin of the newcomer, and he turned his gaze towards the bed.

"You, on the other hand, Susanna, can stay like that forever. Your beauty could bring down an entire empire."

"Your words do not impress me, Melchiades," she answered, hiding her nakedness from his filthy gaze. "I know that what's in your mouth is very far from your heart. You showed me once, and I don't tend to give second opportunities."

Melchiades raised his hand to his forehead and scratched an eyebrow, nervous. He turned around abruptly and walked by Dismas without looking at him.

"Gestas is waiting. Now. I don't think you'll have time to enjoy her," he spat before disappearing into the shadows of the room.

Dismas made a move to follow him, with an urge to break Melchiades's neck right there, but thought twice. He returned to the edge of the bed and grabbed his clothes to get dressed.

"I didn't know you had a thing with Melchiades," he said as he pulled his tunic over his head.

"Oh, yes! But it's not what you think. I don't get into bed with men like him. It was work, and I almost ended up beaten by a—" A sudden cough interrupted her, and she brought her hand to her mouth, lowering her eyes.

Dismas narrowed his eyes as he fastened his tunic around his waist with a rope. He was about to ask more about that, but Susanna found her voice as quickly as that strange cough had interrupted her.

"I have never understood why Gestas has not gotten rid of him," said she, changing the subject as she straightened herself up and tied her black hair into a ponytail with a red ribbon.

"I guess he'd feel bad for his cousin" he answered, looking at her with delight. "After all, Melchiades was the one who put him in contact with Bar Abbas, and Gestas has ended up occupying his position. If I were Bar Abbas, I would have made the same decision too. Gestas is worth a thousand times more."

"It's the weight of family," Susanna nodded; "sharing the same blood always has a price."

Dismas couldn't have agreed more. That was why he had chosen to cut all ties with his, he thought, while caressing the bare neck that peeked out from behind Susanna's ponytail.

"The time has come." Dismas let out a solemn sigh. He looked again at those smooth, delicious breasts that illuminated his darkness.

"I can wait, if you want, so we can finish what we were just starting." Susanna hinted at fantastic worlds behind each of her words.

Dismas sighed as he leaned toward her to kiss her goodbye. "The night is going to be long. You better go,"

Long and dark, like everything around me, he quickly completed in his mind as he vanished into the shadows of the room.

Gestas waited, the firelight of a torch illuminating his restless face.

"Bar Abbas has sent a message. It has to be tonight. Melchiades will accompany you."

At his side, Melchiades stirred like a faithful dog upon hearing his name.

"I thought it was going to be you and me," Dismas answered, ignoring Melchiades's presence.

"Do you trust me so little?" Melchiades stepped forward, hurt by his words.

Susanna's comment flew fleetingly through Dismas's mind. *No second opportunities for Melchiades.*

"Even going with a woman would be more discreet. Although some of them would do it better than you, of course," Dismas kept pushing.

"I don't really know why you hate me!" Melchiades bellowed with disproportionate fury. "I'm sick of you ignoring me. You forget that you're only here because I put you in touch with Gestas!"

"And you are still here because you put Gestas in touch with Bar Abbas, and he is forced to pay you back for the favor," Dismas exploded, barely containing himself.

The flame of the torch behind Melchiades quivered slightly before he lunged at Dismas.

"I'm going to kill you, bastard!" he shouted, the veins in his neck near bursting.

Dismas tried to repel him, but his fury was such that they both fell to the floor, rolling over each other between fists and insults.

"Damned imbecile," Gestas whispered to himself with a sigh of disbelief.

After a few moments of indecision, he leaned over the men, trying to untangle them. He managed to release the twisted neck of his stupid cousin from Dismas's powerful arms—snakes sculpted in marble.

I should have let Dismas kill him, he thought as he pushed Melchiades against the wall.

Melchiades let his body slide until he fell seated on the floor. The sound of his panting, getting air back into his lungs, filled the darkness.

"If your cousin lays a hand on me again, I'll kill him! I swear to you!" Dismas shouted as he stood up, the veins of his arms still bulging.

"Did you hear?" Gestas kicked his cousin in the backside. "And if he doesn't do it, I will! If you kept your mouth shut, you wouldn't ruin the plans, damn it!"

Melchiades didn't respond, his voice muffled, inaudible.

Gestas let his gaze wander beyond the contours of the room. It was obvious that sending both men together was off the table. There weren't many options left if he wanted the plan to succeed. It had taken them too long to get here, and he was not going to allow his cousin's stupidity, his lack of restraint, to send everything to hell.

It was now or ever.

They were about to light the spark that would set everything on fire, a hotbed of resistance in Jerusalem that would ignite the other cities. They'd all follow their example, encouraged by the groups they had infiltrated among the different local authorities, and would turn all of Judea into a great fire that would burn down the yoke of the damned Roman oppressor once and for all.

What the prophets and the great Moses had announced would finally be fulfilled; the Messiah had finally arrived. Men like him and Dismas had made it possible. Not with prayers; not with sacrifices in the temple; not with absurd laws and precepts. No, it had been the sweat of their arms and the blood shed by the enemy that had given wings and power to Bar Abbas.

Yeshua Bar Abbas, the Son of the Father, had come to the world with an idea—to establish a new kingdom of David. But it had been them, men like Gestas and Dismas, who had snatched that idea from the air and brought it down to earth and planted it in the soil, making it germinate in two words: *rebellion* and *death*. Gestas boasted privately of being the one to plant the first with his natural inclination to reject any authority; Dismas had sown the second with his visceral hatred of the enemy.

Gestas looked back into the room. No, that new kingdom of David could not be exposed to failure just now. Nobody was going to twist his plans. Much less his cousin. Blood was important, but that of the Jewish people was worth much more.

"Okay," he said, nodding towards Dismas. "I'll go with you. We'll both go. And you—you'll stay here until we return. Do you hear me?"

Still seated against the wall, Melchiades barely nodded.

"When we return, you'll hear this signal." Gestas hit the wall with his fist intermittently.

"I know, Gestas. I am not that stupid," he growled, raising his head. "It's the same one I had to give."

Losing his patience, Gestas grabbed his cousin by the front of his tunic and, lifting him off the ground, he pushed him against the wall.

"Well, I want to see you repeat it, here, right under my nose, dear cousin!" Gestas tilted Melchiades's head and pressed one of his cheeks hard against the stone of the wall.

"You're hurting me!" Melchiades's distorted voice snorted.

"Repeat the sign, or I swear I'll do it myself with your head until it bursts like a pumpkin!" Gestas spat in his face, without letting go.

With his hesitant hand turned into a fist, Melchiades knocked on the wall behind him, replicating the sign. His entire body writhed under Gestas's pressure.

Dismas looked away from the humiliating situation.

"Again," Gestas ordered upon hearing the correct code.

Melchiades repeated the knocks once more, and Gestas finally let go of him.

"Alright, little cousin. Now stay here and wait for us to return. Will you be capable of doing just that?"

Melchiades dropped to the floor again, dejected, his face hidden under his hands. Dismas thought he heard a low moan escape from him that sounded like a stifled laugh. Gestas turned to him, pushing him towards the exit, adamant.

"Let's not waste any more time. The sooner we leave, the sooner it will all begin. The night will not shelter us forever."

"So, Bar Abbas has decided to do it during Passover," Dismas said with satisfaction.

"Passover, yes. Is there anything more purifying than this feast? Only this time, instead of lambs, we will sacrifice Romans."

Gestas disappeared into the darkness and Dismas made as if to follow him, but before leaving the room, he tilted his head back. His gaze slid over Melchiades, whose face was no longer hidden, and he recognized a smile that the man quickly deleted with his hands. Their pupils met, and Dismas had time to glimpse the waves of rage within him.

He didn't understand that smile at the time, nor the storm pounding in Melchiades's eyes. He would later, though, when it was too late.

The narrow alleys of Jerusalem, on a clouded night that obscured any moonlight, seemed like a labyrinth designed by the devil. The absence of the hustle and bustle that gave life and color to the city during daylight now turned the streets into nameless places difficult to distinguish. The stalls of potters, tanners, and carpenters had disappeared inside the houses like snails during a storm and, although sometimes some sections could be identified by their smells, the only emanations that penetrated with each labored breath of Dismas and Gestas were those of fear and caution—fear of being discovered, caution so as not to attract attention.

Dismas had drawn and walked the route too many times to make a mistake now. From time to time, a fire burning inside one of the homes would filter through the lattices of a window, spilling some light outside that forced them to avoid it. But it was the exception; at that time, Jerusalem was sleeping soundly, resting before the arrival, the following week, of the avalanche of pilgrims who would set upon the Holy City for Passover.

Bar Abbas could not have chosen a better time to start the rebellion. There were many expectations placed on this Passover. There were voices talking about a Nazarene whom his followers wanted to make king during the festivities, and nobody wanted to miss the spectacle. Except for the lambs, Dismas smiled, hearing in the distance the bleating of the hundreds of animals that were penned up on the other side of the wall, waiting to be slaughtered. And all for the greater glory of a god in his temple who spoke through the mouths of priests and Pharisees that became rich with the commissions from the sacrifices.

What a blundering, mischievous lie.

Dismas had to spit to keep from choking on the sudden bitter taste of hypocrisy he felt.

"Damn it, you pig! You almost hit me," said Gestas,

leaning forward behind him. "Are you sure this is the way out toward the Kidron Valley? I'd swear it wasn't that long."

"Soften up, we're fine," Dismas replied with a sharp whisper.

Gestas had good reasons to be uneasy. His mission was too important to fail now. Every revolution needed weapons to be wielded against the enemy, and those had required a lot of money stolen from the caravans, and the effort of forging them all out in secret, sheltered in a place that had once served as King David's hideout.

The final result, very numerous, waited now outside the city, along the Kidron Creek, hidden inside enormous barrels carried by a discreet caravan. Its owner believed he was delivering the wine that would supply the pilgrims in Jerusalem. Only they knew what lay inside—bubbling Roman blood ready to be spilled.

With his heart beating like a hammer, Dismas finally saw the outlines of a wider street that crossed the alley they were walking along. He quickened his pace, eager to clear his doubts. The gate in the wall that opened upon the Kidron Valley had to be at the end of that intersection. He clenched his teeth so hard that his cheeks tensed like the skin of a drum.

"I hope you're right," Gestas whispered at his side, reading his face.

Dismas poked his head out slightly onto the broader road and breathed a sigh of relief; there at the end of its right hand stood the wall, with an empty hole in its entrails. They had chosen that entrance to the city because the Kidron Gate was not usually guarded. The exit route crossed the valley that gave it its name, leading to olive groves and fields of crops that blanketed the land west of the city.

Dismas and Gestas emerged from the shadows of the

corner, but a murmur of voices stopped them in their tracks. Dismas pushed Gestas into the shroud of one of the doorways and both held their breath.

If it was a Roman garrison, they were lost. He was reassured when he recognized the accent, stained by earth and sea alike, of Jewish voices from Galilee.

"Pilgrims here for Passover," he whispered in Gestas's ear.

Dismas peered at them through the thickness of the night. Where were they headed at those hours? They were no more than a dozen, walking towards the exit of the city, led by the torch that one of them held. His attention was drawn to the man walking beside the fire. The glow of the flame on his white tunic injected strength and presence into that figure, as if the light that the others were following came out of him rather than the torch.

They were advancing toward the same place where Dismas and Gestas had placed all their hopes.

"I hope those fools don't endanger our plans," Gestas murmured, his face emerging from the shadows that kept them hidden.

They waited for the strange group to pass through the gate and for their voices to be swallowed up by the night.

Dismas's imagination nervously toyed with the idea of those men exposing their whole plan. What if one of them raised an alarm when the wagons outside the wall prompted suspicions? What if those who were waiting for Dismas and Gestas became nervous when they saw that group of strangers? What if...? Dismas closed his eyes, trying to drown his stupid thoughts until silence fell on them again like a knife. The danger had passed.

They shook off the shadows and advanced with renewed stealth to the gate of the city.

"There's no one here, damn it," Gestas muttered, furious, as he crossed the threshold and saw that the wall was their only company.

The eyes of both of them spread over the black immensity of the valley that opened at the foot of the city. In the distance the waters of the Kidron rushed furiously over the rocky ground and, a little further on, they could still see a point of torchlight vanishing in the distance. That entourage of the living flame remained in Dismas's mind.

At that moment, they heard the sound of heavy wheels scraping through darkness. They turned in the direction it came from, along the left side of the wall, and saw some horns piercing the cloak of night. The heads of the oxen gave way to the wagons the animals were pulling, emerging behind.

Dismas and Gestas looked at each other, relieved. The result of so much effort, so much sacrifice, was finally approaching, and there was no turning back.

Atop one of the wagons, someone extended their arm in greeting, and Dismas responded by raising his. It was the agreed signal. Both waited for the oxen to come near.

As soon as the animals approached, they jumped as if someone had shaken a hornet's nest—from the back of the wagons, figures shining with the pale reflection of a sad moon. Dismas pulled the dagger from his belt, ready to defend himself, but five stingers in the shape of Roman lances on his chest forced him to throw his weapon down. Still disoriented by the surprise, he turned his gaze towards Gestas's cries. His companion was on the ground, trying to free himself from the weight of the knees on his back, struggling like a cornered boar. The Roman soldiers who held him stifled his screams of fury and despair by grabbing his nape and burying his face into the dust he had just bitten.

Dismas looked again at the ring of Roman soldiers that were now surrounding him, their spears prodding his chest, forcing him to bend before them. He resisted, defiant, his eyes burning, but a sudden pang of pain made him look down at his chest. A trickle of blood began to flow from under one of the spearpoints, and he sank to his knees.

They had been defeated before the battle had even started.

The exit to the Kidron, the place that was supposed to mark the beginning of Bar Abbas's liberation, had become a mousetrap.

With his eyes fixed on the ground, Dismas gritted his teeth in rage, thinking of the face of the one who had betrayed them. He let out a cry of hatred, a sound of pain and fury, but the lament died on his lips with a sharp blow to his back. His body collapsed on the ground, and everything became as dark as the imminent future that awaited him and Gestas.

2.

The scraping and rattling of chains brought him back to his senses. His eyes gradually took in the place where he was. The flaming tongue of a torch made shadows dance on a concave wall that became a ceiling when Dismas finally forced himself to sit up on the ground where he lay.

With confusion still clouding his mind, he fixed his gaze on his numb hands. Shackles had lifted the skin from his wrists like onion, and bound him to a chain whose end was attached to the wall outside the cell.

He looked like a dog—no, not even a dog. Dogs were not tied up when they were locked in. He tried to push himself up, using his chained arms on the floor for support, but a sharp sting in his chest made him groan in pain. The damned Roman spear. He felt the rough blood that had dried around the wound, under his right shoulder. He shook his head; he should see a doctor before it were too late. He greeted the thought with a derisive snort. Why bother? By the time the wound festered, he would be dead. Roman law was merciless.

He clenched his fists as he remembered the trap they had fallen into, and his chains twisted violently. If he ever had that rat in his arms again, he would kill him without mercy.

"Dismas?" It was a hollow voice, beyond his cell.

He peered across the iron bars, the golden glow of the torch in the hallway allowing him to see into the cell directly in front of him.

They recognized each other in the fulgent glint of darkness, and Dismas felt comforted by the presence of his friend Gestas. At least they would die together.

"He has betrayed us." The words burned in Dismas's mouth.

"Whoever it is, I would not like to be in his shoes when Bar Abbas discovers it." Gestas spoke with the confidence of someone who still believes he has everything under control. "Then his anger will explode, and vengeance will fall upon the traitor and all the Romans."

Through the bars, Dismas was surprised by the gleam in Gestas's eyes as he spoke. It was heartbreaking how unrealistic his friend was, unable to realize who had undoubtedly betrayed them. But even more pathetic was seeing the hopes he still placed on Bar Abbas, as if he were an omnipotent god. Not even Bar Abbas could escape the treachery they had fallen into.

"I would give everything I have to be there and see that moment!" Gestas added with a smile. "When we reunite with Bar Abbas, we will ask him how he knew about the traitor."

Dismas lowered his head and sank back into the darkness of his cell. Gestas was delirious or, worse still, he really believed that Bar Abbas was the true Messiah who would free them all. He sighed and glanced at his chained wrists. There was an inexorable reality that apparently escaped his friend: neither Bar Abbas nor anyone could free their hands from the weight of those chains without the weapons that the Romans had snatched from them by the Kidron gate.

At that moment, the sound of a bunch of keys rattling echoed from down the corridor. An iron door howled on its hinges and footsteps approached. Dismas exchanged an expectant glance with Gestas. They recognized from the shadow a Roman soldier approaching them.

He stopped in front of Dismas' cell.

"Are you Dismas?" the soldier barked as he released the chain attached to the outside and opened the bars. "They're waiting for you."

The Roman pulled on the chain, and the shackles sank into the raw flesh of Dismas's wrists. Dismas gritted his teeth, trying to avoid any show of pain as he emerged from the shadows.

"What do you want from him?" Gestas bellowed from his cell. "He won't tell you anything! Dismas, be strong!" he exclaimed, gripping the bars in his hands.

The jailer looked at him with a mocking smile and hit the bars with the end of the chain he held in his hands. Gestas barely managed to avoid the metal's lashing.

"You damned animals! Know that your end is near, and it will be with blood, with lots of blood!"

The soldier laughed at Gestas's outburst.

"And who is going to make that happen? Bar Abbas, that smelly bandit you call Messiah?"

He spat through the bars of Gestas's cell and, turning away, walked down the corridor with Dismas following behind him like a dog.

"I think your friend hasn't realized yet the situation you're in," he said mockingly, as the curses spat by Gestas melted in the background.

Dismas didn't answer, his mind focused on avoiding the jerks of the chains on his lacerated wrists.

The jailer left him alone in a room on the upper floor, but not before making sure that his chain was carefully attached to the iron ring that hung from one of the walls.

Dismas, leaning against that wall, slid to the floor while he stared at the blue square framed by a small window above him, out of his reach. Would that be the only sky he would see before dying?

The question put his heart on the edge of the precipice. For the first time, he felt the vertigo of what it meant to be imprisoned by the Romans. The shackles on his wrists did not prevent him from raising his hands towards that blue, trying to touch with his fingers something that was escaping him and that he would never reach again.

The presence of a stranger brought him back to his captivity, and he lowered his arms.

"Hello, Dismas."

Dismas recognized his voice before he saw him.

He looked at the newcomer and, without pulling his back away from the wall, he rose from the floor very slowly. The stranger walked a few steps until he was in front of him, but out of his reach, at the safe distance that the length of the chain provided. He knew perfectly well that, otherwise, Dismas would kill him. Because he was the traitor.

Dismas's entrails began to churn as they had that day under the bed in that brothel.

There was a moment of tense silence between them before Dismas decided to speak.

"I wonder what you have gotten in exchange for your betrayal." The words came out casually, without apparent tension.

A smile crossed Melchiades's face, dripping, mocking, contemptuous.

"You were always the clever man," said he, tasting his triumph. "But this time I won. It's so easy to unnerve you."

"They say you have the rare ability to do that with everyone," Dismas answered without losing his temper.

Melchiades gritted his teeth, and his smile turned into a ferocious grimace.

"That night it was easy to get you hot while that bitch Susanna was warming your bed."

"I thought you came to watch us to get yourself excited."

Dismas's contempt hit Melchiades so hard that he couldn't prevent a brief twitch in his left eye.

"I only needed to press in the right place for you to jump on me like a lion," Melchiades continued, recovering his composure. "It wasn't difficult to get Gestas to replace me in the job. It only cost me this much," he pointed to the bruise on his left cheekbone. "It's a more than reasonable price to have you here, tied with chains, like a dog, in front of me."

"Do you hate me so much as to ruin everything we've been building all this time!?" Dismas could not hide his fury any longer, and Melchiades smiled, at last satisfied.

"Although you may not believe it, it's nothing personal. I must admit that your arrival among our group was a hard blow to my ego. I was the one who had introduced you, betting heavily on you, and all of a sudden I stopped feeling indispensable in the organization. I was no longer useful because you did everything much better. You knew how to plan, how to command, how to fight…. You even predicted the enemy's reaction!" A stinging laugh slipped between his words. "It's a pity you didn't know how to calculate the reaction of a friend."

"You betrayed us out of *jealousy?*" Dismas exclaimed, his eyes bulging. "Because you felt like a scorned slut?"

"Oh, no, my dear friend!" Melchiades shook his head,

with a smile that still hid a secret. "It's true that it hurt me to stop being useful, but that made me less attached to the messiah's cause. And that's when I began to reconsider my situation. If I was already feeling trampled by you, what would happen the day Bar Abbas gained the power he sought? You and Gestas would get all the honors, but what would become of me? Nothing."

Melchiades waved into the air in front of him.

"So I became curious about what the enemy would be willing to offer in exchange for my knowledge. Have you ever heard that Rome does not pay traitors?" His lips vomited an acid smile. "Well, it turns out that's not exactly true. They wouldn't pay much for your head, that I have to admit. But as for Bar Abbas, you cannot even imagine what they were willing to pay for him!"

"Bar Abbas is not with us," Dismas said with a defiant grin.

"As we speak, a Roman garrison is falling on him like a frightened rabbit."

From his crouching position, Dismas pounced like a lion with every muscle of his body, but despite all his momentum, the chains stopped him just inches from where the traitor stood.

Melchiades looked him in the eyes, fearless in the protection the irons offered him.

"And it all started with you. With the way you treated me. With the way you despised me. With the way you ignored me."

And he spat in Dismas's face.

Dismas struggled against the chains, mad with fury, as if boiling oil had been thrown at him.

"So you've come here just to tell me this? To make me feel guilty about your betrayal?"

His screams alerted one of the guards, who looked into the room to see what was happening. Melchiades waved his hand at him, and the soldier disappeared again.

"Oh, no, dearest Dismas! I have come for something else." His eyes gave a hint of the shadow of the secret he was about to share. "I have always found your devotion to the cause of Bar Abbas somewhat ironic. You fell on our side because you wanted to avenge a personal tragedy. Bathsheba, was that her name?"

Hearing her name from that filthy mouth, Dismas twisted in his chains, holding his breath.

A look of satisfaction crossed Melchiades's face when he realized that he was finally touching bone.

"A man who learns how to listen can learn everything he needs to know. You wanted to avenge her death that came thanks to the brutality of a Roman platoon that day, in the eastern part of the city. But what if I told you that it was Bar Abbas who planned it all? Sow chaos, create disorder. Those were his exact words. By giving a false tip so the Roman army would fall upon the population."

Dismas fell to his knees, still not understanding, but fearing everything.

"The objective," Melchiades continued from above, "was to cause the greatest number of deaths, to enrage the people and to generate new blood for the cause."

"Wretched!" Dismas whispered through his teeth.

"Wait, my dear. I'm not finished yet. And I swear to you by the most sacred thing that what I am about to say will change your life."

The dull noise of the chains echoed mournfully against the wall.

Melchiades's face lit up, about to devour his prey.

"Then it came to me. 'Bar Abbas, this is the opportunity

we were looking for to get the blacksmith to join us,' I said, brilliantly. I had seen you that day at the fountain, mad with rage, facing down the Romans because you thought she'd been hurt. And a small seed germinated in my devious little head." He poked at his temple with a naked smile.

With frozen eyes, Dismas remembered Melchiades's face that day in the crowd.

"What if we replicated that same situation, but with a more dramatic ending?" he continued, waving his hands in the air, fascinated by himself. "The mayhem that Bar Abbas had planned to the east of the city offered that opportunity on a silver platter. It was all very simple. The pieces were all on the table: a wedding, the bride, the dowry, exotic merchandise arriving from Syria, and a mother eager to please her son. All that was necessary was to play with them skillfully."

The words fell upon Dismas, and the room became smaller and smaller around him.

"So it was *I*," Melchiades said, gravely, solemnly, cruelly, "who told your mother about the wonders she could find that day on the other side of the city. It was I who got them a guide to take them there. It was I who made sure that once in the eye of the storm, there would be someone willing to end the life of your beloved Bathsheba."

As he spoke, images of that fateful day played through Dismas's mind—of him with Bathsheba, forbidding her to go to that part of the city; of his mother assuring Bathsheba that with that man as a guide, they were safe; of the Roman soldier who, ahead of his own ranks, dealt the mortal blow to Bathsheba; of him stabbing that soldier a dozen times under Susanna's astonished gaze....

"Now is when you should say, with a look of astonishment: 'But Melchiades, it can't be true! That's impossible! It was a Roman who killed my dear Bathsheba, and we don't deal with Romans.'"

He paused a few moments to register the impact of his words on that face that lay, defeated, at his feet.

"And this," he continued, "is when I answer you: You don't know what you can get from a Roman when you promise him the best flesh in town. That bastard almost killed poor Susanna. But you were there to save her and kill him afterwards, am I right? Twists of fate don't exist, my dear friend! Everything is always planned ahead."

The images in Dismas's head were swept away by that of Susanna's face, that day at the fountain, so willing to talk to him; of the last night with Susanna, that sudden cough that interrupted what she had been about to say about her relationship with Melchiades....

A terrible cry emerged from his lungs, and he let himself fall, crushed against the ground like a worm.

In front of him, Melchiades was enjoying the catharsis of the moment.

"Irony of ironies, isn't it? You joined us to avenge the death of your beloved Bathsheba, and the culprits were right behind you. Tell me one thing, good old Dismas: How does it feel to know that you have been fighting on the wrong side?"

As Melchiades enjoyed the taste of his own bitter words in his mouth, Dismas suddenly threw his legs out like a whip, and with a strong kick knocked Melchiades's feet out from under him, dropping him to the floor. Dismas grabbed him by the bottom of his robe and dragged the man toward him. Then he pounced on his body like a caged beast. In an instant his face hung so closely over Melchiades's that Dismas could smell the bastard's foul breath, and he felt as though he could burn the man's eyes out with fire from his own.

It had all happened so fast that the traitor still didn't understand the stupid mistake he had just made, ignoring the limits of the safe distance those damned chains provided.

Something cold surrounded his throat and began to pull, peeling his neck as if it were the head of a garlic. The burning of the raw wound made him want to scream, but he couldn't.

Air—he needed air.

He couldn't breathe. He brought his hands to the bundle of chains that Dismas was pulling tight with arms tense as iron bars, the veins under his skin swollen with the heat of blood that cried out for vengeance. Melchiades tried desperately to get air, his face a dark red now, while his crazed legs began to kick frantically, in search of ground on which to flee.

"I need *air!*" he cried out to himself before losing consciousness.

The links of the chains continued to sink into the raw flesh they had opened, the rust mixing with viscous blood that now flowed down over the body, until a dull snap inside his neck halted everything.

As he watched Melchiades' life fade from his body, Dismas saw again the horrified eyes of his very first victim, laughing at him.

"You will never die!" Dismas moaned with a cry before his strength abandoned him, feeling exhausted. Beneath his body, there was no pleasure, no hope, no life. Only the remains of someone who, in his departure, had left behind only an expression on his face that offered the most absolute nothingness.

The incandescent glow in Dismas's eyes, on his cheeks, all over his body, left him unaware of the hands of the guards falling upon him, pulling him, separating him from the corpse beneath him.

On his blood-stained face, the white line of his teeth traced a desperate smile.

"You wanted to know, didn't you?" cried out a voice from within his own depths. "Well, this is what it feels like to know that you fight on the wrong side! This is what it feels like!"

It took three guards to control Dismas, pulsing with fury, and as they tried to lead him back to his cell, the smile on his lips froze.

No, he still had not attained the vengeance he sought. The idea fell like a stone into a deep, dark, black pit, and splashed in his stomach. The icy air that it unleashed rose from the abyss, went through his throat, and crossed his lips into a vomit: Bar Abbas.

He was the guilty one. He had to pay.

3.

"What happened? Dismas! What happened? Answer me!"

Hidden in the shadows of his cell, Gestas's demands echoed in the emptiness of his soul. Each breath of air that entered his body swept into an infinite windowless space.

For what? What had it all been for?

An unfathomable anguish seized him, and Dismas had to open his eyes just to keep from falling into the abyss.

Gestas's words continued to dance, far away, over his head, as he tried to revive his broken spirit, fill it with some meaning, gather what was left to keep him alive.... He brought once again to his lips the only atonement his life needed: Bar Abbas. He only had to wait.

"Dismas, I know you can hear me! What have they done to you? Did they torture you? Did you tell them anything?"

He turned, his face dimly bathed by the light of the torches burning in the hallway.
Gestas's voice had regained the foreground of his attention, demanding answers that Dismas could not reveal. Not yet. They would be his farewell gift when he arrived. And he would arrive.

"Gestas, shut up! I don't feel like talking," he muttered.

Far from calming Gestas, his words increased his agitation.

"So you've talked! You told them everything, didn't you? Did you betray Bar Abbas? Damn you, Dismas! *Damn you!*"

"Gestas!" Dismas threw himself against the bars of his cell, gripping them as if he wanted to tear him apart. "Shut up for once! Shut up, shut up, shut up!"

The madness in his gaze, in his words, left Gestas stunned, speechless. Despite the bars that separated them, a shiver of terror shook his shoulders, making him fear for his life.

The jangling of keys against the dungeon door captured their attention. Dismas sharpened his ears like an animal about to fall on its prey. The groan of the hinges opening announced the moment he had been waiting for.

Footsteps, mixed with the metallic clatter of chains, advanced toward them—guards accompanying a prisoner. They looked at each other; Dismas recognized the anxiety rising on Gestas's face, as the light of a torch spread like a golden stain over the corridor and approached their cells.

Gestas was the first to see him. His face and his soul both contracted, and he fell to his knees, all the strength abandoning him.

"That's perfect! Prostrate yourself before your liberator," mocked the guard who led the way. "How do you Jews call him?"

"The Messiah!" added the other guard, pulling on the chains that held Bar Abbas by his ankles.

The prisoner stumbled but remained on his feet. The jailers couldn't help laughing at his pathetic dance, but Yeshua Bar Abbas ignored them, not even taking his eyes off the ground. His figure, despite the place he found himself, exuded such extraordinary dignity that it even managed to impress Dismas.

"Aren't you going to say anything to your disciples? Not

a word of comfort to someone who prostrates himself like this at your arrival?" mocked the man carrying the torch, as he left it hanging on an iron ring on the wall.

"Then you'd better bow down," added his companion, pulling the chains hard enough as to make Bar Abbas fall to the ground on his face.

All his dignity was gone. Gestas put his hands to his face, horrified at watching the final collapse of all his hopes.

"While you're lying down like that, maybe it's time to beg your friends for forgiveness. After all, you are the cause of their imprisonment!" The guard kicked his sandal into the prisoner's bare legs.

Bar Abbas howled in pain at the tearing in his thigh, while the guard bent down on his heels to remove the chains from the prisoner's shackles. He stood up again and, without taking his foot off Bar Abbas's calf, passed the chains to his companion. The latter straddled Bar Abbas's back and, taking him by the arms, passed the chains through his wrists. Now shackled by his upper limbs, Bar Abbas was forced to rise, and looked at his captors with a mixture of blood and fire.

"Your fall will be much worse than mine."

His words, grave and deep, formed a thick halo that the guards quickly dispelled with laughter.

"You're very sure of your victory," the older guard said, leaning in so that his face nearly touched the prisoner's.

"It is written," Bar Abbas responded, holding his gaze.

"Do you know what else is written?" He let loose a belch in Bar Abbas's face that was like a thousand storms blowing over a pond of dead frogs. "I'm fucking hungry! Open the door."

"Which cell, sergeant?" asked the young legionary, amused.

"Which one do you think we should put him in?" He looked at his companion as if he were an idiot. "We'll lock him up with this other one, who doesn't seem so impressed with his Messiah."

He nodded towards Dismas's cell:

"You're an old dog, aren't you?"

He slipped his sword unexpectedly through the bars, resting its point under Dismas's chin, but the latter did not even blink.

"I see your capacity for surprise was stolen from you long ago," the Roman sergeant added, peering at him through the bars. "So much the better; you'll suffer less when the time comes."

They shoved Bar Abbas into Dismas's cell and, after securing his chain to the wall of the corridor outside, they left the basement amid laughter and threats.

"Pray to your god, for you don't have much time left!" one of the guards shouted, before the creaking of the bolt on the door separated the three prisoners from the land of the living.

The crackling of the single torch in the corridor was the only sound that was heard for a long time. Huddled before the bars, still on his knees, Gestas tried to understand what it meant to have Bar Abbas among them. Who was going to free them now?

In the other cell, Dismas and Bar Abbas had not even exchanged glances yet, each absorbed in their thoughts, cautiously ignoring each other. Time seemed to have ceased around Dismas, who continued to cling to the iron bars that the fire in his hands could not melt.

Suddenly, coming back to life, Gestas stood up again, extending his arm between the bars, pointing at Dismas.

"It was him! He is the one who betrayed you, Bar Abbas! It was he who talked!"

"Gestas, calm down, brother." Bar Abbas's firm voice sought to restrain him.

"No, you have to listen to me!" Gestas insisted. "They took him with them, they tortured him. He let it slip."

"Enough, stupid!"

Gestas froze at the command of his master.

"The only one who talked," Bar Abbas continued sharply, "the one who betrayed us, is your cousin."

Gestas grabbed the bars of his cell as if he were about to drown.

"What!" In his voice was a combination of disbelief and hatred. "Damn it! I should have killed that bastard with my own hands. I was about to do it!"

"I did it myself."

Dismas's voice pushed back the shadows that surrounded them, and brought with it a silence that made even the crackling of the flame go mute.

Bar Abbas and Gestas both turned to Dismas with astonishment.

"The soldiers brought me out because Melchiades wanted to talk to me," he said slowly, looking at Gestas with ice in his eyes.

Then he turned to Bar Abbas, who noticed for the first time the stains of blood in his tunic; something deep in his brain triggered a spark of alarm that his pride overlooked.

"I choked him with these chains." Dismas raised his arms and looked at the iron around his wrists as if seeing them for the first time. "He died in my hands without anyone to help him."

Dismas could feel the heat of Bar Abbas's gaze on him.

"Dismas, why didn't you tell me?" Gestas asked between

delirious laughs. "Well done! I wish it had been my hands,"

"And what did he say to you?" Bar Abbas interrupted, dismissing Gestas from the conversation.

His voice was hard, dark, lurking. Dismas tilted his face, avoiding it.

"He told me it was him," he said.

Bar Abbas moved slowly until he faced Dismas.

"Strange that he took the trouble to come to tell you."

Dismas gazed into that face. He had always seen poise, determination, conviction behind those features. Now the lines that outlined the eyebrows, the lips, the forehead of Bar Abbas appeared faded, the ordinary face of a mortal man.

"He told me something else." He swallowed slowly, preventing his Adam's apple from giving him away.

"Yes?" Bar Abbas's caution crumbled.

Dismas raised his arms and grasping the sides of Bar Abbas's face between his palms, pulled it towards his own, like two lovers gazing into each other's eyes, fire coming between them.

"He told me that I've been fighting on the wrong side."

Then Dismas thrust his head like a rock on Bar Abbas's forehead, both colliding with the impact of two fierce bulls in a duel of life or death.

They fell to the ground, rolling, tangled in their chains, trying to hold each other—a stunned Bar Abbas bleeding from his forehead as a panting Dismas climbed onto his body and positioned himself astride his chest, a knee on each side.

Bar Abbas tried to shove him off with his hands, with his legs, but Dismas moved his knee forward until it sank into his neck. Bar Abbas lay motionless, without struggle, like a mouse under a cat's claws. His wide eyes looked up at Dismas's face above him, but he only saw veins carved in his throat, rage dripping onto his skin.

"The only thing that ever shed light," Dismas roared, "the only thing that shed light in my life, you turned into darkness, the shadows that surround us. Now you will taste the pain you caused!"

Bar Abbas felt the pressure of the knee on his neck. He tried to scream, kicking like a child in a puddle of urine that was growing larger.

Dismas didn't relent. Behind him, Gestas's shouts alerting the guards merged with the pulsing of blood he felt between his legs. He was powerful, capable of engendering life and death at the same time. Then he drew himself up solemnly and, leaning all his weight onto his knee, sank it into Bar Abbas's throat.

The wretched face suddenly went pale, hints of life sputtering from his lips, pupils devouring the color of his eyes.

Everything around Dismas began to vibrate and spin and lose its contours. Melchiades's face appeared over Bar Abbas's, then the face of the first Roman soldier he'd killed, followed by the faces of all those he had murdered, one after the other. They were all laughing, all laughing at *him*, while he crushed their lives with his knee, again and again and again....

There will always be another, and your thirst will never be quenched.

Dismas collapsed onto his victim, his cheeks on Bar Abbas's, both breathing, their chests riding, one on top of the other, their hearts beating with the force of a thousand galloping horses.

He could hear the sound of his cell door opening, the shouts, the hurried footsteps, and someone grabbing him by the shoulders, throwing him to the ground, both of them face up now, shoulder to shoulder, the point of a spear prodding his throat.

"Evil beasts," the sergeant shouted through the bars. "Did you want to escape what we have been anticipating for you? The cross will dispense well with your worthless lives, you bastards. Take that dying man out of here and put him in the cell with the other fool."

When the guards left, silence fell on those three beaten throats—Bar Abbas's, burning with every breath that entered his lungs; Gestas's, consumed by laments for a nonexistent revolution; and Dismas's, thirsting for a vengeance that would never be satiated.

Lying on the damp floor of his cell, Dismas felt a slight tremor in his body. He had let Bar Abbas's life slip through his hands. He'd lost the courage to finish him off. At least he had the consolation of the cross ahead.

Someone had to pay for the sins he had committed.

4.

The crowd surrounded him in the middle of the square. They shouted at him angrily, pointing their fingers at him. He tried to escape by slipping between them, but someone pulled him back and he fell to the ground. They all swirled around him, a popular outrage demanding his condemnation. He raised his eyes and saw among the strangers the familiar face of the Roman soldier who had started his chain of vengeance.

"You must die too!" he yelled, making his way towards him with a dagger in his hand.

Dismas looked around in panic, in search of a way out. He kicked his legs against the floor, dragging his whole body backwards, while everyone chanted for his death without the slightest compassion.

He awoke with a start, unaware of where he was. It had all been a dream, but the cries of the crowd shouting for his death continued to echo in his ears.

"Our blood will be worth more spilled on that wood than it is in our own veins."

The familiar voice brought him back to reality. He was in the darkness of his cell.

"Death will be the spark that will ignite the rage of all our people." The voice of Bar Abbas.

"Yes!" Gestas's voice pulsed with excitement again. "The signal that our brothers need to start the revolution! We will die for our people."

He didn't know how much time had passed since his confrontation with Bar Abbas, but the emptiness of his stomach told him that he hadn't eaten for a long time. He put his hand to his forehead, confused, and the sound of the chains on his wrists gave away his presence to the others.

"And you, Dismas." It was Bar Abbas again. "Will you die with us too, even if you are chosen?"

The yelling he had heard in his dream returned like a dull clamor in the background, louder, filling the air around them, filtering through the stones of the walls from the square outside. He looked up, not understanding what was happening.

"They are deciding which of us will live. For Passover, the people release one of their prisoners," said Bar Abbas, his face pressed against the iron bars of his cell defiantly, making sure Dismas saw him still alive.

"I don't think they'll choose me, Bar Abbas," Dismas sputtered, getting up. "But even if they do, I will not forgo the walk to Golgotha and have the pleasure of seeing your body nailed to a cross"

The cries of the unseen crowd redoubled in intensity, but he couldn't understand what they were yelling.

"It's a shame that it all has to end like this between us, after everything we've been through. Frankly, I don't understand what you can have against me. I gave you life when you were dead, and we fought for a just cause."

Dismas jumped like a lynx, clinging to the bars.

"My only consolation for not having killed you with my own hands is knowing that you will suffer and pay for everything you have done on that cross."

"We will suffer, Dismas. We will suffer." Bar Abbas said without flinching. "We are in this together until the very end. Isn't that right, dear Gestas?"

The cries outside suddenly ceased—the people had decided.

The echo of footsteps in the distance overlapped with the beating of the three hearts before the dungeon latch creaked.

"Together in this, aren't we, Bar Abbas?" Gestas asked hesitantly.

"Together to the end, brother," Bar Abbas reassured him with a pat on the shoulder.

The same sergeant than before stood now earnestly in their presence again, unable to hide a slight sneer of mockery in his lips.

"Dear prisoners, the people, your people, have decided. Soldier, open the bars," he commanded at one of the soldiers who stood by him, while pointing to the cell where Gestas and Bar Abbas lay.

A sudden anguish gripped Dismas's chest.

"Prisoner Gestas! The people have called for your freedom! You are released," the sergeant bellowed.

Dismas breathed a sigh of relief, and all eyes turned to Gestas.

He raised his head very slowly, his heart pounding wildly in his temples before the abyss of doubt. He looked at Bar Abbas, his chin tense and proud, adamant. Together until the end.

"I reject it," he said with all the dignity which was left on him.

Everyone present was astonished. He was giving up an offer of freedom.

Then the soldiers burst into laughter, spoiling everything.

"All right, all right ," the sergeant was compelled to say

amidst the giggling. "It wasn't true. Go back to your place, Gestas. You weren't the chosen one."

The laughter was like a slap to the prisoner's cheek. He took a step back, confused. If at that very moment he had turned to Bar Abbas, he would have seen a spark lighting up his eyes and his soul.

"Bar Abbas, every son of a bitch has its lucky day. Step forward. You are set free. The people have chosen you."

Bar Abbas showed no hesitation—he crossed the threshold of the cell without a trace of regret.

Behind him, Gestas was startled, not understanding what part of the joke he was missing.

"Bar Abbas, aren't you going to reject freedom?" he uttered, still resisting with his heart what he was seeing.

Bar Abbas, in the corridor now, didn't even turn around, and the soldiers closed the cell in Gestas's face, marked by a look of betrayal. He did, however, look toward Dismas across the iron bars.

"I suppose I should be thankful." A small smile crossed Bar Abba's lips as he bowed his head. "After all, you let me live that I might suffer a terrible death, and look where I've ended up."

Dismas rushed against the bars, wanting to devour them, wishing to get at Bar Abbas's throat.

"Gestas has shown more courage than you! He was willing to die for you!"

"Someone has to die for others to live." Bar Abbas forced a rotten grin. "You, better than anyone, should know that."

Dismas's claws shot out furiously between the bars, trying to snatch him, but one of the soldiers moved faster and struck his arm with his spear. Dismas disappeared to the back of his cell with a heartbreaking scream. The howl raised new laughter among the guards.

"Come on, let's go. We don't have all day." The sergeant pushed Bar Abbas forward hurriedly, while he turned to Gestas. "As for you, don't cry too much. You're going to die crucified alongside another man who also calls himself a messiah. Bah, you israelites! You're all crazy lunatics, waiting for the impossible to happen."

The sergeant moved on, and a bolt of fury pierced Dismas's soul as he watched them leave.

"Bar Abbas! Bar Abbas!" he shouted, red with rage. "I… I curse you! Do you hear me? I curse you completely! May YHWH curse you! May YHWH curse you for everything you've done! YHWH… YHWH…"

The creaking of the door closing in the distance struck Dismas silent. He leaned his back against the bars and let himself fall, his body sinking.

He was a fool. Did he realize what he was saying?

YHWH cursing Bar Abbas? YHWH had just saved him from death!

The only man YHWH had cursed was him.

YHWH, who had created the heavens and the earth and the seas and the birds and Dismas himself, was once again spitting in his face. YHWH had laughed at him with Bathsheba. YHWH had shown him paradise on earth, only to take it away when it was about to be his.

Dismas had called upon YHWH then, trusting that he would save her.

You will see his power. But she had died.

YHWH had turned his back, and Dismas had responded by turning his own. Back against back, for the rest of eternity.

So why was Dismas calling on his name again now? For what? To make him curse Bar Abbas?

A laugh of despair shook him. YHWH had just *blessed* Bar Abbas!

Who would pay for all his crimes now?

"He has only cursed me. He has only cursed me, alone," he could barely hear himself say, as he beat his forehead against the bars, and rivers of fire began to flood his cheeks.

PART FIVE
Crucifixion

I.

Still tangled in the threads of despair that he had been weaving in his soul, Dismas found himself transported to a place under the light of a blinding sun, pummeled by the voices of hundreds of angry throats.

He looked around, bewildered by the change of scenery. Gestas, to his left, stood there, staring absently at the ground, as the soldiers finished loosening his shackles. Dismas looked at his bare wrists and was surprised not to have noticed that they had taken them off of him as well.

In front of them, three soldiers on horseback led the procession they would now be forced to join. They waited impatiently, while at their sides, other guards tried to hold back with their lances the unruly crowd that gathered around them, anticipating the violence ahead. They had come to see the spectacle of a crucifixion, but the focus of their attention was neither Dismas nor Gestas. It was a little further away, behind them. Dismas turned his head over his shoulder to see who was the object of such interest, but a sharp pain on his arm brought him back to reality.

"Come on, you!" bellowed a soldier, brandishing his whip. "Take the wood."

Stung by the lash, Dismas turned his gaze in the direction that the Roman pointed. A bare wooden beam lay at his feet. He remembered seeing men condemned to death carrying the horizontal crossbar of their cross through the streets of the city. Patibulum, the Romans called it. A name too beautiful for such cruelty.

The soldier raised the whip again, and the new lick on his flesh ignited fury on his face. The soldier smiled, threatening him again, and Dismas bent down obediently.

The splintery wooden beam dug into his shoulders, behind his neck. A sharp prickle ran through his body at the first contact with the cross.

Another soldier appeared under his arms extended at both sides and wrapped a rope around the end of the beam, tying it tightly to his wrist.

"Little chicken, little chicken, you can't get away!" he mocked as he tied Dismas to the wood.

He went to the other end of the crossbar and did the same. Dismas felt the weight of the beam bending his back. The muscles in his legs tensed, and he had to spread his feet slightly to find the right balance and not fall on his face.

They set off. The shouts of excitement spread like a wave over the sea of heads surrounding them. The soldiers on horseback leading the march split the crowd in two, making way for the condemned. Jerusalem had become a Red Sea that parted before the cursed sons of Moses.

But the city had not come out into the streets to see the two of them. He and Gestas were the appetizers for a more succulent execution. It was the one behind them who was the reason for so much expectation.

"Come on!" He heard the voice of a soldier, along with the sound of the whip cracking. "You certainly don't seem to have the strength to be the Messiah of the Jews."

Beside Dismas, Gestas burst out laughing wildly when he heard the soldier's mockery. "Bar Abbas was right! The

Messiah is coming to die with us. Hail, Messiah! Hail!" He seemed to have lost his mind.

The Messiah. So that was why there was such a crowd gathered. Another messiah on the list of the Jewish people. He thought of Nathaniel. Maybe this was the man for whom his friend had left everything.

What a disappointment! Isn't that right, dear Nathaniel? Just like mine. Neither of our Messiahs could deliver.

Anyway, what crime had this Messiah committed to share his fate?

The faces in the crowd that surrounded them were drunk with jests and insults. What had this man done to evoke so much hatred?

Spurred by curiosity, he tried to tilt his head slightly to catch a glimpse of the figure behind him, but it was useless. As he moved his neck to one side, the splinters of the wood dug hard into his skin, and the pain forced him to look ahead again.

The weight of his body grew with each step. Time stretched out slowly, and the patibulum on his shoulders seemed to crush him against the ground.

The crying of several women diverted his attention to one of the edges of the multitude.

"Is no one going to take pity on him?" one begged amid the grief of the others, who couldn't restrain their compassion.

"How can you applaud the condemnation of an innocent man?" shouted another, facing a man who overshadowed her and seemed to enjoy the sight of the condemned.

"Shut up, women! You don't understand anything," he answered without even looking at them.

"He's the Messiah, and you're executing him!" another, the youngest, cried in support of her companion.

Dismas licked his dry lips. They were an island in a sea of hate. Brave women. They had been followers of that man, like many of those present, in his days of glory, and now, in the bad times, they were not afraid to show it in public.

If she were still alive, she would be there with them, demanding that man's freedom, clamoring about his innocence. And he would be behind her, looking after her....

The idea suddenly assailed Dismas, point-blank, out of nowhere. He clenched his teeth hard to extinguish the bitter warmth he had just experienced inside.

Who was that man? Was he really innocent? Could he be the messiah that Bathsheba had expected? Dismas felt a renewed desire to see him, but the weight of the wood on his neck made it impossible.

"If we have to wait for him to climb the hill of Golgotha, we'll never be done here."

The voice of one of the soldiers walking behind opened an unexpected opportunity.

"Come on! Get up!" The same soldier was yelling, with the hissing of the whips tearing through the air and the flesh of that condemned man.

He heard the voices of those women again, redoubling their laments, as the excitement of the crowds raised.

"Is no one going to do anything to stop this torture?!"

The clash of voices and the tumult caused the riders at the head of the procession to halt their horses and, with them, the entire entourage. They turned to see what was happening.

The centurion in charge of the execution approached on his horse.

"Can you explain to me what the hell you're doing?" he yelled at his underlings.

Dismas could see his face of exasperation as he looked at what was happening behind him.

"You bunch of useless men! Can't you see he won't make it to Calvary alive like this? Find someone to help him carry the cross, damn it!"

Now that they had stopped, Dismas had the opportunity to move his feet hesitantly, stealthily, turning around while preventing at the same time that the weight of the wood unbalanced him.

"Hey, you! Help your messiah!" he heard the furious centurion shouting.

"I don't have anything to do with him!" protested a new voice, a Jewish one.

"I don't give a damn whether you do or not! I order you to help him, if you don't want something worse happening to you!"

"All right!" the Jew complied, as if he had any choice. "But I want it to be clear to everyone around here that I have no relation whatsoever with this criminal. I'll help him because I'm being forced to!"

Dismas at last found a position from which satisfy his curiosity out of the corner of his eye and get a look at the man.

The Jew who had just spoken was crouching over a wooden beam on the ground, but Dismas couldn't see the man himself. Then he noticed a cloth stained with blood moving under the patibulum, a figure trying to stand with the help of the newcomer.

Despite the anguish and the weight of his own cross, Dismas was struck by the drama that was unfolding before his eyes. The man's body was covered in wounds that were mixed with blood and dust, and he barely had the strength to stand up under the weight of that piece of wood.

How could this man be any messiah? Dismas was ashamed of even having thought such a stupid thing. After seeing this, how could there still be anyone so stupid as to continue believing in him? Those women were crazy! For the first time in his life, he felt relieved that Bathsheba was not there to see it. Her heart would have broken with sadness.

"Hey, you! Do you think you're in the circus or what?" One of the riders drew up close to Dismas on his horse. "Turn forward if you don't want to look as pretty as that criminal!"

The horse snorted out its nose, covering Dismas with its snot.

They resumed their march. Dismas barely had the energy to spit out the slime that the animal had left hanging from his lips. He had nothing left to hold on to except the wood on his shoulders, from which he would soon hang.

What could a man think about when he was about to die that way? The best he could do was to look out into the abyss of nothingness and let himself be dragged to the end, leaving everything suspended there in the empty horizon.

A little further ahead, beside him, he saw Gestas dragging himself heavily under his yoke. His image, pathetic, coarse, dirty, did not move anyone in the crowd to compassion. Was Dismas's own appearance as miserable as that of Gestas? Was there no one capable of pitying him?

He was a nameless man on death row. No one here was crying for him.

And whom would he expect to find, after all? Hadn't he wanted to break all ties with his family? He had only sown power, ambition, hatred, rage. And nothing grew under that arid soil.

Bathsheba, why did you abandon me?

He squinted his dusty eyes under the white light of that sky that was becoming leaden.

They finally left Jerusalem through the judicial gate, and outside the city now, outside the shadows of its walls, the spectacle began to lose intensity. Few stayed to watch the climb of the condemned up the slope of Calvary.

Several isolated groups were scattered along the edges of the road, waiting for the condemned, crying out a final encouragement, a final consolation, a final farewell. None of them were for him.

He forced his mind away from that sad thought by shifting his attention to the stones that paved the tortuous path that other criminals had traveled before him. He didn't want to stumble over any of them and provide satisfaction to the soldiers who brandished in the air with their whips.

Then he recognized her.

She was among a group of women, broken with sorrow, who seemed to envelope someone in a blue cloak that stood in the middle of them. His vision blurred suddenly by a flash of light that seemed to undo his heart, and he tripped, almost falling to the ground.

"Hey, you! I warn you that if you fall, you won't get any help like that sorry sod back there." His stumble had not gone unnoticed by the nearest soldier. "So let's go, keep going. We're almost there!"

But Dismas didn't move; he did not even hear the soldier. His gaze, his attention, his whole being, were focused on that unmistakable face, despite the pain that overwhelmed her... But the tears that lit his sister's disconsolate eyes were not meant for him.

He was overcome by an absolute loneliness. Sara had not recognized him. She had not even seen him, because her gaze was lost somewhere else, behind him. The only person in the world who could shed tears for him was shedding them, instead, for that man—the Messiah.

He cried out in silence to the entire universe, compelled it to force his sister to turn towards him for a single instant and recognize him. Then tears of compassion would flood her cheeks and tell him that she was here by his side and that she loved him and that everything would be as before.

But Sara did not turn.

"Hey! Didn't you hear me?" The guard's voice came back to his ears, and the lash of a whip made the air around him vibrate. "Get going!"

Dismas lowered his head and continued his hesitant step under the weight of the wood.

It was better this way. She shouldn't see him. She should never know that he was dying this way, like a despised criminal. Besides, he was already dead for her and his mother. Why bother renewing the pain?

"Faster! We don't have all day to watch you die!" the guard roared with impatience.

The whip hissed in his ears before it cracked on his torso. Dismas fell to his knees, bent by pain, sadness, and the weight of the wood on his shoulders. The scream that deflated his lungs mixed with the barking of a dog in the distance.

"Come on, stand up if you don't want to get beaten to a pulp," the soldier's threatening voice snorted in his ears. "Hey, get out of here!" He turned to the sharp, dry barking of the dog that had come between him and Dismas.

The mutt growled, showing his teeth defiantly.

The Roman tried to reach him with his whip, but the dog skillfully dodged it and continued its threatening dance around him.

Dismas gathered the last remaining strength he had and, raising one of his knees, dug his foot into the ground in order to rise again. He glanced in the direction of the dog he heard barking: a lump formed in his throat.

Atzel. Despite his long absence, despite the time gone by, Atzel had recognized him. The only one.

"Dogs are your only company," the soldier exclaimed, amused, with the whip waving in the air.

The animal, with its tail raised and its front legs firmly planted on the ground, continued to show its fangs.

"Cassius, don't you know how to get rid of a dog, or do you want us to stay here all day until you decide?" The centurion's voice exploded from the horse.

The mocking glances of his companions forced the soldier to pull his dagger from his belt.

"Come here, little doggy." He leaned towards Atzel with a forced smile while brandishing the metal.

"Atzel, go away. Get out of here," Dismas whispered, almost inaudibly.

The animal didn't move. It continued to bark froth at the soldier.

"Atzel! Atzel! Come back here right now." Sara's voice reached Dismas's ears like a torrent.

"Woman, you better take your dog, or I swear I'll butcher him like a chicken," said the soldier, lowering his weapon.

Sara's figure rushed into Dismas's view. She was untying the rope around her waist with a trembling hand, oblivious of his presence. He turned his head away and closed his eyes with a heavy heart, fighting against the impulse to be recognized by her, to be embraced, to be loved again. A storm shook his eyelids. She could not see him like that, about to be hung on a cross that denounced him as a worthless criminal.

He finally opened his eyes, let his gaze fall to the ground, and with his jaws clenched, he raised his right foot to flee from there before it was too late.

Sara managed to tie Atzel, but the dog, pulling towards Dismas, forced her to turn his way.

"Atzel!" she exclaimed nervously under the gaze of the soldier, who still had not let go of the hilt of his knife.

The stupid dog seemed to have gone mad at the sight of that criminal. Sara grabbed the leash with both hands, ready to pull Atzel hard, but she couldn't do it: the dog had stopped in front of that man and, extending his front legs forward as only he knew how to do, he bent his neck in front of the intruder.

As he had only ever done with his owner. As he had only ever done with her brother.

A shiver ran through her forearms, and her eyes became fixed, frightened, searching the face of the criminal. Atzel's leash slipped from between her fingers and fell softly to the ground, still, motionless.

Time and space threw a blanket over the three of them, pausing everything, and she threw herself at him with open arms.

"Brother!" she exclaimed, her voice breaking against his chest, covering him with kisses, smearing his dusty face with tears.

Dismas's heart trembled, and with it, his entire body.

"Didn't we have enough with one of you scum? Now another Jewish bitch is throwing herself into *your* arms too?"

The hiss of the whip striking the air near their ears brought both siblings back to the hill of Calvary.

Sara turned towards the soldier with indignation.

"Allow us one more moment! He's my brother!"

Atzel renewed his barking at the man who dared to threaten the only two people he bowed to in this world. The soldier gave a look of weariness and, brandishing the whip for the last time, decided that the time had come to end it. The tip tore through the air quickly before drawing a red line on the animal's side. Its cinnamon fur began to stain with blood and Atzel backed away, howling.

"You'll be next, if you don't get away!"

Sara turned to her brother urgently, defying the threats the soldier continued to spew behind her. She put her hand on his cheek. There was so much to say, so much to know! But there was only time for one gesture, for one look capable of setting his soul on fire.

"I *won't* say it again!" the soldier bellowed angrily behind her.

"Dismas, my brother, listen to me! You're not alone." The tears that flowed down her cheeks were only for him. "I'm here with you. And *he* is with you, do you hear me? He is with you! Make Bathsheba proud!"

Hands on her shoulders violently separated Sara from him.

"Let me go! Let me go!" She fought uselessly, while the soldier pushed her away and she struggled to free herself from his grasp. "You are not alone, Dismas! He is with you! Don't lose sight of him! Brother, look to him!"

Sara's voice was lost behind him among the voices of the soldiers who had come to see what was happening.

Dismas's body was still trembling when the soldier returned again, out of breath.

"You should learn from your women. With them alone, you could start a revolution!" The Roman smiled as he licked blood from the small wound that Sara's teeth had left on his hand.

The procession set off again with Sara's words still in Dismas's ears.

Make Bathsheba proud.

Proud of him? Why? What could she possibly be proud of if she could see him now, like this, with a wooden beam spread over his shoulders? Of his condition as a criminal? Of the blood he had shed with his hands to avenge her death? Of the women who had passed through his bed, as he tried to quench his thirst for her? Of the curses and insults he had directed on high, to Almighty God for her absence?

Seized by vertigo, he tried frantically to grab onto his cross so as not to fall into the infinite darkness. A tear struck the dry earth of Calvary at the very moment that the rays of the sun pointed from above to the three crosses that were nailed to its summit. One of them had his name written on it. From all eternity.

2.

Raised on the cross, over Calvary, the vertigo became overwhelming. Suspended between heaven and earth, he was held to the cross by only three nails, three long, pointed irons that had pierced his hands and feet with a sharp blow of the hammer. He bowed his head on his chest and let his gaze wander over the ribs that stuck out like the sticks framing a tent in the middle of the desert. He could count all his bones.

One, two, three, four, five… He stopped counting.

Where had he heard that before?

His eyes sank again into the blurred horizon of blue and ochre before him.

The sharp blows of the hammer brought his attention back down to the ground. He had to blink his eyes several times before he could focus on the Romans nailing the last convict to the cross. The so-called Messiah looked like a bloody worm crawling upon the cross. He, too, had been stripped of his clothes.

Look to him, Sara had told Dismas.

The shadow of a sad smile stirred in his mind. So this was the one whose power he was supposed to have seen.

"Show me your power," he barely whispered, trying in vain to shape with his lips the dark irony he felt.

It was useless. A sudden spasm silenced him, his tongue

stuck to the roof of his mouth. His throat felt as dry as a broken shard of baked clay lying in the sun.

To the left of the Messiah, he thought he saw some soldiers playing dice, with the tunic of that man rolled on the ground beside them. Who in his right mind could be casting lots for the tunic of someone condemned to death?

The vertigo returned, and his whole body trembled. Would the three nails securing him to the wood hold his weight? A feeling of terror invaded him, and he wanted to scream for them to get him out of there. But no, it was not a fall that would kill him. Nor would the pain he felt in his limbs, which seemed to scratch his skin from the inside; nor the horrible thirst in his throat, which cracked; nor the aching of his dislocated bones, and his heart melting like wax, which burned.

Up here, what would kill him in the end, slowly, without haste, was the struggle that his entire body had begun to fight to continue breathing. He felt the iron of the nails rusting the blood in his hands and feet, and the muscles under his skin, tense, pulling at the bones every time a breath of air entered his lungs.

He allowed his gaze to wander, shifting aimlessly through the light of a horizon that offered no comfort. To his left he heard a voice, roaring with fury. Gestas. He was hurling curses into the air, but Dismas barely understood what he was saying.

In the space that separated them, a tree grew now that suddenly rose to the same height at which they hung, interposed between the two crosses. Dismas smelled the freshly cut wood before he saw the Messiah hanging from his beam; some carpenter must have urgently cut that cross at the last minute, since it was the only one of the three that gave off that warm and fresh aroma.

There, from that height, so close to Dismas that he could almost touch him, it was disgusting to look at that man. His executioners hadn't been satisfied with the punishment of crucifixion—they'd tried to tear him apart with the lashes of their fearsome scourge as well. What had that poor bastard done to deserve that?

Those women had said he was innocent. Sara's presence had confirmed it for Dismas. Was that possible? So much punishment just for calling himself the Messiah? Not even Bar Abbas would have been treated so harshly.

Dismas noticed a crown of thorns covering the man's head. The points dug into his temple, causing trickles of blood to flow down his face. Dismas paused his gaze upon those lips that seemed to make the wind blow. He was praying.

"Hail, king of the Jews!" the same soldiers that Dismas had seen betting on his clothes shouted out with laughter. "Here at last, you have the throne you deserve!"

A sound from above caught his attention and, raising his face to the sky, Dismas saw a group of swallows chirping happily, oblivious to what was happening down here. They were fluttering in a circle several cubits over their heads, weightless, as if they were crowning the summit of Calvary.

A crown of swallows over a crown of thorns.

The laughter from below merged with the chirping from above; those unscrupulous, drunken men were laughing at the one who had wanted to be king of the Jews, while above, some birds made him king of the firmament.

Something ached suddenly inside Dismas's broken heart, as if a thorn from that crown was digging into his memory. The flying swallows and the aroma of freshly cut wood from that cross brought him back for a brief moment to that room, to that paradise he had never been able to enjoy.

He smiled grimly, cursing the ironies of fate, the untimeliness of his senses, the cruelty of memory, all conspiring to retrieve from oblivion the aromas of a lost home, precisely there, on Golgotha, a cursed place to which not even God deigned to pay attention.

He saw men pass below his feet who stopped in front of the cross of that broken man. He knew immediately from their clothes that they were priests and Pharisees. Like the ones who had rebuked the prophet John that day on the banks of the Jordan.

"You who were going to tear down the temple and rebuild it in three days—now you hang on a cross?" one of the chief men of the temple asked him in a tone that dripped with mockery. He made his words sound solemn on that landscape of death. "I call upon you, if you are the Son of God, to come down from that cross, and then we will all believe that you are the Messiah. Show us your power now, Galilean!"

The Pharisee's mocking cry pierced Dismas's chest like a lance.

You will see his power.

The words shook his insides again, and a shiver spread through his exhausted body. He looked up expectantly. Could the hour of that oracle that had not been fulfilled for Bathsheba have arrived? Had YHWH reserved it for this moment, and was his Messiah, the man at his side, about to perform the miracle of freeing himself and freeing Dismas with him, so that the whole world would believe in him?

A few moments passed.

Nothing happened.

The Messiah remained on the cross, and looks of relief covered the faces of those Pharisees, as if for a moment they had feared that something extraordinary was really going to happen. Like him. But they were content, while he, dejected, let his face fall again onto his chest.

They were about to leave the hill of Golgotha, satisfied, when they heard a quiet voice above them.

"Abba, forgive them for they know not what they do."

The man had spoken. It lacked the strength and intensity of a messiah, but those words stopped the priests in their tracks. They looked up in disbelief. One of them, the one who had rebuked the crucified man, cleared his throat nervously and hurried the others away as quickly as possible.

Abba. Dismas suddenly felt challenged by that word. The man had called out to his father. And he begged forgiveness for those who had done this to him. Dismas felt ashamed when he heard that. That man had done nothing, but still he forgave them all; Dismas was guilty of many things, but he had not forgiven anyone.

Who was the Abba of this convict, to whom he had pleaded for mercy?

In the emptiness of that moment, Dismas swallowed. He, who had not condemned that stranger, felt guilty of the unjust condemnation.

Then he felt the heat of someone touching his feet; it was brief but warm, very warm, fire advancing like molten iron through the veins. It was a confusing and unexpected sensation, which momentarily rescued him from death to bring him back to life. He bent his exhausted head over his body just in time to see a group of women passing below him. They stopped by the cross of the Messiah, replacing the Pharisees and priests, who had left for good.

He saw the blue cloak he'd noticed among the brave women who were with his sister on the slope of Golgotha. He thought she was among that group and had been the one who had given him that gentle caress on his foot, but he didn't see Sara among the four figures who now stood in front of that cross.

The woman in blue approached the feet of the Messiah and kissed them and cradled them. Dismas knew then that it had been her; he raised his gaze towards the crucified man and could imagine the feeling of infinite comfort that must have reached his soul in those moments of absolute solitude, because one touch of that woman had been enough to burn his heart.

Who was she? He watched her extend her hands again and murmur some words that hardly anyone could hear, not even the people who surrounded her, behind her, sorrowful and silent.

One of them burst into tears, unable to repress her sadness. Dismas, hanging like dead weight, tried to imagine that she was crying for him and that those tears served as a balm for his body. He looked thorough his blurred vision at her. He felt a moment of shock when he recognized in her sorrowful features the young woman he'd once known in Magdala. His mind flew to that stable—he'd had that mouth between his lips, his own legs between hers. He couldn't be wrong. But what was she doing there, next to that pure woman? If that man hanging above were really the Messiah, he would know what kind of woman the Magdalene had been and would not accept such a sinner in his inner circle. And yet...

"Mother."

From the mouth of the crucified came that word, and the sobs went silent.

The woman in blue looked up at her son's face. Beside her, someone stretched out his arm over her shoulders, covering her.

"Mother, there is your son," continued that broken voice, from above.

She followed the direction of her son's gaze to the one who was holding her to his chest, and raising her hand, she caressed his cheek. Her new son pulled down the cloak that covered his head, revealing the astonishment that those words had left on his face.

Dismas, who had mistaken him for one of the women, recognized the clean and handsome young man who had splashed in the waters of the Jordan. He had been one of the disciples of the prophet John. The other John.

You will see his power.

The memory prickled his skin.

"Son, that is your mother." His words were now clear and strong.

The young man held the woman in blue in his arms with a delicacy and tenderness that Dismas felt like a gash within himself.

He had never hugged his mother like that. How badly he had behaved towards her! He had not even asked his sister about her.

"Oh Mama, forgive me!" he muttered, ashamed of himself.

And yet that man hanging on the cross was watching over his own mother even now. He had to be innocent. Someone who cared for his mother in this way could not have committed any crime. That woman's face attested to it. The eyes of the young disciple, John, at her side, reflected it. Even the pure and sincere tears of the Magdalene gave firm testimony to his innocence.

The hollow and shrill sound of bitter laughter broke the moment. It did not come from below.

"Your *mother*? You're giving us your mother?" Gestas's body twisted with each word. "And what are we going to do with her? What we want is freedom! Give us freedom!

Aren't you the Christ? Then save yourself and save us! Do you hear me? Idiot! You're an idiot!"

Gestas's insults flew through the air like flames of hatred.

"Gestas, *shut up!*" Dismas turned to him, hurting deep inside. He couldn't believe what he was hearing from that man's filthy mouth. "Shut up for once! Don't you have a heart? Can't you see either?"

Gestas shook his head like a wild horse.

"What do you want me to see?! Someone who calls himself Christ and yet isn't even capable of saving himself?"

As he screamed, Gestas's eyes were two black holes. With that hatred, it was impossible to see anything. Dismas swallowed, dizzy, and had to moisten his lips with his tongue several times before he could rebuke Gestas.

"Do not even you, who are enduring this same punishment, fear God? This man has done nothing wrong! We... we deserve what is happening to us, the crimes we have committed.... But this one"—he glanced down at the face of the woman in blue—"this one has done no harm. He is innocent."

Gestas didn't answer. His body fell, defeated, all of his weight under his two nailed hands. The wild curses had left him drained, without air to breathe; his chest seemed like an immense wineskin about to burst.

Also weakened by his words, Dismas turned his gaze again toward the mother of the Christ. He wanted to comfort her somehow for the insult she had received, but she didn't seem to notice what had happened; her attention was solely on her son.

The swallows that had been flying above were gone. Clouds had gathered over their heads, as if wanting to hide from heaven what was happening down here, on the summit of Golgotha. The sudden darkening of daylight startled everyone present.

Dismas bowed his head onto his chest, depleted. He had lost all feeling in his limbs.

"Abba, this is the child you saw in that manger." His words were barely a whisper in the mounting darkness that the wind had brought with it. "The light that you saw that night... I had to see his power... You deceived me. You abandoned me. You... you have abandoned me."

The lament died on his lips, and he closed his eyes, abated, all of him swallowed in silence. In the distance, he thought he heard the wind speak. It was returning his words with a new voice.

"*Eli, Eli, lama sabactani!*"

Dismas was frightened to hear the echo of his thoughts. He slowly turned his head toward that man. It was he who had spoken. His lament was the same, almost in Dismas's own words.

The same but different.

They were the beginning of a song. *Eli, Eli, lama sabactani.*

Where had he heard them before?

He closed his eyes, trying to remember, but his memory only brought a deer drinking water on the banks of a river. It was like the place where the prophet John had baptized him and Bathsheba. But there was no one there, only the growing brightness of a dawn that broke as the deer dipped its snout into the clear, clean waters of the Jordan.

The deer of the dawn.

He could hear in his mind that melody he had heard since he was a child.

"The Deer of the Dawn," the song was called. It was very popular among the women who went every morning to wash clothes in the river. As the eve of the Sabbath began, while preparing dinner, their mother had taught Dismas and Sara to pray by singing psalms. There were some popular tunes that served as melody for some of them. And "The Deer of the Dawn" was the melody of Psalm 22. Dismas and Miriam had loved that song.

Suddenly, Dismas's eyes opened as they never had before in his life. They floated brightly in astonishment while his labored breathing accelerated with a sudden excitement.

"*Eli, Eli, lama sabactani*" was the beginning of Psalm 22!

He began to repeat to himself that psalm that he had sung a thousand times in Galilee, in the shadow of his home, with the help of that familiar, haunting melody. The words fell upon his heart like a fine, gentle April rain, and surprise and wonder took hold of the depths of his soul as he recognized himself in many of its stanzas.

Had his hands and feet not been pierced, as the lyrics of the psalm announced? And had he not bent his head over his chest to count his bones beneath the tautness of his skin? Had he not felt his tongue and throat dry as a shard of baked clay? Hadn't he seen himself like spilled water, his bones dislocated, and his heart melted like wax?

Dismas raised his head up sideways, uneasily, as Atzel used to do when he lost sight of his owner. He was the protagonist of a psalm that had been written a thousand years before. How could that be?

Could his feelings, everything he was experiencing nailed to that wooden beam, have been prophesied by King David?

Perplexed, Dismas considered again the words of the psalm without understanding. He couldn't be the protagonist, but he had felt in his own skin the same as its author. He raised his head and slowly looked again to his left.

Who are you?

Silence enveloped the sad figure hanging from that cross that smelled of freshly cut wood.

If He had been the one who had murmured the beginning of that psalm, then only before Him should unfold the true meaning of the words that followed.

The song continued to swirl, incomplete, in his mind. He could not recall all the verses by heart, but he began again.

"*Eli, Eli, lama sabactani,*" he repeated, humming from the back of his mind the melody of "The Deer of the Dawn." The notes of the tune managed to pluck new words from the walls of his memory, and a little tremor stirred the back of his insides when he came to those forgotten verses:

"All who see me mock at me;
they make mouths at me, they shake their heads;
'Commit your cause to the Lord; let him deliver—
let him rescue the one in whom he delights!'"

Holy, almighty God, had not those Pharisees been uttering mockery at the foot of the cross with similar words? Then another phrase of the psalm struck his mind with the force of a lightning bolt:

"They stare and gloat over me;
they divide my clothes among themselves,
and for my clothing they cast lots."

A dry, heartrending, inexplicable sob took hold of Dismas as he remembered the Roman soldiers he'd seen playing dice at the foot of the cross. He searched with weary eyes among those below and saw that one of them was wearing, hanging from his shoulder, a tunic that didn't belong to him. They had been gambling for the clothes of that man, of Yeshua, of... of.... He could not finish the thought.

He looked up and felt an infinite vertigo. Emptied by

darkness, the sky seemed to have no owner, and he had an inexplicable fear of falling into it.

Was that man nailed to the cross beside him really the Messiah?

Bathsheba, would you believe in him? he groaned inside himself.

He shook his head. It couldn't possibly be like that. You'd have to be crazy to believe it.

But Psalm 22 did exist, and it had been fulfilled... *Eli, Eli, lama sabactani.* There they were, both nailed to the cross a thousand years later, to prove it.

"How can you do this to me now, O Lord?" he resisted, turning inward and letting his head fall to his chest, overcome by the sudden doubt that opened an abyss in his heart.

He was delirious, that was what was happening. He was delirious, and in the face of the darkness of death, he was clinging to the words of a prophecy.

A prophecy that he knew had been fulfilled.

You will see his power.

"L... Lord." He was surprised to hear his own voice. The syllables stumbled against the dryness of his mouth and died between the cracks of his lips. He searched the walls of his throat for the last drops with which to moisten that dry mouth, dry as baked clay.

"Yeshua."

A beat.

"Yeshua!"

This time the cry flew across his chest into the open air.

The man, that worm, turned his head slowly towards him. Dismas could hardly distinguish the features of that face, bathed in blood against the darkness that now filled the sky. But those eyes, sunken in pain, seemed to open with an inexplicable brightness, and Dismas suddenly felt as if the entire universe had turned to him and nothing and no one else existed on the face of the earth.

Only the two of them, nailed to their crosses, at the top of Mount Calvary.

"Remember me when you are in your kingdom."

The words seemed to spring from his mouth without even passing through his head, nearly as though they escaped from beneath his skin. He would have said more… That he was sorry. That he wanted to ask forgiveness for so many things, of so many people, of him. But he had no strength at all left even in his lips. It had to be like this. It had to be this way.

"I assure you," He answered with an infinite, unfathomable, indescribable tenderness, only for Dismas's ears, "that today, this very day, you will be with me in paradise."

Dismas heard the words, and he felt himself sink under a blanket of light, as he had on the banks of the Jordan.

At last he was going to enjoy it.

Paradise.

And he closed his eyes, happy.

Made in the USA
Columbia, SC
23 March 2025

5cb34adf-c66a-4e2f-9a91-f6377fcf9da8R01